Pr̶
Ellen To̶̶
The Understudy

She is a stunning new writer, and certainly for anyone in the creative arts—especially live theater—it's a MUST read. I laughed, I cried, and I reminisced for hours because her whole story is so incredibly real, and without even being aware, you become a part of it. I, literally, was there…and because of her, I have had no sleep for the last two days. She is, now, a national gem and to be treasured!

> —Peter White, actor, played Lincoln Tyler, *All My Children*

There are so many things to enjoy about this book. The story of what really goes on in theater…at auditions, opening night, rehearsals, backstage, wardrobe fittings. It's all just like it really is. Breathtaking! Also, the true fellowship actors have for each other as the play gets closer to opening. And falling in love. It's all there—witty, funny, and deeply touching.

> —Joyce Van Patten, American stage, film and television actress

The very PITH of a life lived in the theater!

> —John Glover, Tony, Obie, and Drama Desk Award-winner

I absolutely loved it! I didn't want it to end!

> —Harrison Hulé, artist

Ellen Tovatt Leary clearly and lovingly lays out the high wire act of a woman struggling to balance her acting career ambition with a life fully lived. This well-told story should be read by anyone who wants to get behind the mystique and tabloid clichés of a profession that few outsiders truly understand.

> —Andrew Robinson, stage, film, and television actor

The Understudy is a heartfelt love letter to actors and the New York theater scene of the '70s.

—Will Mackenzie, American actor and five-time Emmy
award-winning television director

Have you ever secretly dreamed of being a Broadway star? If so, then this terrifically entertaining novel, *The Understudy* by Ellen Tovatt Leary, will become one of your favorites. Ms. Leary's debut novel, about the pain and the hilarity of being a part of the "fabulous invalid," as the theater is called, truly knocks it out of the park!

—Karen Kondazian, actor and award-winning author of *The Whip*

I loved it! It took me back to my early days of auditioning and performing and my going on for Betty Hutton in *Gentlemen Prefer Blondes!*

—Patsy Mackenzie, Broadway actress, singer, dancer

Anyone who loves the theater will want to read *The Understudy*. Anyone who loves New York will want to read *The Understudy*. Anyone who loves love will want to read *The Understudy*—an irresistible, truthful, sensual, insightful novel.

—Allan Leicht, Emmy award-winning writer and playwright

I took so long reading this lovely book because I never wanted it to end!!

—Renee Lippin, stage, film, and television actress

Ellen Leary's *The Understudy* brilliantly conveys the essence of what it means to be an actress working in the theater! As a reader, we become totally absorbed with the trials and tribulations of Nina Landau with her loves, her losses, and her ultimate triumph in coming to terms with who she is! It is a must-read for all lovers of theater and artistic expression!

—Stacy Keach, stage, film, and television actor

In her second book *The Understudy*, Ellen Tovatt Leary tells a story revolving primarily around Broadway and the fascinating world of the theater. She writes of this arena with authenticity, accented with fascinating characters, insightful revelations of an actor's triumphs and rejections, and wraps it all up with a cocktail of sparkling humor. I loved this book!

—John Schuck, veteran actor of stage, screen and television

In *The Understudy*, Ellen Tovatt Leary delivers something wonderful: a vivid, funny, and moving look at life and love set against the backdrop of 1970s Broadway. Leary knows the territory, and her memorable novel takes you deep inside a world where actors put everything on the line as they pursue their personal and professional dreams. Note to Hollywood: *The Understudy* would make one hell of a movie.

—Scot Safon, Emmy-winning former Executive Vice President at Turner Broadcasting's CNN and TNT

The true thrill of a life in the theater!

—Val Meyer, Broadway actor, stage manager, and TV director

The sweet, sweet feeling I get while reading *The Understudy* is nostalgic. I revisited the early part of my own career with the familiar rooms, the smells, addresses, situations, nausea, ambience, the romance of a NYC neighborhood during snowfall, the shock of transitioning in an instant from backstage to onstage by merely opening a door, and the terror and joy of being in front of a crowd.

—Peter Friedman, American film, television, and Tony-nominee Broadway actor

The Understudy was very nostalgic. It's the way it really was for me and so many others. And, a terrific read!

—Judy Kaye, Tony award, Obie award, and Drama Desk award-winning actress/singer

If you're a theater lover, you are in for a treat. This book brought me right back to the theater scene in NYC and post-performance cocktails at Joe Allen. And that's a pretty great place to be! Ellen Tovatt Leary has created a wonderful character in Nina. She's smart, ambitious, and lovable while dealing with the work/life balance so many of us struggle with. What an enjoyable read!

—Pamela Fahey, casting director/founder of Pamela Fahey Casting

An exuberant tour of Broadway in the 1970s told with the insight and enthusiasm of one who lived it. The joys of theater are evident in these pages—as are the complex webs of love, ambition, and friendship. One leaves *The Understudy* deeply appreciative of an actor's devotion to craft, and how life and the stage can be so closely intertwined.

—Daniel Mason, physician and author of *The Piano Tuner* (2002), *A Far Country* (2007), *The Winter Soldier* (2018), and *A Registry of My Passage Upon the Earth* (2020)

Ellen Tovatt Leary's *The Understudy* is wonderful. An evocative, nostalgic, charming, and loving love story about the theater, about acting, and all else that goes with it. You will fall in love with Nina Landeau.

—Nancy Dussault, Emmy winner, two-time Tony nominee, Theater World Award, and teacher

Nina is a terrific character, full of dimension, surprises, emotion, and a delicious smattering of irony. Her battles with confidence really pull you along.

—Nancy Meckler, stage director, (Broadway and the Royal Shakespeare Company), and film director

THE UNDERSTUDY

The Understudy

A Novel

Ellen Tovatt Leary

HANSEN PUBLISHING GROUP, LLC

This is a work of fiction. All of the characters, organizations, and events portrayed in this novel are either a product of the author's imagination or are used fictitiously.

The Understudy
Copyright © 2020 by Ellen Tovatt Leary

25 24 23 22 21 20   10 9 8 7 6 5 4 3 2 1

ISBN: (PAPER) 978-1-60182-344-1
ISBN: (EBOOK) 978-1-60182-345-8

Cover design by Jon Hansen
Book interior design by Jon Hansen

Cover artwork, "Half-Hour (The Understudy)"
Copyright © 2020 Harrison Houlé
www.harrisonhoule.com

Hansen Publishing Group, LLC
302 Ryders Lane
East Brunswick, NJ 08816
https://hansenpublishing.com

Author site:
Facebook.com/EllenTovattLeary

For David and for Daniel

Some of the best moments of my life have been spent

holding for the laugh.

—Ellen Tovatt Leary

THE UNDERSTUDY

CHAPTER ONE

The Audition

On the day of the audition, Nina woke before the alarm. The morning sun streamed through the east-facing windows on Madison Avenue, throwing a lopsided rectangle on the floor of the small apartment. She lay in bed for a moment thinking of the difficult day ahead. Then she sat up, turned off the alarm, and headed for the bathroom.

Emerging from the shower, she wiped a swath through the steamed-up mirror and assessed her face. She had her mother's coloring: gray-blue eyes and reddish-brown hair, as well as her flawless skin. And thank God for the good bone structure, she thought, recognizing her mother's high cheekbones reflected in the mirror. No wonder her father had loved her so much—she looked exactly like her mother.

She wrapped herself in a towel and went into the kitchen to pour herself some coffee. As she sat down to drink it, the phone rang.

"I didn't wake you, did I?" asked Tom, nervously.

"No. I'm up and showered and having my coffee."

"Oh, good. I just wanted to say break a leg. Did you finally choose an outfit?"

"Yup."

"Which one?"

"My blue knit."

"Oh! I love you in that! It shows off your figure. What time is the audition?"

"Eleven o'clock."

"Oh, well. Good luck. I mean…break a leg. Don't be nervous. Remember what you always told me: concentration, preparation and confidence."

"I'll do my best. Thanks for calling. Light candles!"

As she put down the phone, it rang again. It was Isabelle.

"I just wanted to wish you good luck."

"Thanks. I'm as nervous as a cat, but I can't prepare any more. I just have to harness my concentration and try to blot out the huge, empty Broadway theater and the people sitting there judging me."

"Well, someone once said to imagine them in their underwear."

Nina gave a short laugh. "It's worth a try."

She put on her makeup and carefully pulled her blue knit dress over her head, zipping the side zipper. The dress brought out the blue in her eyes and showed off her figure. She had tried on at least six different outfits the night before, sitting and standing and walking around in them to see if they were comfortable enough to move in. They now lay in a heap on the living room couch. She looked at herself in the full-length mirror on the back of the bathroom door, turning her head this way and that. She reached into her bra to adjust her breasts, fluffed her hair, and gave herself one last look before she got her purse and tote bag and left the apartment.

It was a beautiful fall morning. The long, listless summer was over. You could feel the shift in the air. Dogs were eager for their morning walks, and people had retrieved their sweaters from the winter storage boxes under their beds. The sun gilded the apartment house windows across the Hudson on the New Jersey side and dappled the sidewalk in front of her. It had rained the night before, but now pink clouds were floating in the sky.

She sprinted to catch the bus just before it was about to close its doors.

"Hold it!" she said, but too quietly for anyone to hear. If I miss it, I'll splurge for a taxi, she thought.

A man saw her running and held the bus for her. She knew from the look he gave her that she had chosen the right outfit for the audition. She smiled her thanks to him and lowered her eyes, grateful for the bus and the vote of confidence. She climbed up the steps and put her token in the farebox, murmuring a soft "thank you" to the bus driver who looked straight ahead.

The school year had already begun, but it was after ten and there was a noticeable absence of shrieking children with their schoolbooks jamming the bus. She made her way easily down the aisle, holding on to the backs of the seats as the bus lurched forward. There was an empty seat next to an older woman with a Channel Thirteen tote bag. As the bus veered to a stop at Seventy-Second Street, she swung into the seat apologizing to the woman for bumping into her. From her bag, Nina extracted a dog-eared script and turned to the scene she was about to perform. Silently she went over the lines once again. The play, *The Second Time Around*, was a new comedy set for Broadway, and she was reading for the lead part of Melanie. The playwright's first play, *Spoiler Alert*, was a Broadway hit, and his second play was eagerly anticipated, especially because Nick Travis was directing again. There was already a great deal of buzz about it in the theater community, even though they had not yet picked a cast.

The trees of Central Park were still green and lush, but a few leaves were already beginning to look singed around the edges as though they had been held too close to a flame. As the bus approached Fiftieth Street, Nina returned the script to her bag, stood, and grabbed onto one of the straps above her. Stepping off the bus, she glanced longingly at the windows of Saks Fifth Avenue before running to catch the Forty-Ninth Street crosstown.

As soon as the bus reached the Broadway stop, she got off and started walking downtown. The wind suddenly kicked up. An empty paper coffee cup with the ubiquitous blue Greek lettering rolled into the gutter, and a page of newspaper wrapped itself around a trash container. Nina slipped on her sunglasses to keep the swirling dirt from her eyes. She made her way toward the Broadhurst Theatre where the auditions were being held, noting the garish neon lights that flared and dimmed and flared again all the way down Broadway to Times Square. Traffic was bumper to bumper, and people pressed together spilling over into the crosswalks as they waited impatiently for the light to change. By the time Nina reached Forty-Fourth Street, she felt her morning crispness ebbing.

Arriving at the Broadhurst, she walked down an alley and found the stage door. She pulled open the heavy, metal door and wrote her name on the sign-in sheet after her time slot. She smoothed her hair before sitting down on one of the folding metal chairs lined up against the wall for the actors waiting to audition. Surreptitiously she assessed the competition. One woman with dark brown hair looked very much like her, only prettier. Let's hope she can't act, thought Nina. She opened her script and read it to herself one more time, moving her lips silently. Her eyebrows raised and lowered with the emotions, and halfway through she felt one of the actors staring at her. She looked up, embarrassed, and smiled. The woman smiled back and quickly looked away.

"Thank you," the stage manager was saying as he parted the thick, black velour curtains and led an actor out of the wings and into the waiting area. "Next?" A lanky blonde rose quickly from her seat, causing her purse to fall in the process.

"Oh!" she exclaimed. Her lipstick rolled noisily down the concrete floor coming to rest under an empty chair. Nina rose to help pick up the articles and return them to the distraught actor. The stage manager waited patiently until everything was recovered.

"Jean Moor?" he asked.

The woman nodded.

"Right, this way," he said kindly, holding the curtain for her and looking down at the concrete floor. "Careful of the cables."

The blonde squared her shoulders and took a last deep breath before heading to the gallows. Nina exchanged silent looks of sympathy with the other actors, and then they quickly returned to their own thoughts. One woman stared into space; another took a round mirror from her purse and gave her face one last check. Nina sat back in her chair and tapped her foot. There was nothing left for her to do.

A few other actors were called in to audition and emerged looking drained. Nina got up and checked the sign-in sheet. She was next. She sat back down and licked her lips.

"Thank you," the stage manager said as the pretty dark-haired actor emerged from the parted curtains.

"Next." He checked his list, "Nina Landau?"

Nina got up, went through the heavy blackout curtains, through the backstage area crowded with props and furniture, and out onto the stage. She put her hand up to shield her eyes and looked out into the audience. Her heart was pounding. There were three people sitting in the front of the orchestra. One she recognized as Nick Travis, the director. The woman next to him was holding a yellow legal pad and sipping from a paper coffee cup. A few seats to the left of them was the playwright George DuPont. They were all looking at her, appraising her. The stage manager introduced her:

"This is Nina Landau."

"Good morning," said Nick Travis. "You are reading for the part of Melanie?"

"Yes," said Nina, a little too quickly.

"Very good."

He sat back in his seat.

"Whenever you're ready."

The stage manager walked to the center of the stage holding a script and waited patiently for Nina to put her purse down on a nearby chair and turn back to him. She could feel the floorboards give as she walked to the center of the stage. How many people have trod these boards? she thought. Brando, Barrymore, Olivier. Her heart was beating wildly, and her mouth had gone dry. The thrill of actually standing on a Broadway stage for the first time momentarily transfixed her. Looking out to the audience from the other side was exhilarating and disorienting at the same time. Her hands were trembling as she opened her script. She cleared her throat quietly and gave a nod to the stage manager.

"Hello, Melanie," he began, "I didn't expect you today."

"I wanted to stop by and see how the patient was doing," said Nina, reading the lines. Her voice sounded strange to her. It sounded at least an octave higher. As she spoke, her mind raced in a silent contrapuntal soliloquy. Better not blow this or I'll never get another Broadway audition.

"That's fine," the stage manager continued in a stilted voice, "but I'm afraid he's asleep. Won't you sit down and let me get you a drink?"

Nina sat in the provided chair and crossed her legs. Suddenly she felt the character shift into gear. Maybe it was the manner in which she sat. Maybe it was the way she crossed her legs. Suddenly the Broadway theater, the three people watching her, the stage manager, all started to fade to the back of her mind and the character of Melanie came to the fore. She relaxed into it, slowly gaining confidence. Then she landed one of the laugh lines, getting a laugh from the three dour people in the orchestra.

When they came to the end of the scene, Nina closed her script, pressed her lips together, and nervously looked out into the audience. The two people on either side of the director, leaned forward and caught each other's eye. The director stared at her, reflectively chewing on his bottom lip.

"Well done," he said finally. "Thank you."

Nina nodded, stood up, and went to get her purse. As she started off the stage, the director called after her.

"Oh! One more thing," he said, looking down at her picture and résumé, "How tall are you?"

Nina stopped. Should she make herself taller or shorter? What were they looking for?

"Five-foot seven," she said, leaving off "and a half."

The director nodded and his assistant made a note on the yellow pad.

Shit! thought Nina, they probably have one of those short leading men. But it was too late. The stage manager parted the heavy curtain and led her out, cautioning her not to trip over the tangle of thick electrical cables.

"Thank you," he said. "Next?"

Another young actor stood up and went through the curtain.

Nina left the theater and sank against the brick wall of the alley. It was over! She had done it! She took a deep breath and slowly let it out. It had gone well. Relief flooded through her. He had asked how tall she was. That must mean they were considering her. Didn't it? Her heart was still pounding. Calm down. Breathe. They had laughed. Thank God!

As soon as she got back home, she called Tom.

"It went well!" she said breathlessly into the phone.

"Oh my God! It went well," he shouted to Brent. "That is great! How was Nick Travis? Did he come on to you?"

"Don't be ridiculous!" said Nina.

"He'll be in your pants in five minutes," said Tom. "He is known to be the worst ladies' man."

"I doubt that," said Nina.

"Come over! We'll celebrate! Brent is making risotto."

"I can't tonight," said Nina. "How about tomorrow?"

"Fine," said Tom, hurt. "Suit yourself."

"Anyway...I just wanted to let you know the good news."

"We'll be going to your opening night on Broadway!" Tom said in a singsong voice.

"It's just a bit premature for that," said Nina. She laughed as she hung up the phone.

What she hadn't told Tom was that she had a date with Paul tonight. She had no desire to deal just now with Tom's disapproval. Paul was the "nice Jewish boy" every mother wanted for their daughter, but she knew Tom didn't like him.

During a recent lunch on the Upper East Side, Nina had complained about Paul to her friend Isabelle.

"Paul asked me to marry him, again, and I turned him down."

"Why? What's wrong with him," Isabelle asked quizzically as she pierced a piece of avocado with her fork.

"He's too perfect," answered Nina.

"You think?" said Isabelle.

"There's just no danger to him. Everything is so predictable."

"Who needs danger when you have a three-bedroom apartment on the twenty-fifth floor of Windsor Tower?"

"Apparently me," said Nina.

Isabelle was a struggling actor who had taken a temp job with the Harris Poll three years ago. It paid the rent. She and Nina had met at an audition that was open to non-union actors, known in the business as a "cattle call." Unlike Nina, Isabelle was not a member of Actors' Equity.

"Boy! I'd take him in a New York minute," said Isabelle. "I'd never have to worry about the rent again or hit the sale rack at Bloomingdales." She paused for a moment. "And look at him, for Christ's sake!"

Nina sighed. "I know. When I first looked into his green eyes, I thought all my relationship problems were finally over. He took me to expensive restaurants like Lutèce. I had never even heard of Lutèce. I was surviving on canned tuna. He is the most thoughtful, most attentive, and most tender man I have ever known. All he wants is to give me things… and do things that will make me happy. And the more he does, the guiltier I feel."

Nina stopped talking and looked down at her salad.

"Why do you think he does that?" asked Isabelle.

Nina sighed, "I guess he's trying to make me love him."

"It would work with me!" said Isabelle.

"Oh, Isabelle. You can't make someone love you if they don't love you."

"You can't?"

"Of course, not! The heart wants what it wants."

Why didn't she just end the relationship? Loneliness, of course. New York was lonely in winter, and as much as she loved the fall, Nina found that she was dreading the approaching winter. New York was a hard place to live in during any of the seasons. Garbage trucks and fire engine sirens jolted you awake at two almost every morning. The twenty-fifth floor in Windsor Tower could seem extremely attractive. She had recently told Paul they could no longer be lovers, just friends. And they were.

At exactly seven the doorbell rang. With some irritation, Nina realized that Paul had probably been waiting down in the vestibule, watching the second hand of his Cartier watch pass the twelve mark before ringing the bell. She knew him too well. Putting aside her impatience, she opened the door and greeted him warmly with a kiss on the cheek.

"You look great!" she said.

"Just back from a week in Puerto Vallarta. You really should have come!"

Nina smiled, lowered her eyes, and gestured for him to come in.

He always looked somehow out of place in her cramped rent-controlled apartment in his Pierre Cardin suit and Cartier watch. Tonight she was glad to see him because she felt like celebrating.

They took a taxi to Café Des Artistes, their favorite restaurant, housed in the old Des Artistes Building on Sixty-Seventh Street and Central Park West. When she told him of her successful audition, Paul immediately signaled for the waiter and ordered a bottle of Veuve Clicquot. Maybe it was the champagne. Maybe it was all those naked ladies gallivanting in the Howard Chandler Christy murals that adorned the walls of the restaurant. Maybe it was because the day had been stressful, and she felt she deserved it. Whatever the excuse, Nina gave herself permission to abandon her moral principles and did not object when Paul leaned over and kissed her in the taxicab on their way home. She welcomed the tip of his tongue as it searched for hers and opened her lips to kiss him back. A muscle twitched between her legs. When their lips parted, Paul gave the driver his address. She closed her eyes, rested her head on the back seat of the taxi, and smiled—enjoying the dizziness, the lack of constraint, and the anticipation of the sex to come. She concentrated on how his new tan made his green eyes dazzle and how skillful a lover she knew him to be.

She spent an enormously gratifying, self-indulgent night at his apartment. No garbage trucks reached her on the twenty-fifth floor.

CHAPTER TWO

The Callback

P aul put her in a taxi early the next morning as he was leaving for work. She was thankful not to have to brave the school kids and the businessmen on the bus in her low-cut, green silk dress and her high heels. She kissed him, gratefully, on the cheek, refusing the twenty-dollar bill he thrust into her hand.

"Thanks, I'm fine," she said. She smiled at him despite her hangover.

Once back in her apartment, she kicked off her shoes and struggled out of her dress. Opening the refrigerator, she poured herself a big glass of cold water. Always hydrate and you won't have a hangover, she reminded herself. It was a trick that a dermatologist had taught her once: when he was in medical school, a surgeon had gotten very drunk at a party one night. He was scheduled to perform surgery the next morning. A few interns put him on a gurney and hooked him up to an IV of fluid, and when he woke up, he was ready to operate.

The phone rang.

"Hold for Susan," the receptionist said. She held the receiver to her ear, her pulse quickening.

"Nina?" bellowed her agent, "You got a callback. They want you to read next Thursday, eleven a.m. Same place:

The Broadhurst. You are to prepare the scene that begins on page thirty-three. Okay?"

"Oh!" said Nina, "Did they say anything else?"

"What did you want them to say? That you were talented and beautiful? You are. Page thirty-three. Okay?…Okay?"

"Okay," said Nina.

With that she hung up.

Nina slowly placed the receiver in the cradle and put her hand up to her mouth. A callback. My God! Thursday. It was now Friday. That would give her a week to prepare the scene. She would work on it. She would memorize it. She drank the water and went into the bathroom. Looking in the mirror, she saw that her eyes were puffy and had dark circles under them. Annoyed with herself for getting drunk, she vowed to get into her best shape ever by Thursday. She had to knock them dead! Despite the circles, she thought she still looked pretty good. She had never played on Broadway before, but she had played leads in many regional theaters on the East Coast and even once Off-Broadway. Maybe that's where Nick Travis had seen her.

She heard the phone ring again but decided to let it go to message. Stepping into the shower, she tilted her face up to the showerhead and closed her eyes letting the hot water pour over her hair and body. She soaped her hands and smoothed them down over her hips and breasts and between her legs, remembering Paul. The guilt, however, could not be as easily washed away as the grime, and she felt a thin film of it still clinging to her body after she emerged from the shower. Stupid to get drunk and end up in bed. But, oh, Paul was such a good lover! He satisfies me all the time. Why couldn't they just be occasional lovers satisfying that urge when it arose and then go on with their lives? But that didn't work when only one of you was in love.

She dried off and wrapped herself in a towel. In the living room, she played the message on the machine: "It's

Tom. Where the hell were you last night? And where are you now, you slut? Call me."

Nina smiled and decided to turn the phone off and look at the new audition scene before calling him back. But as soon as she opened the script, her mind wandered to what she would wear for the callback. She knew the conventional wisdom was, if you got a callback, you wore the same outfit that you had worn for the first audition. That would cement you in their minds. They saw so many actors. But Nina felt it would also show a certain desperation. She wanted to appear more…laid-back. She decided she would wear a completely different outfit.

The scene she read for the first audition was good, but largely exposition. The scene she was to read for the callback required a lot of emotion. It would be difficult to pull out all the stops in an audition. Especially with the stage manager reading in that wooden voice. God! Why didn't they pair her with an actor? She read the scene aloud. The tears did not come. She was not one of those actors who could cry on cue. She could laugh on cue, but not cry. She sounded phony and affected. What if that happened at the audition? She felt her anxiety begin to mount. Then she remembered a role she played that called for her to break down in tears the minute she arrived on the stage: Estelle Hohengarten in Tennessee Williams's play *The Rose Tattoo*. There had been no time to build to the emotion. She solved the problem by going off into the wings ten minutes before her entrance, closing her eyes, and recalling the death of her father. Just as the tears began to well up, she would hear her cue, make her entrance, and collapse on the stage, weeping. It had worked every time. But how did you do that in an audition…?

She decided to take a break and called Tom back.

"Hi. It's me."

"Where the hell were you?" Tom said, "I called twice last night. You could be lying in a ditch somewhere!"

"I was out with Paul."

"Oh, Paul. I should have guessed. I thought that was over."

"Anyway," said Nina, "The agency just called—I got a callback."

Tom's attitude changed instantly.

"A callback? That's fantastic!" Then he spoke loudly to someone in the next room.

"No. It's Nina. She got a callback. No...she's not dead; she was out with Paul," his voice dropped with distaste.

He spoke into the phone again.

"A Broadway Baby! We're going to see your name up on the marquee, Nina Landau! In lights on the Great White Way! Come over tonight; we'll celebrate. Bring wine. We have leftover risotto. It's fabulous!"

"Okay," said Nina, "but no wine for me; I'm in training."

Nina took the bus across Seventy-Ninth Street and caught the 104 up Broadway. At Eighty-Fourth Street, she walked over to West End Avenue where Tom and Brent lived. The apartment was dark with wine-colored walls and enormous gilt-framed paintings. Their bedroom was painted a deep red and had stark, white lacquer moldings. An original poster from *Gone with the Wind* hung on the wall.

Brent was a successful stage manager and Tom was an actor. She and Tom had met in an Off-Broadway play years before in which he had a small part. His warmth and humor had cut through her customary shyness. Grateful to have someone to eat lunch with, their friendship blossomed into a close and protective relationship. Even though Tom was gay, it didn't prevent him from falling in love with her. And she loved him, too. There just was no sex. He took her to hear Barbara Cook at the Carlyle and to all the Broadway musicals that Brent got comps for. Dinner parties at their apartment were always something to look forward to. Brent was a great cook, and they inevitably included fascinating personalities. Best of all, Tom was always there for her when things got rough. He had seen her at her worst and loved her anyway.

Their Schnauzer Gus greeted her at the apartment door, wagging his tail and jumping up on her.

"Gus! Down!" Tom shouted, sharply.

The dining room table was set with a white tablecloth and gold chargers under Spode plates. Ornate silverware gleamed on white linen napkins. There were candles in silver candleholders and cut-glass goblets.

"Wow! Who's coming?" asked Nina.

"You! We're hosting a Broadway star!" said Tom.

"I wish you would stop saying that," Nina said, annoyed. "It puts so much pressure on me."

"Oh, Nina! You know I love you no matter if you get that job or not. We just wanted to celebrate the good news."

"Well...I appreciate your support," said Nina, relenting.

The risotto was scrumptious, and the conversation was risqué—who was sleeping with whom and what plays were having problems staying open after the influx of summer tourists had ground to a halt. Nina allowed herself one glass of wine. "Hair of the dog," said Tom.

"I think Nick Travis is still married to Fiona de Groot," noted Tom, helping himself to another portion of risotto.

"And that would be of interest to me...why?" asked Nina.

"You never know," said Tom, raising his eyebrows, suggestively.

"What happened to your diet?" asked Nina.

"Oh, I decided that if God had meant me to be thin, he never would have invented the overblouse."

Nina laughed.

"Look, all I want is a chance to be in a Broadway show," she said. "I will even play the maid. There is a maid, by the way. I am not interested in Nick Travis or anyone else at this point."

"All I am saying is that I think he is still married," said Tom, defensively.

"I am very happy for him!" said Nina.

For the rest of the week she shut herself in her apartment working on the audition scene. First, she read the whole play through again to get an idea of the context of the scene. Then she read the scene a few times over, underlining Melanie's words in red ink. She started memorizing the lines, reading them over and over until she knew them without looking at the script.

Isabelle came over on Sunday to cue her.

"You sound good!" Isabelle said after they had read the scene through.

"Thanks," said Nina, "I want it so badly. I know I shouldn't, but I can't help it."

"Oh, I understand," sighed Isabelle, "but remember what you always told me about auditions: 'Do 'em and forget 'em! Otherwise the rejection is too hard to take.'"

"I have a wheelbarrow full of rejections," said Nina wryly. "I should be inured to them by now, but I never get used to them. It is not a profession for the thin-skinned. It's such a dichotomy. They want actors to be vulnerable enough to portray complex, sensitive characters and yet remain immune to rejection and criticism."

"Well, maybe you'll get this one," said Isabelle, consolingly. "You really sounded good."

"Did you believe the tears?" asked Nina, apprehensively.

"Yes!" said Isabelle, "I was worried about you for a minute."

"Oh, good" said Nina.

"Have you had any auditions lately?"

"None," answered Isabelle. "I keep wondering if I should keep pursuing this acting thing…?"

Nina hesitated. "Well, of course, Uta Hagen says if you have to ask the question—don't."

Isabelle looked down.

That night, before she fell asleep, Nina thought about Isabelle and the plight of all the actors in New York City who didn't quite make the grade. What would become of Isabelle? The city just ate you up and spat you out. How long could she continue to try to make ends meet working at the Harris Poll? How many more years of stress and anxiety could she take before she caved in and went back to Indiana…to do what? Teach acting? Nina realized how lucky she was to have the opportunities to work. She had to do everything in her power to get this job and stay in the race.

Thursday dawned, bright and sunny. Herringbone clouds hung low in the September sky, portending a change in the weather. Nina woke early and prepared herself for the callback. She washed her hair and got into her audition outfit, smiling at herself in the full-length mirror and softly saying to her reflection, "Nina Landau. Yes, nice to see you again, too!"

Then she blew loudly through her lips a few times to loosen them up and read through the scene again before she put the script into her tote bag.

There was surprisingly little traffic, and she found herself at the Broadhurst early. She decided to go in and see how many people were waiting to read. She pulled open the heavy metal stage door and was startled to see only one person in the waiting area, a man. He stood as she walked in.

"Hi. Are you reading for the Nick Travis play?" he asked.

"Yes," said Nina.

She recognized him from somewhere. Maybe TV. He had tousled, sandy-colored hair, a boyish charm, and was about six feet tall. But the most striking thing about him was his sparkling blue eyes.

"Oh good. I was hoping I'd get to read with an actor and not the stage manager" he said, grinning.

"Are we reading together?" asked Nina.

"I think so. Are you..." he looked down at a name written on his script, "Nina Landau?"

"Yes," said Nina, "Who are you?"

"Matt Ryland," said the man, offering his hand.

Nina took the hand in hers but looked puzzled.

"Did someone tell you that you would be reading with me?" she asked.

"Yes, my agent."

Nina had the sudden feeling of being left out of the loop and a mild annoyance at Susan for not letting her know.

"Well, that's great," she said, recovering quickly. "Do you want to run through the scene? We're early."

"Sure," said Matt.

They read the scene together, quietly. Nina kept the tears in reserve, just below the surface, but she felt confident that she could call them up when the time came. Matt read extremely well. As he read, Nina realized that she had seen him either on television or in the movies, but the name was not one she was familiar with.

"Wow!" said Matt, when they finished. "I thought we sounded good."

"Let's hope they do," said Nina.

They both sat down on the metal chairs to wait.

It wasn't long before the stage manager came out through the curtains and asked them if they were ready to read. They rose, as a unit, and walked onto the Broadway stage.

"Hey, Matthew!" called Nick Travis from his seat in the orchestra, "Good to see you, man. Thanks for making the trip."

"No problem," said Matt.

Nina put her purse down at the corner of the stage. The feeling of being excluded welled up in her again: so, they know each other.

"And Ms. Landau," said Nick Travis, "nice to see you again. Are you ready?"

"Ready?" asked Matt, looking at her, with raised eyebrows.

Nina screwed up all her courage. She knew she had to get rid of these negative feelings and focus on the part.

"Can you give me just one minute?" she asked, apprehensively.

"Sure," said Matt. "Take as long as you want."

Nick Travis shifted in his seat.

Nina turned her back. She pressed two fingers of her left hand to her temple to help her focus, ignoring the Broadway theater and the same three people who were sitting there. She tried to ignore her anxiety about making them all wait and to take herself mentally back to when her father had died. She loved her father, and his death hit her hard. Her mother died when she was very young, and he raised her. She could see his face in the hospital bed, thin and pale. Her father. Sturdy and strong. Her father, who always told the story that he had never had to ask for anesthesia when he was at the dentist's office. "I can take a little more," he would say. And the dentist would work and stop and look at him. "A little more," he would say until the whole procedure was completed without any anesthesia at all. But in the hospital, he had so much pain that he wanted to throw himself out of the window. How awful that he had to die that way! She missed him every day. She missed his voice on the phone. And the sound of his laugh. She felt the tears start to well up in her eyes. They threatened to spill over and run down her cheeks.

"Ready," she said, turning.

The scene went well. The tears had come. God! thought

Nina, what actors do to themselves! The last thing she wanted was to relive her father's agony. *Anything for the part*, she thought, with some distaste. *Here I am, pimping out my own father.* She walked to her purse and took a tissue from it. Nick Travis sat up in his seat.

"Very nice," he said. "Very nice. Thank you for coming back. Thank you both. We'll be in touch." Then he said to Matt, "Take care, buddy."

"*Thank you*," Nina gushed, sounding to herself like an idiot. She exited quickly to the waiting room.

Seated on one of the metal chairs was the lanky blonde whose purse had spilled its contents the week before. Nina glanced at her but couldn't bring herself to smile. Instead she blew her nose and headed for the door that led out to the street. Matt was behind her. As they went out, a tall handsome man was preparing to come in. He had a quizzical look on his face and a piece of paper in his hand.

"You're in the right place," said Matt, in a friendly tone. "Good luck."

"Thanks," the actor said, breaking into a relieved smile.

They walked down the alley and exited into the bright sunshine of Forty-Fourth Street.

"Do you…want to have a drink?" asked Matt, tentatively.

"That sounds great," said Nina, trying to keep the desperation out of her voice.

"Shall we try Joe's?" asked Matt.

"Sure," said Nina.

They headed to Forty-Sixth Street and Ninth Avenue. Nina had been to Joe Allen, the theatrical restaurant, many times before, but it was always a welcoming place to sit and have a drink, especially on a Thursday afternoon when it was practically empty.

As they entered the dark restaurant, the hostess greeted Matt warmly.

"Welcome back to New York, Mr. Ryland! What are you doing on the East Coast?"

"Oh, just here on spec," said Matt.

She took two menus from a pile, smiled at Nina and showed them to a small table in the back on the bar side. The walls of the restaurant were famously hung with framed posters of Broadway shows that had been monumental flops.

They ordered wine and Nina turned to Matt.

"I'm really embarrassed, but…am I supposed to know who you are?" she asked.

"Probably not," said Matt, "Unless you watched a series called *The Crescent Moon Café.*"

"The Western thing?" asked Nina.

"Yeah, cowboy stuff. You probably never saw it," Matt said, dismissively.

"I'm so sorry," said Nina. "I guess I didn't. And you're here from…California?"

"Yeah, I did a television thing out there that Nick directed about a year ago, and he called my agent when he was holding auditions for this play. So, I flew in yesterday. I'm staying with a friend. What about you?"

"Oh, I'm a New York City girl, born and bred."

"Wow!" said Matt, "I didn't know people were actually born here; I thought they just arrived at the bus terminal."

Nina laughed.

"Well, there are a few of us," she said.

Nina realized that she must have seen him on TV a hundred times. He had unruly, blond hair that implored you to reach out and pat it back into place, deep-set blue eyes, the kind that sparkled when he laughed, and a masculine crease along his jaw line. He was movie-star handsome, and Nina realized with some irony that he probably was, indeed, a movie star.

The drinks arrived and they talked about the play and

actors they knew in common. Nina let the wine slowly flow through her body and relax her. She sighed and leaned back in her chair, taking in the coziness of the dimly lit bar and the sound of the bartender shaking mixed drinks. Matt looked at his watch. Nina was suddenly afraid he was going to say he had to leave, but instead he said, "I'm starving. Shall we get some lunch?"

"Sure," said Nina. "I didn't eat any breakfast. Too nervous," she added.

A Cobb salad and a burger later, they were laughing and more at ease with each other. They split another glass of wine, and Nina was feeling the familiar buzz in her brain from the alcohol. She was happier than she had been all week. Go slowly, she reminded herself: breathe, unwind. It had been a long, tension-filled week. Auditions were dreadful. She was happy to have it over with and to feel that it had gone well. She was happy to be in Matt's company. He was so handsome. And so charming. I'm sure he belongs to some lucky girl, she thought.

As they finished, Matt called for the check and signed it, adding his house account number. Nina started to object.

"Please," said Matt, "Let me get this. I'm so happy not to have to sit here by myself."

Fat chance of that ever happening, thought Nina. But she smiled and acquiesced graciously.

As they headed out the door, Matt said, "Well, I hope we'll be working together on Broadway."

"That would be nice," said Nina.

She was wishing he would ask for her phone number, but instead, he asked if he could put her into a taxi.

"No, I'm going to grab the 104," she said, "but thanks, anyway."

"Okay, then," said Matt. "See you at rehearsal" and he winked.

Nina laughed and they went their separate ways.

See you at rehearsal. How wonderful it would be to play that part opposite him on Broadway! She let her mind wander lightly over that beguiling landscape before catching herself up short: "Do 'em and forget 'em!" That was the mantra regarding auditions, she reminded herself. *Still...he wasn't wearing a wedding ring...*

CHAPTER THREE

The Offer

"Okay, here's the deal," Susan said on the phone the next morning. "They liked you, but they want a name. They have an offer out to Diana Lawrence to play Melanie. However, they would like you to understudy the part and also play the part of the maid."

Nina said nothing.

"Look, honey," Susan continued, "I know you're disappointed, but let's look at it this way—it's a chance to be on Broadway and to work with Nick Travis. He is very loyal to his actors and always uses them again. The pay is a standard equity contract with "Favored Nations," which means no one gets more money than you. Everyone gets the same: Equity minimum, even Diana Lawrence, but, hey, Broadway minimum is not chopped liver."

Nina remained silent. Diana Lawrence. She had heard of her, of course. Diana had played parts on Broadway, but she was hardly a name. It was the same old vicious circle: you couldn't work on Broadway unless you were a name, and you couldn't become a name unless you worked on Broadway.

"Look," said Susan, "you can think about it and let me know, okay? Your decision. But I think you'd be foolish to turn it down. Okay? Nina? Are you there?"

"Yes. Yes, I'm here," said Nina, dully. "I'll think about it. I'll let you know."

"Don't take too long," said Susan in a warning tone, and she hung up the phone.

She didn't get it. She came close, but she didn't get it. The pain went through her like a punch in the stomach. Play the maid? That was…humiliating, wasn't it? Her mind was in turmoil. She had gotten into a Broadway play. She should be happy. But what a crushing disappointment. She knew how to play the part of Melanie better than anyone. Better than fucking Diana Lawrence. She had played lead roles at Long Wharf, an hour and a half from Broadway. Why couldn't she play them on Broadway? How could they…Oh, it was useless to cry and argue with the gods. But the tears came. She wiped them away angrily and rose to make herself a cup of coffee.

She couldn't face Tom, but she had to talk to somebody. She picked up the phone and dialed Isabelle.

"Oh Nina! I'm so sorry," Isabelle said. "I can imagine how you feel. So, so disappointing."

"I think I'm going to give it a pass," said Nina.

"Turn down a Broadway play? Really?"

"I know, but it's so…humiliating."

"To work on Broadway with Nick Travis? Humiliating?" said Isabelle, amazed. "And to understudy the lead? I don't think that's humiliating at all!"

Nina reminded herself that Isabelle was the one who thought she should stick with Paul just to have financial security, even though she wasn't in love with him.

"Well, maybe I could just understudy and not have to play the maid." said Nina.

"But then you'll be sitting in the audience the whole time and watching the actors up there on the stage. Don't you want to be part of it all? Be part of the ensemble? Get to be in costume and makeup and share in the excitement?"

Nina sighed. "I don't know what I want."

"Look," said Isabelle, "I can't talk now. I've got to go to work. Why don't I come over later and we can hash it out?"

"I would appreciate that," said Nina, her voice filling with emotion.

She hung up and paced around the small apartment. She felt injured and angry. After all that. All the preparation. All the nerves for the auditions. And it had gone well! I read well! And it was all for nothing. She would have to go back on unemployment, along with the rest of the out-of-work actors. At least she would have a claim, she thought. She had worked all summer in an Off-Broadway theater and that, combined with the two days she had worked as an extra on a film, would give her enough weeks to collect unemployment. Wouldn't it? She wasn't sure if the extra job would count as a week. Thank God her father had left her a bit of money, so she didn't have to panic and take a job waiting tables.

The phone rang. She hesitated but decided to answer it. It was Paul.

"Hi," he said in his deep voice, "How's it going?"

"Oh, not too good, I guess."

"Why? What happened?"

"I just heard back from the callback audition, and I didn't get it. They want me to understudy the part."

"Well," said Paul, "that's still good, isn't it? I mean you could be the *All About Eve* girl and sabotage the leading lady, right?"

"I don't think so," said Nina. That was the extent of Paul's acquaintance with the theater world, she thought bitterly, the movie *All About Eve*.

"They also want me to play the…a small part," said Nina.

"Well…Okay then," said Paul, considering. "Doesn't sound too bad. You didn't hit it out of the ballpark, but you got a bunt, right?"

Nina smiled. Sports and real estate. Those were the two things that Paul could relate to.

"Yeah. A bunt. Like you didn't get the Trump Condo deal, but you got the Hell's Kitchen fixer-upper."

"Hell's kitchen is an up and coming neighborhood," said Paul with conviction.

"Oh, Paul. I'm so disappointed," said Nina, and the tears began again.

"Oh, sweetheart," said Paul, "I know you are. What can I do to cheer you up?"

"I wish there were something. I really do," said Nina. "I just have to make the decision if I'm going to take the job or not."

"You mean you're thinking of turning down a Broadway job?" asked Paul.

"That's what Isabelle said," Nina said, sniffling.

"That girl has a lot of common sense," said Paul. "Look. Why don't I pick you up tonight, and we'll go somewhere special for dinner? We can both get plastered."

"I can't tonight," said Nina, "Isabelle offered to come over and help mop up the tears."

"Oh, okay. How about tomorrow night?"

"That would be so lovely, Paul," said Nina, gratefully, and she felt the tears well up in her eyes again. Sure now, she thought, now the tears come easily. Why did she have to work so hard for them when she was on stage?

She hung up and dialed Tom's number. The machine picked up.

"Oh, no!" said Tom's familiar voice on the answering machine. "I can't believe I've missed your call! I'm gonna be so upset. Don't hang up. I'm probably out walking the dog. Leave your name and number. I'll call you right back. I promise."

"It's me," said Nina, dejectedly. "Call me back."

Tom picked up before she could hang up.

"I'm here! I'm here! I was just in the shower. What's the matter? You sound like death."

"Susan called. They want me to understudy the part of Melanie and play the maid. Oh, Tom, I'm so miserable. I don't know what I'm going to do."

There was a pause.

"I'll tell you what you are going to do," said Tom, "You're going to take it! You'll be pulling in a Broadway salary and working with Nick Travis. You'll be cutting your Broadway teeth, and learning a lot, and mingling with the best of the best theater people, and letting them get to know who you are, and having every weekday free, except Wednesdays, to go out on commercial calls, and have the casting people say, 'Oh, aren't you one of Nick Travis's girls?' And because you are going to play the hell out of the maid!"

Nina stopped sniffling and reached for a tissue. She blew her nose, loudly.

"You really think I should do that?" she asked, nasally.

"Of course, I think that. Because it is what you should do!" said Tom.

"Oh, but Tom," said Nina, "The maid? It's like a…a joke part. I think she has only one line!" Her tears threatened to rise again.

"Listen, honey, a part is what you make it. You know that. You know there are no small parts only small actors. Hold your head up high and sign that contract! You are going to be on Broadway, Nina Landau!"

Nina sniffed. "I told Susan I would think about it and call her back."

"Call her back! Tell her yes, yes, yes, yes and yes! Give me that contract! I'm going to work with Nick Travis, honey, I'm going to Broadway!"

Nina stopped crying. "I guess I was just so hurt…so… disappointed…that I didn't get the part. I mean…you know how much work I've done. I've played leads at Long

Wharf, for Christ's sake! I've played leads Off-Broadway. Why can't I play a lead on Broadway? Tell me that? Why do they have to cast fucking Diana Lawrence?"

"Oh, wow!" said Tom, "They cast Diana Lawrence?"

"Oh, God! Please don't say that was a good idea, Tom, I couldn't take it."

"Of course not, honey," said Tom, "You are a much better actor than Diana Lawrence. But she is…more of a name."

"Don't you think I know that? Oh, Tom, It's so unfair!"

"Of course, it is, honey, but that's show biz. That's what you signed on for when you went into this business. Remember? No one promised you a rose garden. You always told me that you were strong enough for the business. Remember?"

"I guess…" said Nina.

"Go call her back. I'm here if you need me."

"Okay," said Nina, considering. "Thanks."

Of course, they were right, thought Nina. Her three best friends. They knew her well. She stood up and blew her nose. She dialed the agency and accepted the job. She was going to Broadway!

CHAPTER FOUR

The First Rehearsal

The rehearsal hall was located in an old corner building on Broadway near Times Square. High up on its brick wall facing Forty-Fourth Street, there was a painted advertisement that once read "Buy O'Reilly's Soap." Now most of the letters were faded, and it read, "Bu O'Reil oap."

Nina took the elevator up to the fourth floor. Her high heels echoed down the long hallway as she looked for room 427. She had dressed in one of her most attractive outfits, the blue knit dress that she had worn to her first audition. A door along the hallway opened; two young dancers in leotards came out and headed down the hall. Through the open door, Nina could hear a piano. Someone said, "Let's take it from bar sixteen..."

When she arrived at room 427, she took a deep breath before turning the doorknob. The large room was empty except for an old brown rehearsal piano at one end and some metal folding chairs. A few chairs leaned against the windows on the street side. One of the walls was mirrored from floor to ceiling. The mirrors reflected the windows making the room seem even more spacious and sunny than it was. They probably use this room for dance rehearsals, thought Nina. People were gathered in small groups, talking and sipping coffee.

She spotted Matt sitting next to the director by the windows. When he saw her, he rose and broke into a wide smile.

"Hey," he said, walking over to her, "I heard you were going to be in the cast! Great!"

Nina smiled back, startled again by his blue eyes.

"Thanks," she said. "It didn't quite turn out the way I had hoped, but what can you do?" She shrugged.

"Nothing," said Matt.

"I am glad that you made the cut," said Nina. "Are you playing Martin?"

"Yes," said Matt, "the one we read."

"Well, that's terrific!" said Nina, genuinely happy for him.

"Come, let me introduce you to Nick," he said.

They walked over to where Nick Travis was sitting, giving notes to his assistant. At a pause in their conversation, Matt leaned over, "Nick, I think you know Nina Landau."

Nick sprang to his feet and took her hand in both of his, smiling warmly.

"Welcome. Welcome. I am so delighted to have you in the cast."

"Thank you," said Nina.

The warmth of his smile washed over her. Nick Travis. He oozed testosterone. He was not particularly tall, probably around five-ten, but he was muscular with dark brown curly hair and hazel eyes. He gave the impression that he had never suffered a moment's doubt in his life. You just knew that once you put yourself into his hands, nothing could ever go wrong. A good quality for a director, Nina thought. He seemed to move around in the center of a magnetic field that drew people to him. Nina could feel herself lit by the reflected glow of his smile and felt the electricity in the touch of his hands. Remembering Tom's comment, "He'll be in your pants in five minutes," Nina blushed in spite of herself.

She often developed a crush on her directors. By now she figured it was just part of her process. A good director was a father figure, a psychologist, and a lover all rolled into one. He spoke with you about the intimate emotions of your character. He showed you the door to walk through to achieve a genuine characterization but never told you how to do it, just led you in the right direction and gave you the tools, the confidence, and the encouragement you needed to find it yourself. Nick Travis was notorious for having affairs with his leading ladies. Nina wondered, briefly, if he also had affairs with the maids?

The door opened and a tall dark-haired woman in her late thirties walked in. Her perfume preceded her. Designer sunglasses were perched on the top of her head, and her nails were painted the same fire engine red as her dress. So were her lips. She had on three-inch high heels made of clear plastic with sparkles inside them. She carried a Louis Vuitton tote bag, a real one, not the knock off that Nina had purchased from a street vendor on the corner of Seventy-ninth Street and Second Avenue. Nick excused himself and went to greet her. All the attention in the room shifted to Diana Lawrence, and Nina walked over and sat down on one of the metal chairs. Matt came over and sat next to her. "Diana Lawrence," he whispered to her. She nodded.

Diana Lawrence made a point of going around and extending her long, red-tipped fingers to each person in turn. She was wearing a stack of gold bracelets that clanked every time she raised or lowered her arm. She was perfectly coiffed. If Central Casting had been asked to supply an actor to play "the leading lady," Diana's name would have been first on the list. She smiled with a bright but cold smile. She pressed her long fingers lightly into each hand, looked intently into each person's eyes, and said her name, as though they didn't know it. *Noblesse oblige,* Nina thought.

When her turn came, she met Diana's gaze with a smile, squelching the urge to curtsey.

An older man came into the room cautiously, as though he wasn't sure he had arrived at the right place. He is probably playing the lawyer, Nina thought. Nick rushed over to greet him.

After everyone had arrived, Nick walked to the center of the room.

"Okay," he said, clapping his hands for attention. "Will everyone please take a seat." He waited for everyone to be seated.

"I am happy to welcome you all to the first day of rehearsals," he said. "We have a very exciting play and an extremely talented cast. The casting process was done with great care, and I hope you know that those of you who are sitting here are the very best! Give yourselves a hand."

There was a smattering of applause, and the actors smiled nervously at each other. He then went on to introduce his assistant, a woman named Kelly; the playwright, George DuPont; the stage manager, Wallace; the assistant stage manager, Kelsey; and John Tatten, the set designer. Nick then introduced the cast. Nick introduced two women as Renee Ballinger, playing Martin's wife, and Charlotte Ways, who was understudying both the wife and the maid. Nina was thrilled at the thought of having an understudy! There were two African American men: one was playing Tony, Martin's best friend, and the other was his understudy. Nick introduced them as Demond Daniels and Shawn Johnson, respectively. As Nick turned his attention to Nina and announced that she would be understudying the part of Melanie and playing the maid, she felt the color rise in her cheeks. She nodded gamely and smiled.

"Okay, now John will explain the set to you. John? It's all yours."

Nick sat down and picked up his coffee. The set designer,

a short, slight man, came over to the piano and uncovered the model of the set that was sitting on top of it. There was a gasp from the group. There sat the living room of an elegant Upper East Side, New York City duplex apartment, complete with a stairway going up to the second floor and doors going off, stage right, stage left and upstage center. On the floor was a miniature Oriental rug, plush furniture upholstered in a pale chartreuse, and a chandelier. It was stunning! The cast burst into spontaneous applause. John smiled and inclined his head before he explained where each of the doors led and then returned to his chair.

"Okay," said Nick, "we'll take a ten-minute break. There's a soda machine down the hall, and if you are desperate for coffee, I'm sure Kelly can call down to the coffee shop and have some sent up. We'll resume in ten with a full read-through of the play. Any questions?"

No one spoke. They all stood gathering their things and readying themselves for the read-through. Diana made a beeline for Nick and together they walked over to the model of the set and were deep in discussion, gesticulating to various doors and pieces of furniture. Nina only had one line, so there wasn't too much preparation she could do.

Matt turned to her, "I've been looking for an apartment to sublet. You don't happen to know of any, do you?"

"Not off hand, but I'll keep my ears open," she said. Then she had a sudden thought.

"Why don't you put your name on the bulletin board up at the Equity office? There are often sublet apartments posted there. You know, people who are going out of town."

"Good idea" said Matt. "I'll stop by after rehearsal. Is that the one on...Forty-Fifth Street?"

"Forty-Sixth," said Nina, smiling, "I'll take you, if you'd like."

"Thanks!" said Matt. "I'd appreciate that!"

When the ten minutes were up, they were asked to

bring their chairs into a semicircle. Matt and Nina dragged theirs, scraping and squeaking, and sat down next to each other. Nina took her script from her tote bag and opened it. Laughter trilled from Diana Lawrence's throat as she hugged Nick and took a seat in the center. The stage manager asked if everyone was ready to begin. There was silence.

"Okay then," he said, and he started reading the stage directions: "Music. Lights come up on a living room in an Upper East Side apartment in New York City. The stage is empty. The music builds to a crescendo and Tony, Martin's best friend, enters from down stage right. The music fades as Tony speaks."

"Martin? Are you here?" read Demond.

"I'm in the bedroom," said Matt, loudly, as though speaking from another room. "Make yourself comfortable. I'll be out in a minute."

All of a sudden the sound of Diana's clanking bracelets broke the mood. She made a show of how embarrassed she was, hanging her head down to her knees and letting her hair fall forward over her face. Then she sat up and mouthed, "I'm sorry," pointedly taking the bracelets off, one at a time, and placing them in her purse. She put her index finger against her lips. Matt smiled, good naturedly, and continued.

"Tony! So good to see you. Thanks for coming 'round."

As the reading continued, Nina noted how good all the actors were. They had a professionalism, a certain patina about them that had obviously been acquired from experience. When they reached the second act and Nina's part, she sat forward in her seat.

"Sir, there is someone at the door who wishes to see you," she said.

"Show them in," said Matt, as Martin.

She sat back. She was done. She listened until they came to the end of the play, concentrating on the part of Melanie. Diana read her part well, with a calm, sophisticated elegance. She had a patrician beauty, and every time she bent over the script, her hair fell seductively over one side of her face. She would flick it back with a toss of her head or sometimes tuck it behind her ear with her long red fingernails. She crossed her legs often, pulling down her short skirt each time. But it crept right back up again, revealing toned, tanned thighs. Nina saw Matt's eyes travel to her legs and felt a pang of jealousy. Matt brought the part of Martin to life, making him both funny and virile, much more so than the script revealed, Nina thought. She could see, immediately, why he had been cast.

When the reading ended, they all applauded themselves. The actors rose and stretched. Nina looked at Matt with admiration.

"You were wonderful!" she whispered to him.

"Thanks," he replied, smiling, sheepishly.

"Excellent!" said Nick, applauding. "Excellent! That will do it for today. I have some meetings. Go home. Get some rest. We'll meet here again tomorrow, ten. Good work."

Diana stood up and bent to put her script back into her tote bag, exposing the back of her legs all the way up to her panty line. Nina watched Matt's eyes taking it all in.

"Do you want to go over to the Equity building now?" she asked him, pointedly.

"If it's no trouble," he said, shifting his gaze to her.

"None at all; it's right up the block. Come. I'll show you."

They left and walked to Forty-Sixth Street where the Actors' Equity Association Office was located. Up in the Membership Department actors were sitting around, scanning *Backstage* and the other professional papers, drinking coffee, and chatting with their fellow thespians. The receptionist handed Matt an index card which he filled out with his name and telephone number and tacked it up on the bulletin board. Then he started to read some of the available listings.

"This looks good," he said, pointing to an index card on the board: "Wanted: single person to house-sit and cat-sit for four months. Rent low (because of the cat). Four thirty-five East Seventy-Seventh Street." There was a phone number.

"That's not far from me." said Nina.

"Even better," said Matt, writing the number on a piece of paper.

"Come. Let me buy you a drink to thank you for your help."

"I'd love to have a drink," said Nina, "but you don't need to buy it."

"We'll argue about it later," said Matt. "Let's go! I could use a drink!"

They headed west to Joe Allen and were greeted warmly by the same hostess who had been there before. She sat them at the same table in the back, on the bar side. They ordered two glasses of wine. Nina's heart was buoyed up and beating fast. As they took their seats, a middle-aged, heavy-set woman came up to Matt.

"Excuse me," she said, "But aren't you Matthew Ryland?"

"That's me," said Matt.

"Oh, I loved you on *The Heart Knows All!*" said the woman. "Would you mind signing my program?"

She offered Matt a playbill.

"Sure!" said Matt and took the program from her, fishing in his jacket pocket for a pen.

"What's your name?" he asked, leaning over the table.

"Lisa," said the woman. He wrote "To Lisa," on the program and added his scrawling signature.

"Thank you!" said the woman, studying the autograph. Then she flurried back into the adjoining room.

Nina sat and stared at Matt for a moment. "You were on *The Heart Knows All?*"

Matt nodded.

"I thought I knew you from somewhere!"

"Oh," said Matt, "You never saw *The Crescent Moon Café* but you saw me on *The Heart Knows All?*"

"I guess so," Nina said, embarrassed.

Their talk turned to the read-through, Nick Travis, and the set. They finished their drinks, and Matt excused himself to go to the phone booths and check his answering service. When he returned, he sat back down at the table, smiling.

"Any auditions?" asked Nina.

"Nah, just a message to call my girlfriend in California. I'll call her when I get back to the apartment."

"Mmm," said Nina, nodding and smiling gamely. Her heart plunged like an elevator that had slipped its cable. Matt insisted on paying. As they left the restaurant, Nina said hurriedly, "I think I see the 104 coming. That's my bus. I hope you don't mind if I run to catch it. I have to get home and…work on my line."

"Sure" said Matt, grinning. "See you tomorrow."

CHAPTER FIVE

The Move to the Theater

The next morning at rehearsal Matt told Nina he had taken the Seventy-Seventh Street apartment. He'd gone to see it and said it was a great space in an elevator building, exactly what he was looking for.

"How's the cat?" asked Nina.

"Never saw him. He was hiding under the bed."

All the metal chairs in the room had been moved against the wall except for those that were representing the couch and the armchairs on the set. Nick Travis began blocking the play. The actors were getting up on their feet and figuring out their moves. Nina took down Melanie's blocking. She probably wouldn't get many understudy rehearsals, so she needed to get the lines and the blocking memorized quickly and be ready to assume the role the moment she was called upon. She watched intently whenever Diana was working on a scene with Nick and listened to their discussions of the character and her motivations. She knew she had been hired to step in and take over in case of an emergency, not to bring her own personality to the part. Her obligation was to create a whole character while not straying too far from the portrait created by Diana. This was the dilemma of being an understudy, and Nina knew it well. She could become a character as easily as she used to playact as a child. But she would need to rein in some of her own instincts in order to conform to Diana's performance and not throw off the rest of the cast if she were suddenly called upon to go on.

Nina was an instinctive actor. She had never taken an acting lesson per se. She had studied theater at college and had taken lessons in voice, fencing, and movement. If you didn't know how to use your voice and your body, you wouldn't be able to sustain a performance for eight shows a week. Each performance she did on stage had sharpened her acting skills. Acting is like gardening, Eva Le Gallienne had said, you couldn't learn it from a book. You had to get out there and do it. Nina had talked at length about different methods of acting with all her theater friends. Everyone had a different theory about what worked for them. They were all valid. There just was no such thing as "one size fits all" when it came to acting. You had to pick and choose whatever process enabled you to do that magic thing of slipping into another person's skin without any self-consciousness.

For Katharine Hepburn, understanding a character was key. Once you had steeped yourself in a character, things would emerge, unspoken things that would bring it to life. Nina found that advice extremely helpful. The great acting teacher, Uta Hagen used to insist—find out what the character wants! Nina asked herself the question: What did Melanie want? What was her motivation? What had made her come back to this husband she had divorced years before? The answer was simple: Melanie wanted to have a baby! Not just any baby, but a baby with the right person. And that person was her ex-husband.

Some actors worked from the inside out, rummaging around in their psyches, dreaming up backstories for emotional connections to their characters and imagining what was inside the purse or suitcase they carried onto the stage.

Others worked from the outside in, needing to know what the character looked like, padding their breasts, coloring their hair, adding glasses, hairpieces, or false noses. Looking like the character sometimes made it easier to feel like the character. Nina once ran into a friend on the bus and was startled to find that he had one green eye and one brown eye.

"What's wrong with your eyes?" she asked.

"I'm playing the part of a psychotic killer in a film," her friend said, "and I want to look disconcerting. So I got one green contact lens."

Whatever worked. As long as your character was built from the inner part of your own soul, your own understanding of how he talked, moved, looked, thought...as long as you revealed that part of yourself that was like the character, it would prove to be a genuine portrayal.

Nina had no trouble relating to Melanie. She had always had an intense desire for a warm family life that included children. Her childhood dreams featured a station wagon full of kids. However, another part of her wanted to be an actor. She believed in her talent and knew that, given the chance, she could show that she was as good as the best of them. It was a driving force within her. Did it outweigh her desire for children? She was thirty-two. She didn't want to go through her life childless. How much longer could she concentrate on her career at the expense of her biological clock? So many of the actors she knew had chosen their careers over motherhood. And so many had regrets. Were the two mutually exclusive? She was determined not to have regrets. She wanted it all!

The weeks flew by. Rehearsals were intense and exciting. As the cast watched from the sidelines, emotional truths were revealed, and comic breakthroughs achieved. The characters slowly began to come alive.

The weather had turned cooler. The beeches, elms, oaks and maples in Central Park each began their own, unique sacrament to fall, with burnt offerings of reds and browns and purples. Fall in New York brought not only a crispness to the air but an excitement in the theater community about the upcoming Broadway season, especially the new Nick Travis play.

Nina dressed in jeans and sweaters. Diana was still wearing short skirts that showed off her legs. A lot of the actors were already off-book. The stage manager, Wallace, watched the rehearsals, taking down changes in blocking and monitoring the words, ready to interject if anyone cut a speech or needed a line. Being off-book made it so much easier for the actors to play the scenes.

Nina cued Matt on his lines whenever they had a spare minute. They went out into the hall to run his scenes. They usually took the bus home together since her stop was the one right before his. And when Nina boarded the bus in the morning, she frequently found Matt sitting there. His face lit up as he watched her making her way down the aisle to him. It was impossible not to smile back. As she sat down next to him, her arm would occasionally graze his, causing a frisson throughout her body. There was no denying the attraction they had for each other. Nina found herself checking the mirror, adding lipstick and a little eye makeup before she left the apartment to do her errands...on the chance that she might run into him in the laundromat, the grocery store, the drugstore...

Finally, after weeks of rehearsal, the day arrived for the cast to make the move from the rehearsal hall to the theater. The excitement was infectious. They were going to be performing in the Barrymore Theatre, on West Forty-Seventh Street, the heart of Broadway. There was a sign-in sheet at the stage door with a pencil dangling next to it. The names of all the cast members were printed on a grid that listed the rehearsal schedule. As Nina took the pencil carefully initialing the spot next to her name with a large "NL," a thrill went through her. Excited, she made her way into the auditorium, smiling at the busy stagehands and put her bags down on one of the velour seats. The Barrymore! The Ethel Barrymore Theatre! The famous actor had performed here, on this very stage. A portrait of her hung in the lobby. The heavy crimson curtain was open, and a tech crew was working up on the stage. The banging and sawing and clanking sounds spread through the theater. The smell of sawdust was in the air and some had settled on the plush seats nearest the stage. High above the apron that protruded out into the audience, lights were being hung on a metal grid. Cables, dimmers, heavy instruments, and gels were strewn over the dark, claret-colored seats. In the back of the auditorium, a balcony rose up to a ceiling covered with gilded designs and mosaics. A giant crystal chandelier was suspended over the middle of the auditorium. The whole theater pulsated with lights and gold and anticipation.

The cast had been assigned their dressing rooms. Nina's was up three flights of metal stairs. "Ms. Landau" was printed on a small placard on the door. Opening the door to her own dressing room and sitting down at her makeup table with bright light bulbs surrounding the mirror, Nina felt like a movie star. On the wall of the dressing room was an intercom, a "squawk box," that transmitted the sound from the stage into every dressing room, so the actors could hear the play and know when to prepare for their entrances.

Matt arrived at her dressing room out of breath.

"You're going to have to learn how to play the harp!" he said.

She laughed. She didn't care. She spread out her purple towel in front of the mirror and on it she placed her pancake makeup and sponge, eye shadow, rouge and brushes, lipstick and eyebrow pencil, brush and comb. Matisse must have felt just like this, she thought, laying out his paints and paintbrushes before he created his canvas. Her face was her canvas, and she loved painting it before each performance to look like the face of her character.

Diana was in the star dressing room, just offstage right, so her costume changes could be accomplished quickly. It consisted of two rooms: a spacious sitting room with a couch and easy chairs for visitors and an adjoining room which contained the makeup table and a rack for her costumes.

The heat was on in the theater, and the clanging and hissing of the old steam pipes was a contrapuntal addition to the excitement. Cold weather was coming, the first preview, the holiday season.

Nick gathered the cast in the front of the auditorium.

"I have some notes before we get up on the stage for the first time," he said. Behind them, a tech crew was noisily working. They had set up a large white board over the tops of the seats in the auditorium and the lighting design was taped to it.

"Guys? May I have quiet for a minute, please?"

The crew quieted down.

"Okay, Matt? Where are you?" Nick looked up from his notes.

Matt raised his hand.

"Matt, I would like to excise that speech, beginning on page twenty-two, your speech to Tony."

Matt reached for his script.

"Excise?" he said, "As in to cut?"

"Yeah," Nick said, "I'm afraid so. They play is running long and we all have to make some sacrifices."

Matt winced. Nina reached for her own script and made the cut. She cast a quick, sympathetic look at Matt. Their eyes met. That was the speech he had worked so hard to memorize the night before. More speeches were cut after that. Nina noticed that Diana retained all of hers.

"Also," Nick continued, "Matt and Diana, the scene between the two of you at the end of the play? It's the denouement. All the threads are coming together. It should be sharp, quick, building to a crescendo. As it is, it's dragging."

"You mean faster?" asked Diana.

"No. Not so much faster as…tighter. Pick up your cues." Matt and Diana nodded.

"Renee, watch that you don't steal focus from Matt during his speech. You are awfully busy. Can you keep the movement down to a minimum?"

Renee nodded.

"Okay, then. Any questions?" asked Nick.

Diana raised her hand.

"I wonder if I could be further stage center when I give that speech to Martin in the second act," she asked. "The one that begins 'the divorce was your idea…' I think it's a pivotal moment in the play, and it's getting lost with me stuck behind the couch."

Nick hesitated. Then said, "Let's try it today and see how it looks. Anything else?" No hands went up.

"Okay," said Nick, "If there's nothing else, rehearsal will begin…" he checked his watch, "in ten minutes."

The first rehearsal on the stage did not go smoothly. The play seemed to sag like a collapsed soufflé as the cast struggled to adjust to the new cuts and the new surroundings. The stage manager had meticulously reproduced the measurements of the set on the rehearsal floor, in chalk, but once they were on the Broadway stage, the distances seemed much greater. They now found themselves on a raked stage, which was entirely different from walking on a flat surface. They also had to get used to the set. Sitting on the upholstered couch was totally unlike sitting on the three metal chairs that had stood in for the couch in the rehearsal hall. Using the actual props instead of the rehearsal props also stymied them. Real coffee cups clattered on their saucers, unlike their Styrofoam stand-ins. Many of the actors were so rattled the lines flew out of their heads. Gone were the laughs. Gone were the touching emotional moments. By the end of the rehearsal, everyone was ready to quit show business. Theater was like gossamer, Nina thought: the slightest thing could skew the magic and make it fizzle out.

"Well," said Nick, with a sigh, "they say the French throw away their first pancake. We'll try it again tomorrow. Get some sleep."

"We may end up on Joe Allen's wall after all" Matt whispered, as he passed Nina in the hall.

Nina was changing out of her rehearsal skirt when there was a knock at the dressing room door.

"Come in," she said, quickly pulling on her jeans.

Nick Travis came through the door. He closed it behind him.

"I wanted to run something by you," he said.

"Oh, okay," said Nina, apprehensively.

He pulled up a chair and sat down. Nina sat down at the makeup table and waited for him to speak.

"I need you in the beginning of the play."

There was a long pause. Nina tried to make sense of his words.

"I need an actor I can depend on, on the stage, in the beginning. I need to establish that it's a comedy. I'm not sure how. I have to play around with it. Are you on board?"

Nina nodded slowly, puzzled.

"You have a good sense of comedy. The audience has to know, right off the bat, that they are allowed to laugh. That this is not a mystery, like George's first play, *Spoiler Alert*."

Nina nodded again, slowly. Then she spoke. "So, you mean…after the music stops, I enter and go to answer the doorbell?"

"Exactly!" said Nick.

"Before Tony comes in?" asked Nina.

"Yes," said Nick, "Can you do that for me?"

"Sure," said Nina, slowly drawing out the word.

Nick stood up. He put a hand on her arm.

"You're awfully good, you know," he said, looking into her eyes. "Come early tomorrow. We'll rehearse it before the run-through. Okay?"

"Okay," said Nina.

Nick paused, looked at her for a moment, then, as if changing his mind, said, "See you tomorrow." He patted her arm, winked, and left.

She sat for a moment, thinking about what he had said. He wanted her to open the play. I can do comedy, she thought. I'm best at comedy. But how do you make a comedic entrance with no words? She stopped her reverie, grabbed her jacket, and ran downstairs to tell Matt.

CHAPTER SIX

The Dinner Date

Matt was waiting for her by the stage door.

"I'll buy you dinner if you can run some of the scenes with me. I need to learn those cuts."

"You don't need to buy me dinner," said Nina, "I have to learn Melanie's lines so that would actually be a big help."

"Terrific!" said Matt, "Done!"

They left the theater and caught the Fiftieth Street crosstown bus to the East Side. On the ride home, Nina told Matt about the conversation with Nick.

"How are you going to make something funny without any lines?" Matt asked.

"Ha! Good question!" said Nina. "I have no idea. I'll have to think of something…" But she wondered how she would accomplish it.

At Third Avenue, they caught the uptown bus to Seventy-Ninth Street. They looked in the windows of a local Italian restaurant.

"Looks good," said Nina. "Let's try it. I'm starving!"

Red and white checkered tablecloths were on the tables along with candles in raffia covered Chianti bottles; low sconces illuminated the black and white photographs of Italy on the walls. They sat down at a table, and Matt ordered a bottle of wine. The menu was written on a blackboard on the wall, and they both studied it.

The waiter brought over the wine and poured them each a glass, setting the bottle on the table. Matt sighed and sat back in his seat.

"Diana is driving me crazy," he confessed. "She upstages me all the time. Every time she speaks, she takes a tiny step upstage. In order to answer her I have to face away from the audience. The audience is never going to know who's playing Martin unless they look in the program!"

"Why don't you take a tiny step upstage every time you answer her?" asked Nina.

"We'll end up at the back wall of the theater by the end of the scene!"

"Well, maybe then Nick will have to say something to her!" said Nina.

"Oh, Nick will let Diana get away with anything."

"Well," Nina sighed, "I suppose there are advantages to sleeping with the director."

Matt picked up his glass and held it out toward Nina. She quickly picked up her own glass.

"Cheers!" said Matt.

The waiter returned with a basket of bread.

"Do you know what you want?" asked Matt.

Nina nodded and the waiter took their dinner orders.

"She couldn't get away with that on a film set," said Matt, reaching for a roll. "If she moved away from her mark, she'd be out of focus."

Nina laughed.

"That would serve her right!" she said.

"And all those big gestures of hers. You've done film work, right?" asked Matt, buttering a roll. "I mean the camera probes your inner thoughts. It records everything in such minute detail. It is right there, two inches away! Not a hundred feet away, like in the theater. You just can't get away with those large gestures."

"Actually," said Nina, "I've hardly done any film work at all. The only time I did a television show, I was scared out of my wits! I took the scenes home, memorized all my lines, and when I arrived for work the next morning, they took away my script and handed me a whole new one...on a different color paper! We had about an hour to learn the new lines and then shoot the scene. I was practically catatonic!"

"Yeah, but if you screwed up, the director yelled, 'cut' and you got to do it again. In theater, there is no such thing. It's over. You've screwed up in front of hundreds of people!"

Nina smiled. "You'll be fine," she said, sympathetically. "You'll learn how to recover."

"I'm not so sure. I'm not so sure." Matt said dubiously, sipping his wine.

"I guess stage is more of an actor's medium. Once a stage director finishes the rehearsal process, he leaves. Film is the director's medium. In film, it's the actor who goes away once the scene is in the can, and the director stays on to tinker with the product."

"But the character still has to come from the same real base, right?" asked Nina. "I mean, you still have to create a whole human being."

"Of course!" said Matt, agreeing. "Arguably more so in film. But there are so many differences! In film, you have to allow the camera to come to you. What I mean by that is, you can't be acting for the audience as you do in the theater. You have to let the camera do that work for you. It's completely different." He sat back and put down his wine.

"There's an old Alan Ladd story," he said. "He came back from a long day of shooting out in the dusty Arizona desert, with his spurs and, you know, his hat, and someone said, 'Did you have a good day, Alan?' 'Yup,' he said, 'a couple of good looks.'"

The waiter brought their food to the table.

"I don't know. I think I may be in over my head. I've never acted on Broadway. I'm used to doing one or two takes and then you go home and have a beer."

Nina nodded, sympathetically, put a napkin on her lap, and helped herself to a roll. They sat quietly eating.

"Mmm. This is delicious," said Nina, looking up. "How's yours?"

"Great!" said Matt, with a mouthful. "We'll definitely come back here." He reached for his wine.

"What did you order?" asked Nina, looking at his plate of food.

"Rigatoni Bolognese," said Matt. "Want a taste?"

"Mmm," said Nina, nodding. Matt speared a piece of rigatoni with his fork and held it out to her. Nina hesitated for a moment and then put her lips around the fork and withdrew the pasta.

"Yummy," she said as she chewed, "Want a taste of mine?"

"Sure" said Matt.

Nina stabbed a piece of her pasta and held the fork out to Matt.

"What is it?" asked Matt, skeptically, looking at the food.

"Fiocchi," said Nina.

"What is that?"

"I have no idea," said Nina: "I like to experiment. I think it's got ricotta in it. Go on. Try it. It's delicious."

Nina watched as his lips closed around the pasta. A shiver went through her. She withdrew the fork and waited for his reaction. He chewed, slowly. Nina tried to tear her eyes away from his mouth.

"That is really nice" Matt said, suggestively, looking at her face.

Nina could feel herself blush.

"To us" Matt said, amused by her nervousness, raising his glass and winking at her.

"Matt," said Nina, "Honestly? I think you're worrying way too much. I'm there at rehearsal every day. I see what you're doing. You are so good in this part. You're going to be fine. I think you're just experiencing nerves that come about this time in rehearsal when people are putting their scripts down and the whole thing is suddenly starting to look real…like it's not just a rehearsal anymore—you're actually going to be doing it in front of an audience."

Matt sighed, "Yeah, okay, but how about a long run? How do you make it real after you have said those lines a hundred…two hundred times? How do you keep it from getting stale? You tell me! I've never done a long run. What the hell am I going to do?"

Nina laughed, "Let's hope that's going to be a problem that we will have to deal with," she said.

Matt leaned in, suddenly, and reached for her hand across the table.

"Come out to California with me," he said, urgently. "Act in front of a camera. I'll teach you. You'd be wonderful."

Nina looked into his eyes for a long moment. They were so brilliantly blue. She caught her breath. *Oh God! Don't look at me with those blue eyes!*

"I think we'd better get to work on those lines," she said, retrieving her hand. Her heart was thumping against her chest.

They finished their meal, and Matt reached for the check. Nina insisted they split it. As they got up to leave the restaurant, one of the waitresses approached Matt, shyly.

"Excuse me. Are you Cal Danforth?" she asked.

Matt nodded and smiled.

"That's me," he said.

"Oh, I thought so!" she said excitedly, looking around at two other waitresses giggling and peeking around the kitchen door.

When they walked out of the restaurant, Nina turned to Matt, "Cal Danforth?" she asked, puzzled.

"Yeah, the television series," explained Matt. "The one you never saw."

"Well, there you go!" said Nina, "Talk about the differences between film and stage! Nobody recognizes me, and I must have done at least…twenty plays"

"They will," he said.

They went up to Matt's apartment. Nina had seen it briefly once before. It was a large, open, one-room loft with a skylight and a kitchen at one end. The windows faced east, and through them you could see the boats on the East River. It was a spectacular apartment, and Matt knew how lucky he was to have found it. It was a four-month lease from a director who was doing a film for television in Canada. Murray, the cat, came to greet them at the door. Nina excused herself and went into the bathroom. She looked at herself in the mirror, freshened her lipstick, and combed her hair. She wasn't going to let this moment pass her by. Life was short, and Matt's girlfriend was far away in California.

They both got their scripts. Nina slipped off her shoes and tucked her legs under her on the couch. Matt paced back and forth in front of her. They worked for about two hours, reading the scenes over and over with the new cuts. By ten thirty, they were both able to play the scenes without their scripts.

"I don't think I can fit any more words in my brain," Nina said as she stood up and put her shoes back on.

Matt stretched.

"Thanks so much," he said, yawning, "I feel much more confident about the lines. Now if I could only find the character…"

"Are you crazy?" Nina said, adamantly. "Listen to me, Matt. You have that character knocked. You are so good in it. I see the whole scope of Martin's personality in your portrayal. It is so full, so true. You're wrong if you don't think so!"

Matt smiled at her enthusiasm.

"You are so sweet," he said.

"I mean it," said Nina, opening her eyes wide for believability.

"Yes," said Matt, "I know you do."

He reached out a hand and touched her cheek, gently. He studied her face, then dropped his eyes to her mouth, absently wetting his bottom lip with the tip of his tongue. Nina's heartbeat quickened. If he doesn't kiss me, I'm going to die, she thought. Suddenly he dropped his hand.

"You better go," he said, looking down.

Nina stood still for a moment and then got her coat from under the cat who had been sleeping on it. Matt helped her brush off the cat hair. She stopped, abruptly, and closed one eye.

"I think I got something in my eye," she said.

"Probably a cat hair," said Matt.

Nina carefully stretched her upper eyelid over the bottom one and then blinked.

They both waited.

"Nope," she said. "Still there."

Matt moved closer to her.

"Let me see."

He bent over, put both hands on her face and gently pulled down the lower lid of her eye.

"Look up," he said.

Nina looked up.

Matt bent and moved his face sideways and closer to Nina's.

"Hold on," he said, "I think I see it..."

Licking his middle finger, he gently wiped the cat hair from her eye.

"Try now," he said, pulling back a little.

Nina blinked.

"I think you got it," she said.

She looked up at him. His lips were much too close. She felt a gravitational pull to close the small distance between them. Every part of her body ached with desire for him. *Oh God, kiss me, please kiss me!* Matt searched her eyes and then lowered his gaze to her mouth again. He put both his hands on her face and slowly, gently pressed his lips to hers. She closed her eyes and felt a rush of warmth flood her body, as though someone had injected her with a vial of cocaine.

Oh, God! thought Nina, *I want to feel like this forever.*

They pulled apart slowly and Matt gazed at her.

"See you tomorrow," he whispered.

Nina mouthed, "…tomorrow."

CHAPTER SEVEN

Nick Travis

The cast was assembled in the auditorium for notes. When the note session ended, Nick pointed to Roger, Matt's understudy, and to Nina.

"Roger and Nina, before you leave the theater tonight, I need you two to meet me in the costume room to discuss your understudy costumes."

The cast gathered up their belongings and went to their dressing rooms to change into their street clothes. Nina put on her slippers and silk kimono that she used as a makeup robe and went down the stairs to the costume room.

Roger was already there. They talked for a while about learning lines and getting together to run their scenes and their eagerness for understudy rehearsals to begin. Roger had the same physique as Matt, and he didn't think that he would have a problem fitting into Matt's costumes. But Nina was about an inch shorter and more curvaceous than Diana, and she was concerned that Diana's costumes might not fit. By the time Nick finally walked in, most of the people had gone home, and the theater had an empty ring to it.

Roger easily fit into Matt's first act costume. Nick nodded and said they could forgo trying on the rest. Roger wished them a good night, and the door clanged shut behind him. Nina suddenly felt vulnerable, standing there in her kimono in the cool, empty room, alone with Nick. But he smiled, putting her at ease.

"Okay," he said, "Let's start with the first act costume, the suit, shall we?"

Nina went to the costume rack and found the hanger that had the red wool suit on it. She took it behind the screen that was set up for changing. She slipped out of her kimono and hung it on a hook. Reaching up to take the suit off the hanger, she had a strange feeling at the back of her neck that she was being watched. She glanced over her shoulder and saw Nick standing at the open end of the screen. She looked at him. He stared at her. Then he turned, went to the door of the costume room, and locked it. Nina's mind started to race. What should she do? Nick returned and walked through the opening of the screen. He put his hands on her bare shoulders and bent to kiss her, lightly, gently brushing her lips. Then he stopped, pulled away and looked at her, quizzically, as if to ask permission. Nina felt a shiver go through her entire body. She closed her eyes and tilted her face up to his. Why not? she thought. *Give me one reason why not?*

He kissed her again, lingering for a longer time and then pulled back.

"Take your bra off," he said, softly.

Nina's arms started to reach behind her and then she hesitated.

"Shall I take it off for you?" Nick asked.

Nina gave a barely perceptible nod. Nick reached behind her and unhooked her bra. The straps fell down on her arms. He slowly peeled the bra off, and her breasts sprang free. He ran his fingers over them and kissed each one, cupping them in his large hands. Nina felt her nipples harden. She closed her eyes. He kissed her lips, again, with more urgency. Suddenly, she pressed her lips to his and felt his mouth open. The tip of his tongue was soft but insistent.

Her heart was pounding in her chest. She parted her lips and let him into her mouth, into a deep, long, greedy kiss. She pressed her breasts into his torso, grinding her hips into his pelvis, feeling the rough texture of his shirt and jeans on her tender skin. She wanted to be consumed by him. They broke apart. Nick looked at her.

"Take off your panties," he whispered.

There was no going back. It was done. Over. Apparently, he does have affairs with the maids, she thought. Other women have done this, why shouldn't I? You don't have to be a good girl all of the time. She reached down and stepped out of her lace thong. As she stood back up, her chest felt constricted, and her breaths short, but she held his gaze.

"Nina," said Nick, allowing his eyes to trail over her body from head to toe. "Look at you! Look at your body! You are so beautiful!"

He took her hand and led her out from behind the screen. He backed her up against the costume worktable. Nina gasped as he lifted her onto the table. He kissed her deeply, stopping just long enough to undo his belt and unzip his jeans. He was breathing hard.

"Spread your legs," he whispered.

Nina felt all the juices of her body release. She was ready for him. He eased himself into her and stopped only for a moment before he slowly started to thrust. She threw her head back. *In, in, in,* was all she could think. The rest of the world receded. There was only Nick and the need for him to fill her. She gripped his hips with her fingernails. Thrusting harder and faster, the table started to move, the steam pipes began clanging and hissing, the garbage truck squealed, and the clanking of the garbage cans came up from the street outside her bedroom window and she woke.

She lay staring at the ceiling. It was a dream. A dream. Her heart was still beating rapidly, and she reached down between her legs. She was all wet. She sat up in bed and rested her forehead on the heel of her hand. *What in the world?* She stayed like that for a while, going over the dream. She shook her head to clear it, got out of bed, and went into the kitchen. She opened the refrigerator and took out a pitcher of cold water, poured herself a glass, and drank it by the light of the open refrigerator. Then she sat down at the table and stared out the window as the dawn gradually started to prepare for the arrival of the sun, with florid colors of pink and orange.

CHAPTER EIGHT

The Understudy Rehearsal

Nina left for the theater early, hoping to work with Nick on the new opening for the play. She had come up with an idea and was anxious to show it to him. But once at the theater, she heard him immersed in a heated discussion with Diana behind her dressing room door. She had left too early for Matt to be on the bus that morning. When she finally saw him come into the theater, her heartbeat quickened, but she avoided looking at him, and with a studied nonchalance, she made a point of talking and laughing loudly with another cast member. She was keenly aware that his eyes were on her. When she finally turned and met his gaze, their eyes locked in a long, searing look and time stood still in the echoing theater.

The first audience was due in a little over a week and tensions were running high. They were nowhere near ready for an audience. The cast gathered in the auditorium for notes before the rehearsal, all except for Diana who was nowhere to be seen. Nick faced them, leaning against the proscenium.

"Roger and Nina," he said, taking off his glasses and looking up from his notes. "Right after rehearsal, will you two report to the costume room for your understudy costume fittings?"

Nina felt a flush rise to her cheeks, recalling her dream. "Renee?"

Nick looked up and sought out the actor playing Martin's wife.

"Watch those sight lines. The rule is, if you can see the audience, the audience can see you. I could see you standing in the wings before your entrance."

Renee nodded.

"Leonard, project, please. You have to fill the whole theater with your voice. We are no longer in the rehearsal room."

"Demond," Nick continued. "Louder and clearer in the first act. Enunciate, please. You are at the top of the play. The audience is just getting used to hearing words coming from the stage. We need to understand you."

"Got it!" said Demond.

Nick looked around. "Props, can we please get a wedding ring for Matt to wear? The play is about the fact that he is married…"

Kelly nodded and made a note for the prop people.

There was a loud commotion in the wings, and Diana appeared on the stage. Her hair was in pin curls under a stocking cap, in preparation for a wig. She was carrying the wig in her hands and waving it around. She took a stance in the center of the stage and shouted at Nick.

"I am not going to wear this…this thing on my head! It is repulsive. It makes me look like…Golda Meir!"

She threw the wig across the stage floor.

Suzie, a transgender Trinidadian woman who was in charge of the wigs, came flying out of the wings.

"Oh, please! Please, Diana," she said, rushing to retrieve the wig.

"You tell…her…him…whatever it is," Diana continued, "I am Miss Lawrence to her." Then she turned to Suzie "Don't you Diana me, you…you…"

"All right, all right," Nick said quickly cutting her off and coming up the stairs with his hands held, palms up, in front of him. "Let's all calm down."

"I don't have to listen to her talk to me that way," said Suzie, in her thick, Trinidadian accent. She wheeled around and exited to the wig room with the wig, muttering under her breath. Nick wrapped his arms around Diana like a straitjacket. Diana burst into tears. He started to walk her slowly off the stage to her dressing room, speaking over his shoulder to the cast.

"Get into your costumes, please. We will have a run-through with props and costumes as soon as the stage is cleared." After a moment he turned back and added, "No wigs."

The cast was stunned. Robot-like, they got to their feet, exchanged silent glances, and left to go to their dressing rooms. No one spoke. Nina walked up the three flights of stairs and slumped into her makeup chair. There was such tension in the air; she wondered how they would ever do a run-through. She got out of her street clothes and put on her maid's costume. The assistant stage manager knocked on the door and came in to collect her valuables for safekeeping. Nina put her wallet, her ring, and her earrings in the basket. She sat back down at the makeup table, and there was another knock at the door.

"Come in," she said to the reflection of the door in the mirror.

Nick walked into the dressing room and shut the door behind him, leaning against it.

"Look, we have a problem," he sighed. He stepped into the room and sat down on the empty chair.

"Diana is going through a very tense time. This often happens at this point in rehearsals. There is a lot of pressure on her. Television interviews, newspaper interviews, photo shoots, so she is naturally on edge. Her nerves," he sighed, again, "…her nerves have never been good, and… well, we're going to try to do whatever we can to placate her. Paul Huntley is making her a new wig, and everything will be fine. But for today…I sent her home to have a massage and get some rest. Can you do the run-through for me? Charlotte can play your part. If you go down to the costume room, Teddy will have a rehearsal skirt for you to wear."

"Of course," said Nina, trying to keep her voice level and not reveal the shock she was feeling. That's what she had been hired for, right? To take over in an emergency.

"That's my girl," said Nick. He rose, winked at her, and turned toward the door.

"Ah…I haven't forgotten the maid thing," he said, turning back and pointing his index finger at her. "We'll work it first thing Tuesday morning. Okay?" He managed a smile in her direction but left the room looking grim.

Nina sat for a moment, staring at her face in the mirror. She could do this. This is what she had wanted from the beginning, wasn't it? She quickly got out of her maid's costume and went down to the costume room in her kimono. Teddy, the costume mistress, got up heavily from her chair.

"Here," she said, "try on this skirt. I think Diana's first act blouse will fit you."

Nina put on the clothes and looked at herself in the mirror. She was walking back up the stairs to her dressing room when Matt spoke to her through his open door.

"Show 'em what you've got!" he said.

Nina gave him a quick, nervous smile.

She sat in her dressing room going over the script. I know these lines, she thought. I'm going to try it off-book. She took another look in the mirror and ran a brush through her hair. She heard the stage manager announce over the intercom that the dress rehearsal would begin in five minutes. She went down to the backstage area, taking her script with her in case she lost her nerve. She had never played the part. She had not yet had an understudy rehearsal, but she had worked so hard on the lines with Matt, and all of her scenes were with him.

When the rehearsal began, she stood in the wings watching Charlotte play her part and taking deep breaths to calm herself. When the cue came for Melanie to enter, she started to go out onto the stage, holding her script. Just before she cleared the sight line, she dropped the script.

"Hello, Melanie," Demond began, "I didn't expect you today."

"I wanted to stop by and see how the patient was doing," said Nina.

It was the same scene she had done in her first audition. Her nerves were just as taut, but she refused to let them get the best of her.

"That's fine," replied Demond, "but I'm afraid he's asleep. Won't you sit down and let me get you a drink?"

Slowly she relaxed into the scene and the character began to emerge. Slowly she began to have fun. She finished the first act, flawlessly from memory and gathered her confidence to attempt the second act. Because she was so familiar with the words, she was able to concentrate on the character. She played the part as Diana played it but brought her own unique personality to it. At the end of the rehearsal, she had performed the entire play off book. Nick seemed pleased.

"Well done," he said, applauding from the audience.

Going back up to her dressing room, Nina felt elated. At least she had shown them that she was talented enough to play the lead. She had vindicated her position in a Broadway cast. She had proved to Nick and to everyone else involved that she was up to the job she'd been hired for. And she had done it without the script! She sank down in her makeup chair with relief. Matt knocked at the door and stuck his head in.

"Knock, knock. May I come in?" he asked. "I am so proud of you!"

Nina smiled.

"Whew. Thanks," she breathed.

"Want to come celebrate? Or are you too tired?" he asked.

"Never too tired to celebrate," said Nina, "but I have a costume fitting."

"I'll wait," said Matt. "Meet you downstairs."

She got out of her rehearsal skirt, put on her kimono, and went down to the costume room. She was pleased to find that all of Diana's costumes fit her, although a little snug in the waist and about an inch too long. They could easily be adjusted. They wouldn't have to make a whole new set for her. She went back up to her dressing room, changed into her street clothes, and went excitedly down the stairs to meet Matt.

They walked out onto a rainy Broadway. The streets were shiny and slick, and the potholes had turned into pools. The streetlights had misty halos around them, and you could see the rain slanting sideways in their glow. Taxis sprayed arcs of water as they sped by, soaking pedestrians at the curbs. Rain always caused traffic to back up. Horns were honking, intersections were blocked, cars had their lights on, and windshield wipers clicked back and forth. Matt looked up to the sky, squinting.

"Can you make it to Joe's? Maybe this won't last long. Unless you want to just try to get the bus home?"

"We'll sit in traffic no matter what we take," said Nina. "Unless we take the subway."

"The thing that runs under the ground?" asked Matt.

Nina rolled her eyes.

"Let's try Joe's," she said.

They dashed in the rain, two long blocks, sprinting from the shelter of one theater marquee to another. As they crossed Eighth Avenue, they zigzagged around the taxies stuck in the intersection. One driver rolled down his window to swear at another in Arabic, who swore back at him in Punjabi. A mounted policeman in a black rubber raincoat tried to steer his horse around them. Nina laughed. Nothing could dampen her spirits today. Finally, they flung themselves into Joe Allen's doorway, stomping the water from their shoes and peeled off their drenched coats which they handed to the coat-check girl. She took them gingerly between her thumb and forefinger, holding them far away from her body. She handed Matt a ticket, and they were shown to their usual table.

Nina collapsed in a chair, plunked down her purse, and dried her face with her cloth napkin. Matt ordered them two glasses of wine. Nina leaned over the menu as Demond and his understudy, Shawn, came into the restaurant. They closed their dripping umbrellas, leaving them in an umbrella stand by the door and walked over to Nina and Matt.

"You were terrific!" Demond said to Nina.

"Thanks," said Nina, rubbing her hair dry with the napkin.

"No," said Demond. "I'm not just saying it. You were really good! Everyone is talking about it! Not only did you get all the laughs, but you aced the emotional scene."

"Too bad you're not playing it," interjected Shawn.

"I'll say!" concurred Matt. "Do you want to join us?"

"Ah, thanks, man, but we're meeting someone," said Demond pointing through the archway to the larger room. "Have a good day off. See you Tuesday," he added as they walked into the adjoining dining room to meet their friend.

The drinks arrived and Matt held up his glass.

"Here's lookin' at you!" he said.

They clinked glasses and drank. Nina sat back in her chair and slowly let the wine relax her. She was relieved the rehearsal had gone well; she was glowing under the compliments and grateful to be sitting in Joe Allen's with Matt.

At a nearby table, a young woman was sitting alone, reading a book and eating a salad. Between forkfuls she would turn the page. Nina stared at her. She had sat alone in Joe Allen's. She had eaten a salad while reading a book. It was a pathetic attempt not to look lonely. How many times had she done that? How many times had she gone to the ladies' room and quickly repaired her makeup in the mirror before returning to the table, feeling self-conscious and alone?

"What are you thinking?" asked Matt.

Nina broke her reverie and smiled at him.

"Just that I'm happy."

"You should be! I can't believe you pulled that off!"

"Well, I have to say, I'm extremely grateful we spent all that time going over the lines," said Nina.

"Yeah, but it was more than just the lines. You really brought that part home."

Nina was pensive for a moment.

"I can't say I wasn't nervous, but to tell you the truth, before I went out on that stage, I said to myself, Nick Travis thinks you're talented enough to play this part. He chose you over many other actors who auditioned because he knew you could play it. He has confidence in you. This is your chance to show him that his faith in you was not misplaced. Don't let him down."

Matt took a sip of his wine and set the glass back down on the table.

"So much of it is about confidence, isn't it?"

Nina nodded.

"I once heard a story," she said, "that took place during a dress rehearsal for *Death of a Salesman*. Lee J. Cobb was playing Willy Loman, and he was upset because the dress rehearsal hadn't gone well. He went up to Elia Kazan, who was directing, and said to him, 'I don't know what I'm going to do. I can't fix it. Can you help me?' Kazan apparently turned to him and said, 'How can I help you? You are the greatest actor in America...maybe the world.' After that Cobb was fine. He just told him how much he admired him. That was enough."

Matt shook his head slowly. "Great story," he said.

"I think all actors are such a complex combination of enormous ego and enormous insecurity, don't you?" asked Nina.

Matt stared at her for a minute.

"So how do you come by all this ego?" he asked.

Nina looked down at the table, absently fingering the stem of her wine glass. "My mother died when I was very young," she said. "I think that affected my whole life. I mean..." she looked up at Matt and gave him a wry smile, "it had to, right?"

"How did she die?" Matt asked, his brow furrowed.

"A drunk driver hit her. Going the wrong way on a two-lane highway. It was a head-on collision. She died instantly."

There was silence.

"How old were you?"

"Four years old. Three and a half, actually. I don't remember too much about her. Occasionally I have glimpses of her in my dreams...and I have photographs, of course, but..." she trailed off.

"How awful for you," said Matt.

"Well, my father was wonderful in that he took over the parenting job and gave me so much love and attention that I never felt deprived. I grew up feeling loved and secure and...with the feeling that I could do anything I wanted to do. But I also have this other thing..." she took a sip of wine.

Matt remained silent, listening to her.

"I have this…deep sense that…life is fragile and precious. I mean, it can go away in an instant! I need to…lap it up. You know…'Happiness, knowledge, not in another place but this place…not for another hour, but this hour.'"

"Walt Whitman," said Matt.

Nina looked up sharply. She studied his face.

"How do you know that quote?"

Matt ignored her.

"And that's your philosophy of life?" he asked.

"Pretty much," said Nina, raising her eyebrows. "Wear your good clothes!" She smiled.

Matt nodded slowly.

"Is your father still alive?" he asked.

Nina shook her head and looked down at the table.

"No. He died three years ago. Prostate cancer."

"Any brothers or sisters?"

"Nope."

"So, you're all alone in the world?"

Nina paused.

"Well, I wouldn't characterize it that way…I have a lot of close friends and…an aunt somewhere in Vermont…let's just say, I'm pretty self-reliant. What about you?" she asked.

For a moment, Matt sat silent. Then he breathed in deeply through his nose.

"Well, I guess you might say, the polar opposite of you. Big, blonde, boisterous California family, two younger sisters. My mother was a nursery school teacher. She just retired. My father taught high school English and coached the soccer team. I played lacrosse in high school…so as to stay as far away from the soccer team as I could," he winked at Nina. "Got into UCLA where I did a lot of theater. A scout saw me there, and when I got out, they offered me the part in a soap opera."

"Sounds like a charmed life," said Nina.

"It was, in a way…" said Matt. "Most of it. Although…"

He hesitated, "None of us gets through life scot-free, do we?"

He smiled at Nina, looked down at his hands and then abruptly changed the subject.

"Are you hungry? Shall we get some dinner, or do you want to head home?"

"I'm starving!" said Nina.

By the time they finished dinner, the rain had stopped. Matt hailed a cab that was just pulling up in front of the restaurant to let off a fare. As they sat down in the back seat, he looked at Nina and held her gaze as he gave the driver his address. She did not object. They went to Matt's apartment. They walked in the door and took off their wet shoes and clothes. Shivering, they got into bed and snuggled under the quilt for warmth. Matt's phone rang. He extracted one arm from the covers, reached over and took it off the hook. They kissed, relishing the feel of their naked bodies touching for the first time. Matt's skin was smooth, and his mouth tasted of red wine. Thankful for the warmth, the darkness, the quilt, and the exquisite luxury of finally being alone together, they explored each other's bodies tentatively and made grateful, gratifying love until both were spent. Matt's whole body started to tremble. She held him in her arms and soothed him.

"Shhh. It's okay" she whispered into his hair. "It's okay."

She held him until he finally stopped trembling and fell asleep. She knew she could hold him forever.

CHAPTER NINE

The Day Off

Nina closed her eyes and pulled the pillow over her head as the sun poured in through the skylight. She smiled as she relived the intimacies of the night before. It was so lovely to slip back into a blissful sleep, remembering them. When she finally woke for good, she marveled at Matt's broad shoulders and muscular back protruding from the sheets next to her. She smiled, feeling incredibly lucky. Eventually, Matt sat up in bed and ran his fingers through his hair. She propped herself up on one elbow and looked at him. He smiled at her.

"Look at you. You are so beautiful," he said, letting his gaze fall on her breasts.

She reached out and pushed back a lock of his hair with her fingers. He caught her hand in his and kissed it. They embraced, breathing in the fresh morning air and relishing the fact that it was their day off, and they didn't need to be anywhere.

Nina kissed him quickly, got out of bed, and walked naked to the bathroom, conscious of her long limbs and shapely body. Twisting her hair into a knot on the top of her head, she got into the shower. By the time she emerged from the bathroom, she could smell the coffee brewing. Matt was standing barefoot at the kitchen sink looking sexy in jeans and no shirt. She slipped one of his T-shirts over her head and sat down at the kitchen table.

"I used your toothbrush," she announced.

"I'll keep it forever!" said Matt.

He poured her a cup of coffee.

"Who's Paul?" he asked.

"Paul?" asked Nina startled. "Why do you ask?"

"You said his name in your sleep last night."

Nina looked stunned.

"I did?"

"Yes."

"He's…an old boyfriend," she said.

"Old?" asked Matt, "as in past?"

"Yes," said Nina.

"But…you still dream about him?"

"I…we're still friends. Matt are you jealous?" asked Nina.

"Should I be?"

"No."

"Then I'm not."

They sat in silence and drank their coffee. Nina could sense an unaccustomed tension between them.

"Who ended it? You or him?"

"I did," said Nina. "He asked me to marry him, and I turned him down."

"Why? What's wrong with him?"

Nina sighed. "Absolutely nothing," she said. "He is a tall, handsome, successful businessman, and he also happens to be very nice."

"Then why didn't you marry him?" asked Matt.

Nina thought for a moment.

"Because I knew I didn't want to have his children," she said.

She was startled to realize that this actually was the reason she had ended the relationship with Paul.

Matt sat and drank his coffee, mulling over her comment. Finally, he said, "If you were mine, I'd never let you go."

"He didn't have a choice in the matter," said Nina. "I was the one who left."

"I would find some way to get you back," said Matt.

Nina just looked at him. She was about to ask about his girlfriend in California, when Matt suddenly stood up and said, "Here I am in one of the greatest cities in the world, and all I have seen of it is a rehearsal hall and the Barrymore Theatre!"

"Are you hungry?" asked Nina.

"Of course!"

"Then I will take you for a Chinese breakfast."

"What do the Chinese eat for breakfast?" asked Matt.

"You're about to find out!" Nina answered.

They got dressed and headed to the Lexington Avenue subway, taking it down to Canal Street. Matt had his camera slung around his neck like a tourist. They made their way through the small, winding streets of Chinatown. Bright red signs with gleaming gold Chinese calligraphy were suspended above almost every shop. Crisp brown ducks minus their heads hung by their feet in the windows, and jars of Chinese spices and pickled vegetables sat below them on wide, dusty window ledges. They dodged Chinese families with young children going about their Monday chores. They turned into Doyers Street and arrived at a restaurant with red booths in the back and metal tables up front. The Nom Wah Tea Parlor was practically empty. They sat down in one of the booths. A waiter brought out a steaming pot of tea and set it on their table, along with two short, thick, white ceramic cups. He left and reappeared, carrying a tray containing various food items on differently shaped plates. Nina looked them all over carefully and pointed to some round and some oblong dishes that the waiter then placed on the table. She asked a question and the waiter answered in monosyllables and quick nods of his head. Matt watched her carefully and put on his own plate whatever she put on hers. He ended up eating everything. Sitting back, he put down his chopsticks and watched her polish off not only her own food but all the food that remained on the serving plates. She sat back triumphantly and returned his grin. The waiter came by with another large tray and set it down on the corner of their table offering to unload more of the delicacies.

"Oh, no, no!" said Nina, waving him off.

"Oh, go on," said Matt, "you can fit another one of these buns under your belt." The waiter looked questioningly at her, holding up a plate of bao, but Nina shook her head, laughing.

"No, no, we'll just have the check, please," she said.

"Check?" the waiter asked. Nina nodded. The waiter counted up all the round dishes on the table and wrote some Chinese characters down on a little white pad. Then he counted all the oval dishes and did the same thing. He added the two numbers together and ripped the paper off, placing it on the table. Matt reached for his wallet.

"No," said Nina, "My treat."

She put a twenty dollar bill on the table, added three singles and they got up to leave.

"Thank you," said Matt, "That was delicious!"

They took the subway up to the Lincoln Center stop. As they emerged at Sixty-Sixth Street, they could see the circular fountain in the center of the complex spouting water. Just beyond it were two huge Chagall paintings, one red and the other yellow, high up in the windows of the Metropolitan Opera House. Nina pointed out the State Theater to their left where the New York City ballet was housed and the New York Philharmonic to their right. They walked up to the building in the center, The Metropolitan Opera House, and went inside. Matt was immediately taken with the beauty of the starburst chandeliers.

"They were a gift from the Austrian government," said Nina.

"They are extraordinary!" he said.

"Someday," said Nina, "we'll go to the opera and you can see the same chandeliers inside the theater. When the house lights go down, they retract, slowly, all the way up to the high ceiling."

"I would love that," said Matt, smiling at her.

"You like opera?" Nina asked, enthusiastically.

"I don't know. Never been to one," said Matt.

"They don't have opera in Los Angeles?" asked Nina.

"Not that I know of."

They walked to Sixty-Fifth Street and caught a cross-town bus that was just pulling up to the curb. It hurtled across Central Park, bouncing over the potholes, as Matt and Nina clutched the metal bar above them, swinging violently to-and-fro. The bus squealed to a stop on the East Side, right by the Central Park Zoo. They got off and made their way into the zoo, following a trail of balloons held by a group of young children and their mothers. A woman came up to Matt and asked for his autograph.

"You're like chum in the water," Nina said when the woman left. "Take you out in public and women from miles around come up and take a nibble."

Matt laughed.

They watched as a zookeeper threw fish to the sea lions.

"Stand over there and let me take a picture of you," said Matt.

Nina posed, smiling, with the sea lions barking in the background. Suddenly she spotted a shiny penny on the ground and stooped to pick it up.

"Head's up! A good luck penny!" she said cheerfully as she plopped it into her purse.

"Are you superstitious?" asked Matt, intrigued.

"Oh, not really," said Nina. "I think all stage actors are

superstitious to some extent...probably because a stage performance is so precarious. I know one Broadway leading man who has to stand outside the theater before the show. He can't go inside until he has gotten the exact combination of numbers from the license plates of the cars going by. I'm not that bad, but there are some things I won't do. I would never whistle in a theater, for instance."

"Why not?" asked Matt.

"Are you kidding? Because it's bad luck."

Matt smiled, enjoying her enthusiasm.

"What else?"

"Well," said Nina, thinking, "you must never, ever quote from, or even mention the title of Shakespeare's Scottish play."

"Macbeth?" asked Matt.

"Shhhhhh" said Nina, quickly. "What are you trying to do? Ruin the opening?"

Matt laughed.

"And don't ever wish someone 'good luck.' Saying 'good luck' is bad luck."

"What should I say?" asked Matt, continuing to be amused.

"Well," said Nina, "you could say, 'Break a leg,' or you could say what the French say, '*Merde!*'"

"Merde!" said Matt, loudly.

"Shhhhh," said Nina, looking around and laughing. "Matt!"

"What else?" asked Matt.

Nina thought for a moment. "Never put a hat on a bed," she said, in a warning tone.

"Well, I know that one" said Matt.

"You do?" asked Nina, with some surprise.

"Of course! What kind of an idiot would put a hat on a bed? You might squash it!"

Nina narrowed her eyes and looked at him, shaking her head.

"I should have known better than to have believed you."

Matt laughed heartily.

They took a circuitous route through the zoo, stopping to admire the large cats lounging in the sun and the monkeys eating oranges. Eventually they ended up at Seventy-Fourth Street and the Loeb Boathouse.

"How do you manage to find your way around this place?" asked Matt.

"I know it like the back of my hand," said Nina. "Growing up, this was my backyard. I grew up in an apartment building. Central Park was my escape from bricks and concrete. My father loved the park. He took me to every part of it: the zoo, the Dairy, Belvedere Castle, Bow Bridge, Bethesda Fountain. He used to take me ice skating at Wollman Rink. The carousel was a big favorite. I know it all. I know the park better than Frederick Law Olmsted."

"I bet you do!" said Matt, enthusiastically. "Who is he?"

"He designed the park!"

Even though the air was cool, they chose an outdoor table at the boathouse, overlooking the lake. They ordered hot chocolate and scones and warmed their hands over the steaming cups. Nina gazed out over the water. The majestic Manhattan skyscrapers loomed up at the far end of the lake like stalagmites.

She turned to him. The cold had made his cheeks ruddy, and the sunshine highlighted his blond hair and made his blue eyes sparkle. The red, yellow and blue were so startling it made her catch her breath. He was so handsome!

"We'll come back in the spring and rent a rowboat," she said. "Maybe we'll go skating at Wollman rink. You skate, don't you?"

"Ice skate?" asked Matt.

"Of course, ice skate," said Nina. "Don't Californians ice skate?"

"Well...I know how," said Matt, hedging, "but there weren't too many opportunities to do it."

"There is so much I have to teach you," Nina sighed.

"Well," said Matt, his ego bruised, "Can you ride a horse?"

"Ride a horse?" exclaimed Nina, "I don't even know how to drive a car!"

"You don't drive?" Matt asked, astounded.

"Why would I drive a car? I grew up on the fourteenth floor of an apartment building on Eighth Avenue and Twelfth Street!"

"But...but how did you...get around?"

"My father said that by the time I was three I knew how to hail a taxi."

Matt sighed and shook his head, "There is so much I have to teach you," he said.

Nina looked at him for a moment.

"Shall we go on? Or are you too tired?" she said sarcastically.

"Lead on, Macduff!" said Matt.

"Matt!" exclaimed Nina, her eyes and mouth wide with alarm.

Matt laughed.

They got into a taxi and Nina asked the driver to drop them at Fifth Avenue and Eighty-Second Street. They got off in front of the Metropolitan Museum of Art and walked up the many steep steps to the entrance. As they entered the Great Hall, their voices echoed in the marble vastness. They went up to the second floor where the permanent collection was housed. Walls and walls of Impressionist paintings greeted them: Cézanne, Monet, Matisse, Renoir, Picasso, Cassatt, Degas. They sat on a low bench in the center of the room in front of a Childe Hassam painting called *Geraniums*, depicting geraniums and watering cans outside a farmhouse. They were silent for a long time looking at the painting.

"There is just too much beauty to take in," said Nina.

"Certainly not in one day," answered Matt.

They moved on, barely glancing at the Rodins in the majestic sculpture garden and passing by the Ming Dynasty vases.

"We'll come back," promised Nina.

Outside the museum, Matt looked around, trying to get his bearings.

"Where are we? Fifth Avenue and Eighty-Second Street? I actually have a friend who lives near here. Do you mind if I give him a call?"

"Of course not." said Nina.

Matt went to a corner pay phone and called his friend, who invited them to stop by. He was taking care of his one-year-old child while his wife was at work. He greeted them warmly, apologizing for the mess in the apartment. They accepted a glass of wine and sat on the couch while he talked to them from the kitchen where he was busy preparing food. The child, a little blonde girl, was in a playpen in the center of the living room. She regarded them with suspicion. Suddenly she burst into tears. Matt got up. He found two stuffed animals lying on the floor and took one in each hand. He then looked around for a third. Wedging it between the first two, he formed a stuffed-animal chorus line for the little girl. The child stopped crying and looked with fascination at the three dancing animals. She broke into a wide smile and reached for them. Matt handed the toys to her, and she sat down happily playing with them. Something shifted in Nina. *How could you not fall in love with a man who did that?*

When they left the friend's apartment, Nina spotted a hot dog vendor on the corner of Madison and Eighty-Sixth Street.

"Let's get a dirty-water dog" she said.

"Ah...I'm good," said Matt.

"Come on, you can't fully experience New York without eating a dirty-water dog!"

She went up to the cart and ordered a hot dog from the vendor. He added mustard and sauerkraut and handed it to her. She walked back over to Matt, who looked at her in amazement, shaking his head.

"I do love a girl with a good appetite!" he said.

Nina offered him a bite. Matt hesitated but then took a small bite of the hot dog.

"Mmm, good!" he said with his mouth full.

They taxied back to Matt's apartment. Nina went to the phone and dialed a number.

"May I have a reservation for two at eight o'clock?" she asked. "For tonight, yes. That will be fine. Landau. Perfect. Thank you." And she hung up.

"Where are we going?" asked Matt.

"It's a surprise," said Nina.

"How will I know how to dress?"

"Wear your good clothes," grinned Nina, raising her eyebrows.

They collapsed on the bed, exhausted and happy.

"Kiss me," said Matt.

Nina obliged.

They fell asleep almost immediately. When they woke, Nina kissed Matt quickly and left for her own apartment to change into her dress clothes.

She showered and tried on a few outfits. Oh, God! Why does everything make me look dumpy? She wanted to look spectacular tonight. It was important. She settled on a black Diane Von Furstenberg wrap dress, black high heels, and added a string of pearls and earrings that had belonged to her mother for good luck. This was going to be a classic New York night. Matt picked her up in a taxi.

He was in a tie and jacket. She had never seen him out of his jeans and T-shirts. He looked breathtakingly handsome!

"You look particularly beautiful tonight," said Matt, staring at her. "You are glowing."

"Don't talk to me," said Nina, "I have been in every outfit I own."

Matt laughed.

She gave the address to the driver. "Twenty-one West Fifty-Second Street."

The cab pulled up outside of the 21 Club. On the balcony above the famous wrought iron gate, a line of colorful cast iron jockeys stood waiting, each with one arm out ready to hold the reins of the horses from the famous stables. Inside, the walls and ceilings were covered with antique toys. Nina and Matt were ushered into the back room and seated at a table in the dark, romantic lounge. There was a wood fire burning in the fireplace.

Nina leaned over to Matt, "This used to be a speakeasy called Jack and Charlie's 21 during Prohibition," she explained. "There's a famous wine cellar."

"Great!" said Matt. "Let's order a bottle!"

Matt looked over the wine list and ordered them a bottle of Montepulciano d'Abruzzo.

"So!" said Matt, sitting back, "You've shown me music, opera, dance, wonderful museums, Chinatown, Central Park, a zoo and now excellent dining. What are you? The Chamber of Commerce?"

"I just love New York," said Nina. "And I want to share it with you."

"You have to give me a chance to reciprocate in Los Angeles."

Nina smiled, "I would love that!" she said.

A waiter came over, opened the wine, poured a small amount in Matt's glass, stepped back and waited. Matt sniffed the cork, swirled the wine around in the glass, and then tasted it.

"Mmm. Very nice," he said, nodding to the waiter.

The waiter filled the two glasses and set the bottle in the wine bucket by the side of the table.

They clinked glasses.

"To us," Matt said.

"To us," said Nina. They drank.

"Mmm. That is so nice," said Nina, appreciating the wine. They sat back and looked at the roaring wood fire.

"Do you miss Los Angeles?" she asked.

Matt thought for a moment. "No. Not really. I miss the driving. I miss my Mercedes, but other than that, no."

"Oh! A Mercedes!" said Nina. "Elegant, classy, and lots of money."

"It was a gift from the producers at the end of the series," said Matt. "It's five years old, but a very nice little car. Convertible. Good, reliable, and very easy to drive. It would be a good car to learn on." He looked at her, suggestively, raising his eyebrows.

"You're gonna wanna Sherman tank," said Nina.

They sat drinking the wine, gazing at the fire and observing the people in the restaurant. They were actors, always engaged in people watching, always noticing and stockpiling speech patterns, styles of walking, how people carried themselves, hairdos, laughs, gestures—absorbing people by osmosis and tucking their observations away for possible use some day in a character, next to their library of emotions. They ordered steaks and devoured them, as they traded stories of their childhoods, their relationships, and their professional experiences—often laughing, and at times commiserating. It seemed they would never run out of conversation.

As they were finishing their meal, a couple about their age was shown to the table on the opposite side of the fireplace.

They ordered wine and clinked glasses. As Matt and Nina watched, the man reached into his jacket pocket and pulled out a small, light blue velvet box. The woman set down her wine glass and put her hand over her mouth. He placed the box on the table, squarely in front of her, and pushed it forward. Then he sat back, watching her, nervously. She looked at him incredulously and opened the box. It was a diamond engagement ring. She slid the ring on her finger, looked at it, and smiled up at him, her eyes brimming with tears. She reached across the table for his hand and they kissed.

Suddenly Matt said, "Let's get out of here."

He signaled for the waiter and handed him his credit card. Nina was startled into silence.

In the cab going home, she asked cautiously, "Are you all right?" She had never seen him so agitated.

"Yes," said Matt, "I'm sorry I…I didn't mean to spoil our day. I just…" His voice trailed off. He reached down and squeezed her hand, but his eyes looked straight ahead.

"Maybe I'd better head back to my apartment," said Nina.

"Please don't," said Matt, "Please."

At Matt's apartment, they undressed and got into bed. Nina lay very still, far over on the edge of the bed, waiting for Matt to speak. After about five minutes, he reached over and with both hands, slid her body across the bed to him.

"C'mere, why are you so far away?" he asked.

"I wanted to give you some space," said Nina.

"I don't want space. I want you close. Always."

The light from the moon shone through the skylight and lit the room.

He traced her lips, slowly, with his fingertip and then kissed her.

Murray sprang onto the bed and scampered over them in a sudden feline frenzy to get to the bookcase behind them.

"That's it, Murray," said Matt, "Help yourself. Read any of the books."

Nina laughed.

Looking into each other's eyes, they made slow, sensuous love, while the cat smirked from the sidelines.

CHAPTER TEN

Tech/Dress

At the theater the following morning, the atmosphere was highly charged. Things were progressing at a breakneck speed. People were running in all directions getting ready for the first tech rehearsal. The crew had worked around the clock to get the set finished. The furniture was covered with sheets to protect it from the sawdust, and the technicians were still working on focusing lights, but it was all beginning to come together.

Nina approached Nick, shyly.

"About that entrance we talked about on Sunday...um, for the maid?"

"Yes. Yes," said Nick, "I haven't forgotten."

"I've been thinking," she said, haltingly, "would it be possible for me to come in from the second floor?"

Nick thought for a moment. "I don't see why not," he said, "Show me. Hold on. Hold on." Then he shouted, "Guys, can we clear the set, please? Thank you."

Nina went up the backstage ladder, opened the second-floor door and peered around it.

"Um...Could I have a doorbell?" she asked.

Nick called to the stage manager, "Wallace, may we have a doorbell, please."

After a minute, a doorbell rang. Nina opened the second-floor door, bounced airily down the stairs, drying her hands on an imaginary apron. On her way to the front door, she noticed the open box of chocolates on the coffee table, downstage center. She stopped short, did a double take, looked right and left to be sure she was alone. Then she walked over to the chocolates, plucked one from the box, popped it into her mouth, and sprinted offstage to answer the doorbell.

"I love it!" said Nick, "We'll work it a few times this afternoon during the tech rehearsal and then put it in tonight. I'll let Demond know not to make his entrance until after you exit."

The poster for the play was ready. Nick had brought one to the theater to show to the cast. "*The Second Time Around*, a comedy by George DuPont, directed by Nick Travis," it announced in white letters on a bright purple background. The cast was listed in alphabetical order, according to the contract. No one person was over the title. Nina filled with pride. It was the first time her name was on a Broadway poster! Diana looked like she had just found sand in her spinach.

They were getting ready to integrate the lighting and sound cues, along with the scene and costume changes into the play. Nick had chosen the music: "O mio babbino caro," a beautiful aria from Puccini's *Gianni Schicchi* sung by Kiri Te Kanawa, to open and close every act. Now, all that remained was for the photographers to take photos of the cast for the newspapers and the front of the theater. They were scheduled for the following afternoon. Everything was falling into place.

After searching theatrical makeup stores for a pair of thick false eyelashes and finding none, Nina decided to make her own out of black construction paper. She cut two small strips, the length of her eyelids, and then cut one edge of them into a fringe. She bent the strips and glued them to each of her eyelids. Sitting back, she looked at herself in the mirror. She had the thickest, darkest eyelashes, and they made her blue eyes sparkle with vitality. She had finally found her character!

Before the tech rehearsal began, Nina went to the pay phone in the hall and called Isabelle to ask if she wanted to come to the invited dress rehearsal that night. She knew she didn't have the money to buy a ticket. But Isabelle, with some embarrassment, told her that Paul had gotten them both tickets to see one of the previews.

"Don't tell me when you are coming!" Nina said with alarm.

Some actors loved to know when people were in the audience. It seemed to energize their performances. Nina was part of the group that hated to know who was sitting out there in the dark. It made it that much harder for her to focus her attention.

"Actually," said Isabelle sheepishly, "I'm glad you called. Paul has asked me to go to Café des Artistes with him tonight. I know it's your special place, and he is just trying to make you jealous. What should I do?"

"Go!" said Nina "Don't be a fool. The food is fabulous. Poor Paul. I haven't even had a moment to call him."

"Are you sure?" asked Isabelle anxiously.

"Sure, sure, sure," said Nina, "Have fun. Give him my love. Gotta run."

She hung up and stared at the wall for a moment. She felt a twinge of melancholy. She was used to taking Paul for granted, thinking that he would always be there. Whenever one of her love affairs fizzled, he would prevent her from falling into that chasm of loneliness. She made it clear that she wasn't interested in a relationship with him. She planned to tell him about Matt. It was only fair, so he could move on to someone else. But...Isabelle...? It felt a bit...incestuous. Nina wondered ruefully if Paul would order Veuve Clicquot and if they would end up in bed to-gether? But the announcement over the intercom that the tech rehearsal was about to begin interrupted her thoughts, and Nina went up to her dressing room to change into her maid's costume. They would tech the play all day long and then perform it for a few invited guests that night.

The tech rehearsal turned out to be extremely bumpy. The stopping and starting of the scenes to incorporate the sound and the light cues rattled the actors. Matt, always so even-tempered, was succumbing to the pressure. He forgot a line and stood for a moment, his head down, clenching and unclenching his fists. You could see the color rise in his face.

"Line, please?" he asked, through clenched teeth.

Wallace, who was busy setting light cues, was not on book. Nina knew the line but decided she had better re-main silent.

"What's the fucking line?" Matt yelled.

There was a flurry of paper, and Wallace nervously shouted the line to Matt.

Diana came on stage for the third act wearing a rehearsal skirt, and in the middle of a speech, she stopped and threw a tantrum because her third act costume wasn't ready, and she wouldn't have a chance to rehearse in it before facing an audience.

Nick, who was normally the one to keep the calm, was uncharacteristically yelling at the tech crew.

"For the tenth time, bring up the goddamn lights? This is a comedy, not Stonehenge. Kelly, tell John if he can't make that scene change any faster, we will just have to cut it. We can't sit around all night waiting for the stagehands to clear the clutter off the set. That is not what people pay to see. Teddy, Diana's third act costume? Do I have to send out to Eaves and rent one? Or will it be finished? Props? Where the hell is the wedding ring for Matt? Do I need to give him mine?"

The performance that night was going to be for a small group of invited friends and family members, so the actors could get some idea of the how audience would respond. It was difficult to time a laugh if there was no one out there laughing. But when the tech rehearsal finally ended, there were still many unanswered questions swirling in the atmosphere. The actors passed each other, silent and tense, on the stairs. Would they know their lines? Would the sound and the light cues work? What if Diana's third act costume still wasn't ready? What about that fast scene change that the stagehands were having trouble with? Suddenly a cry came from Diana, who rushed out of her dressing room in her short makeup robe as though she had seen a tarantula. Apparently, some unwitting stagehand had brought her a spray of peacock feathers for luck.

"Get them out! Get them out!" she shrieked.

The nonplussed stagehand shrank back against the wall holding the offending feathers.

"I forgot that one," Nina whispered to Matt as they went up the stairs. "Peacock feathers. The evil eye. Bad luck."

By five things finally started to fall into place. Diana's third act costume was finished, and she came out on stage wearing it for Nick to approve. It showed off her cleavage, so she was pleased with it.

"Fabulous!" Nick said, smiling.

The lighting designer had raised the settings on the first act set, and John Tatten had come up with an ingenious trick to make the set change quicker: he had thrown an invisible netting over the couch, the chair, and the coffee table. Attached to the netting was all the clutter from the party scene. In the dark of the scene change and with the music playing, the stagehands had only to lift off the netting, and in less than a minute, the set was pristine. Theater was magic!

"Okay," said Nick, "Let's set the curtain call. Ah, can someone please get the pizza box off the set?"

A crew person ran across the set to retrieve the box like a ball boy at a tennis match.

"Okay, Nina, our maid is first. Nina, enter from the downstage left wing, please...followed by our lawyer, Leonard, downstage right. Renee, come from stage left and stand next to Nina...Fine. And then let's have Demond, from stage right. Matt, come in from stage left and join Renee...good. And may we have Ms. Lawrence, please, from stage right."

Diana entered looking sullen and stood next to Demond.

"Okay," said Nick, viewing the lineup. "All join hands. And...take the bow from Diana...and...bow. Now let's try it looking like you're happy."

The cast bowed again, all smiling except for Diana.

"Alright, we'll run it once with the music. Nina, wait for the light cue before you enter. Wallace, can you give Nina a light cue, stage left please?"

Nina went off in the wings and waited. The closing music started up.

"Applause, applause," Nick shouted from the audience, while clapping his hands, "and..."

Nina saw a little red light go on. She walked on to the stage standing just a bit in from the curtain.

"Come further on stage, Nina," Nick shouted over the music. "The point is to see you!"

Nina shuffled sideways, crab-like, a few inches to her right. The rest of the cast emerged, clasped hands and bowed, watching Diana out of the corner of their eyes.

"Okay," said Nick "...and the curtain comes down... once...maybe it goes back up again...we don't know... Okay, applause, applause, and bow again, please. Together, please. You look like a comb with missing teeth. That's better, but let's have some smiles, please. This isn't a police lineup. And the curtain comes down...Good."

"There'll be a break for dinner, and we will resume at half-hour, seven thirty" said Wallace over the intercom.

The cast dispersed. Diana waylaid Nick, and they could be heard arguing in her dressing room.

"She wants a solo bow," Matt whispered to Nina on the stairs.

"Do you think she'll get it?"

"Hard to say. He'll probably want to avoid a total meltdown before she faces her first audience."

They went to their separate dressing rooms to get ready for the dress rehearsal. Sandwiches, fruit, and coffee were laid out on a backstage table. That would serve as dinner for the crew and any of the actors who chose not to leave the theater.

At seven thirty the stage manager called half hour, the time, by Equity union rules, that all the actors had to be present and accounted for, which meant ensconced in the theater and signed in. Tonight, they had all been there long before, and most of them were already in their costumes and makeup, nervously pacing the halls.

Nina came down from her dressing room early to prepare for her new entrance. She had on her maid's costume, her wig, and her thick, black construction-paper eyelashes. She stopped and checked herself in the full-length mirror, set up in the wings. When you put on that costume and that makeup and wig, she thought, something magical happens—you become that character.

She went to her place by the back, brick wall of the theater. Over the intercom, you could hear the hum of the audience as they were entering the theater and taking their seats. It sent chills through Nina. The coughs, the murmurs of conversations, all made her heart race. She heard the call for "five minutes, please" come over the intercom, and her mouth went dry. She climbed up the backstage ladder heading for the little platform like a tightrope walker in a circus, except there was no safety net. How in the world did she imagine she could open the show and make it funny?

What was she thinking? She had barely even had a chance to rehearse the bit. What if it fell flat? She would be making a fool of herself in front of so many people.

Just then something caught her eye at the bottom of the ladder. Demond was standing there giving her a thumbs up. Suddenly she knew she had to make this a success because it wasn't about her—she was part of a team. She couldn't let the rest of the cast down. She managed to give him a quick smile and started blowing short breathes out through her lips as though she were doing a Lamaze exercise.

"Places" was called.

Nick's voice could be heard addressing the audience from the apron of the stage.

"Hello and welcome! Thank you all for coming. What you are about to see is a dress-tech rehearsal and not a finished product. What that means is that we may have to stop from time to time to correct things that aren't working properly. The actors, in some cases, are just getting used to their completed costumes, and there might be other technical elements that we will have to stop and iron out. But the cast is ready for an audience, and you can do your part by providing them with the kind of responses that will help them. So please sit back, relax, and enjoy the show."

There was applause. Nina licked her lips. Her pulse quickened. She heard the music start up, Kiri Te Kanawa's beautiful voice singing the Puccini, and her heart started pounding. This was it. There was no turning back. Standing in the dark on her precarious wooden perch high above the theater, she smoothed her maid's apron with both hands. Her legs felt wobbly, as though they might give way. The music built to a crescendo. She could hear the sound of the curtain going up. There was an audible gasp from the audience when they saw the set. This was a good sign, thought Nina. The music began its diminuendo. As the music trailed away, the doorbell rang. She cleared her throat, softly and, with a shaking hand, reached for the door handle. She opened the door, entered, and went jauntily down the stairs as though she hadn't a care in the world. Crossing the stage, she suddenly noticed the box of chocolates, did a double take, looked right and left, and went downstage to take one from the box. She popped it into her mouth and gaily scampered off, stage right. The audience laughed. Her heart was beating fast, but she felt euphoric. *The bit had worked!* Demond was in the narrow space in the wings, readying for his entrance with his head down, like a thoroughbred in the starting gate. He brushed by her on his way to the stage. She waited a moment to hear him say the familiar lines:

"Martin? Are you here?"

His voice was strong and confident.

"I'm in the bedroom."

That was Matt!

"Make yourself comfortable. I'll be out in a minute."

Nina broke into a wide grin and climbed the stairs to her dressing room, pleased that she had managed to do what Nick has asked of her, pleased that her comedic instincts had come through for her. She had no more entrances in the first act, so she sat listening to the play over the intercom. Matt's scene with Demond was going well. The audience was laughing.

Filled with too much nervous energy to sit in her room alone, she decided to go down to Matt's dressing room and wait for him to come offstage. Sitting down at Matt's makeup mirror, surrounded by his things, a sense of happiness came over her. Next to the mirror, she noticed a note in a feminine handwriting. She looked at it for a moment, trying to resist reading it, but eventually gave in to her curiosity.

"Matt Dear," the note read. "Sending this four-leaf clover, for luck on your first audience. Can't wait to see you! Love, Sharon."

Nina stared at the four-leaf clover that was taped to the card. Her heart sank like a stone. She quietly got up and left the room, closing Matt's door behind her. She went back up to her own dressing room. The first act was just coming to an end. She sat at her makeup table and listened to the intercom. The audience began to applaud. They liked it. At least there was that.

The second and third acts went as well. When the third act came down the cast hurriedly went to their respective places for their curtain call. Diana was nowhere to be seen. The music started, and the curtain went up. Nina's cue light came on. She entered from the stage left wing, smiling, and stood on the stage. The audience applauded. She could not see the people over the bright footlights, but she could hear them. Out of the corner of her eye, she saw Leonard enter from stage right. Then Renee, then Demond and then came Matt. There was a noticeable increase in applause. There were some cheers of "Bravo!" Nina felt pride surge through her.

Then from the second floor, the upstage center door opened. Diana emerged, swept down the stairs and onto the stage to great applause. She passed the waiting cast members, and at the apron of the stage, she sank into a deep curtsey with her head bowed and one hand over her heart. She rose, grandly, smiled and nodded, first to one side of the orchestra section and then to the other. Then she looked up to the few people in the balcony and threw kisses. Renee squeezed Nina's hand and suppressed a giggle. Diana then backed up, joined hands with the rest of the cast and together they all bowed. The curtain came down. The applause was still going, and Wallace signaled for the curtain to go up again. The cast took a second bow. They had done it!

The stage manager's voice came over the intercom: "Rehearsal tomorrow at ten. First preview tomorrow night at eight."

You could hear the groans from the cast members on their way to their dressing rooms. It was ten thirty. By the time she got home, Nina thought, it would be almost midnight.

CHAPTER ELEVEN

Charlie's

Nina got out of her costume and hung it up. Teddy would be coming to get it, to iron it for the next performance. She put on her kimono and sat down at her makeup table. Slowly, she pulled out the hairpins and took off her wig. She placed it carefully on the wig stand on her dressing table where it resembled a bust of Beethoven. Suzie would be coming to take it down to the wig room to freshen it for the first preview. Then she carefully peeled off the false eyelashes and put them in their box, saying a silent farewell to her character for the night. She could probably get a week's worth of performances out of them before needing to make another pair. She took a cotton ball and wiped off her thick stage makeup with some cold cream from the jar by her mirror. Once her face was clear of makeup, she peeled the nylon stocking cap from her head, and one by one, undid all the bobby pins, and combed out her hair. It felt good to get out of the tight pin curls. This slow, dismantling of the character was part of the process of decompressing after a performance. But tonight, her heart was unusually heavy. There was a knock at the door, and she felt a sudden rush thinking it might be Matt, but it was Kelsey coming to return her valuables.

"Good job!" she said to Nina.

Nina smiled. "Thanks."

She pulled on her jeans and a sweater, took one last look in the mirror, dabbed on some lipstick, and started down the stairs with her suede jacket over her arm. Matt's dressing room door was closed. A feeling of anxiety welled up in her as she passed it. She continued down to the ground floor and walked across the stage to the stage door. The ghost light had already been set up by the stagehands. It was a single bulb on a pole stand that stood in the center of the empty stage, eerily lighting the stage and the first few rows when the theater was not occupied. Some said it was to appease the ghost that every theater is thought to have.

"Way to go, Nina!" Demond said to her, "You started us off with a laugh!"

"Thanks," said Nina, "Your scene with Matt sounded terrific!"

She went outside. Matt was standing there, signing autographs and talking with some of the audience members. He looked up at her.

"Joe's?" he asked.

She nodded, relieved.

They walked over to Joe Allen, but there was a long line to get in the door.

"Let's try Charlie's," said Matt.

They walked to Forty-Fifth Street, between Broadway and Eighth Avenue and entered the restaurant just as a couple was vacating a table. They sat down and ordered drinks. As they were waiting for them to arrive, someone spotted Matt from across the room and came over to the table.

"Hey, Matt" he said, "I heard you were on this side of the continent."

"Yeah," said Matt. "Doing a play at the Barrymore."

"So I hear!" said the man. He looked at Nina, waiting for an introduction.

Matt cleared his throat. "This is Nina Landau," he mumbled, reluctantly. "Nina, uh, Pete Mandel. We did a series together."

"Nice to meet you," said Nina, smiling.

"Yeah. You too. Don't want to intrude," said Pete, backing away, looking from Matt to Nina. "Good luck on the opening."

"Thanks," said Matt, tightly.

Pete started to walk away and then turned back.

"Say hi to Sharon," he said, pointedly.

Nina looked down at her hands.

"Asshole," said Matt, under his breath. The drinks arrived and they clinked glasses. Nina smiled bravely.

"To us," said Matt, looking at her intently.

They drank in silence.

"I have something to talk to you about," Matt said finally.

"That sounds dire," said Nina.

"Not really," said Matt. "It's just that…" he paused and took a sip of his wine, "How to begin?" He cleared his throat.

"I wasn't exactly the clean-cut California kid I may have given you the impression I was. I mean…being the only son of Doctor Ryland, head of the English Department at Calabasas High, there was a lot of pressure to…succeed. And I did. Succeed, I mean. But not in the academic world of my father. It was clear to me from the start that trying to compete with him in that world would get me nowhere. There was less pressure on the girls, I guess. One of them did become a teacher…anyway. I took a different path, one that wouldn't pit me against him, one-on-one. I became an actor. He did not approve. Actors in Hollywood, to him, were people who got into drugs and threw away their lives on dissolute marriages. But I persevered. I got into UCLA, got more and more successful in the theater department there, and, I think I told you, a scout saw me and hired me right out of college to do *The Heart Knows All*." Matt sighed, "Well…long story, short, I got a lot of exposure, a lot of money, and a lot of fame pretty quickly. Too quickly."

He paused and took a long drink of his wine. He looked at Nina, trying to gauge how she was taking this information. But she just held his gaze, waiting.

"Drugs were offered at all the parties," Matt continued, "Cocaine and…well…I was always the someone who was up for trying new things, so I tried them and…you can't just *try* that stuff. It gets you." Matt looked down at the table. "At first I thought I could handle it. I did just enough to make me feel confident in an unfamiliar environment, but the demands of the TV show got more and more arduous. They wanted me in practically every scene…there was a fan club and…the *Soap Opera Digest*, and, you know, after a few months, the pressure got pretty bad, and I started to use it to…smooth out the problem areas. I don't mean to excuse myself, but doing an hour show every day is almost impossible. Even with a teleprompter, you have to know your lines."

He looked up at Nina who was listening intently. She nodded, slowly. Matt went on.

"I got hooked. Just as my father had predicted. And the thought that I had fulfilled his prophecy made me so angry that the only way to dull the pain was…more coke. Basically, I spun out of control. I was rail thin…I think I was down to 130 pounds. I hardly ate. I slept only about…two or three hours a night. My money was going out as fast as it was coming in—a lot of money."

Matt stopped and stared into the distance with a pained expression on his face.

"People started to take notice. Not in a good way. After a while, I was fired from the soap."

Matt paused. A muscle in his jaw pulsed. He drank from his glass. He did not meet her eyes.

"My father helped to keep it out of the newspapers and to keep me out of jail. He got me into rehab, but he never trusted me again. And once trust is gone...No one would hire me and...this...person came along...and she wasn't angry with me, like my family. She was...kind and patient...very patient...and somehow she knew that this wasn't the person I wanted to be...and she helped me to... get back to who I was."

Nina sat still, looking at him.

Matt moistened his lips and looked up at her.

"It took more than one time," he said. "Ha! Many more. It's...very tough shit. But she hung in long enough. She never gave up, and I finally...she finally made me get there."

"Sharon." said Nina.

Matt nodded.

"So," he continued, with a sigh, "I owe her a lot. My life, really."

"And now?" asked Nina."

"What? Drugs, you mean? Oh, I never go near them. I can still drink a bit," he said, with a nod to the glass of wine, "but I have to be careful there, too. Once an addict, always an addict."

"How long has it been?" asked Nina.

"That I've been clean? Oh, let's see, about...five years," said Matt.

Nina sat back in the chair and studied him.

"Well, that's...quite a story" she said, finally. "I'm glad you told me."

"Well," Matt said with a deep sigh, "That's not all."

There was a long pause.

"She was pretty upset about my leaving for New York. So, I had to...I promised her..."

Matt looked down at the table.

"...that...when I came back...we'd get married."

He looked up at Nina with a pained expression.

"I see."

They held each other's gaze for a time. Matt dropped his eyes and played with his wine glass.

"She doesn't know anything about you and me."

He sighed and looked back up at her. "I spoke to her last week. She wants to come to opening night. I...couldn't say no. I...hope you understand. I owe her a lot."

"So you said. Your life," said Nina.

Matt nodded. "Yeah."

"And you plan to pay her back with your life," said Nina.

Matt looked at her and frowned, "What do you mean?" he asked.

"Do you love her?"

Matt looked down at the table. "I thought I did. Sometimes it's easy to confuse gratitude with love."

Nina said nothing.

"My family is coming around slowly, but they're still wary. My dad's a tough old bird. They're very grateful to Sharon, of course, especially my Mom...but they still keep their emotional distance," Matt said in a cynical voice.

"Why do you think that's so?" asked Nina.

"Why? In case I have another relapse. You know, once bitten, twice shy. That kind of thing."

"Are you afraid that might happen?"

"Oh, God," said Matt, suddenly sitting straight up and shifting in his seat. "You never know with that stuff. I hope not. I am so glad to be free of it. The TV work gradually picked up again. Nick hired me to do a guest star bit in a TV movie, even though he knew about...the problem. And then I got the Western series. And that led to this play. And..." he looked into Nina's eyes, "I've never been happier in my life!"

Nina nodded, imperceptibly.

Matt reached for her hands across the table.

"Nina. Whatever I had to go through, including all that shit...if it led me to you, I wouldn't change a thing."

They sat for a while in silence, drinking their wine. Finally, Matt cleared his throat.

"So, anyway," he said, "I spoke to…her last night. I…I couldn't tell her over the phone. It just didn't seem fair. She hasn't done anything wrong. I have to at least tell her face-to-face. I owe her that."

"Tell her…?" asked Nina.

"I told you, she doesn't know about you and me."

"Matt," said Nina, "you do what you have to do. I knew from day one that you had someone in California. You didn't hide anything from me. Believe me, I never wanted to cause you problems."

"Nina," said Matt, shaking his head, "I'm in love with you. I never knew what love was until now. I want you in my life. Always."

Nina swallowed. Her eyes started to glisten with tears. *He loved her!* He had never said it. But just as quickly, fear gripped her. He would see Sharon again. She would be here, in New York. In his apartment. In his bed. Nina drained her glass.

"Let's go home," she said. "We have to be back at ten."

They left the restaurant and hailed a taxi. Matt gave his address and sat back in the cab.

"I really should head home," said Nina. "I am dead tired."

"Sure," said Matt. He leaned forward and gave the driver Nina's address.

They sat in silence. When the taxi pulled up at Nina's building, Matt reached out and held her arm, preventing her from opening the door.

"Please stay with me tonight," he said.

Nina hesitated, and then sat back in her seat. When they got to Matt's apartment, Nina quickly washed, undressed, and got into bed.

"I'm sorry," she said, "It's just been a long, emotional day and I'm exhausted."

"Go to sleep," said Matt. He kissed her on the cheek and pulled the covers over her, tucking her in like a child. Not long after, she could feel him crawl quietly into bed alongside her. They lay there, in silence, for a long minute. Both knew the other was awake. Finally, Nina reached over and touched his arm. In the darkness and the quiet, came Matt's soft voice.

"I don't want to spend any time away from you. Not tonight. Not ever."

Nina smiled as welcoming, restorative sleep swallowed her whole.

CHAPTER TWELVE

The Elevator

Nina woke in the middle of the night unable to get back to sleep. Her mind was agitated. She lay awake and thought about everything Matt had said. She thought about Sharon. The promise of marriage. She thought about the note and the four-leaf clover. Then, to ease her mind, she tried to concentrate on her new entrance and the laugh she had gotten. She changed positions every other minute and tried to get back to sleep but after an endless, nerve-racking hour she finally gave up.

She slipped out of bed quietly and walked to the kitchen. Wanting to make herself a cup of tea, she gingerly placed the kettle on the stove and went to the cupboard for a cup. The cupboard door squeaked when she opened it. She froze and glanced quickly over to the bed. Matt stirred in his sleep and turned over. Reluctantly, she turned the flame off under the kettle and sat down in the armchair. It wasn't fair to wake him. He had a lead role, and he was facing his first preview that evening. She sighed and tapped her fingers on the arm of the chair. What should she do? She wished she had the bottle of Ativan the doctor had prescribed for her when her father had died, but it was back at her apartment. She wanted to get dressed and go home, but she was afraid to go out on the street at that hour. She knew she had to get some sleep. It would be her first preview, too. Maybe, she reasoned, if she stood right by the front door of the apartment building and hailed a taxi to take her the four blocks to her home... She got up, dressed, noiselessly, scribbled a quick note to Matt and tiptoed out the door, closing it softly behind her. She rang for the elevator and when she didn't hear it start up, she glanced at her watch. It was two thirty. She wondered briefly if the elevator stopped working at some point during the night. Then she heard the motor grind into gear and the steady, smooth sound of the car rising and clunking to a stop. The door slid open. She got in and pressed "L."

The elevator descended and stopped at the lobby floor. As she pushed the outer door open, a muscular man shoved her back into the elevator. Nina's heart leapt in shock. *This couldn't be happening!* In a desperate effort to reason with him, she blurted out the first thing that came into her mind.

"What about your mother?" she asked, inexplicably.

He pinned her against the back wall of the cab with one arm, while he pressed the button for the door to close. Nina frantically tried to break free. She flailed around for the button panel, slapping at it, pressing buttons wildly. The elevator started to go up. Then stopped. The door slid open. And then it closed. It started to go down. The man punched her in the jaw. In a surge of adrenaline, she hit him back, striking his shoulders with clenched fists. He punched her again, sending her head sharply sideways. Shocked and terrified, she kicked at his legs and tried to knee him in the groin. He stepped back. She lunged for the button panel again, violently pressing whatever button she could reach. *Get out!* was all she could think. He grabbed her arms and angrily yanked her away from the panel. He held her roughly against the opposite wall of the elevator. His left fist connected with her jaw, sending her head sharply to the left. He's trying to knock me out, she thought, dully. *Keep fighting!* She felt herself slipping into a semiconscious state, desperate to stay awake. But it was as if a huge wave had struck her and the undertow was sucking her down, down to the bottom of the ocean. Kicking and flailing for the surface, her arms and legs worked violently to propel her toward life. But which way was that? Maybe she was kicking toward the bottom? She was completely disoriented and running out of breath. She was going to drown. She was going to die. Suddenly the elevator clanked to a stop, and she regained consciousness.

The inside door slid open. She shoved her way toward the door, and he slammed her head against the back wall. With all her might she fought him. She scratched at his neck with her fingernails and tried to reach his eyes. The elevator went down. Her heart banged against her rib cage. She marveled at her own strength. Once more, the elevator jerked to a stop and she heard the inner door slide open. She ripped herself from his grasp and flung her body against the outer door. It opened. She ran out. He ran after her. She realized they were on the lobby floor. She started screaming for help and running to the apartment doors, frantically ringing the bells. The man started to take off. He paused for a moment, and when he saw that no one was coming to her aid, he headed back toward her. Nina dove at the nearest apartment door and rang the bell, again and again, as hard as she could. The door opened a tiny crack. The man backed away, turned, and ran out of the building.

"I saw him! I saw him!" said an elderly lady, as she peered over the chain. Cautiously, she undid the chain and opened the door a little wider. She wore a faded bathrobe and a hairnet. Nina pushed passed into the apartment and collapsed on the nearest chair. She was breathing hard and shaking all over. All the blood had drained from her face.

The woman shut the door and locked it.

"Are you all right?" she asked, turning toward Nina.

Still breathless, Nina managed to nod.

She closed her eyes and pressed on her heart, in an effort to stop it from pounding.

"Do you want a glass of water?" asked the woman.

"Yes, please," Nina whispered.

When the water came, her hand was trembling so hard she was afraid she would spill it.

"Thank you," she breathed.

"Do you want me to call the police?" the woman asked.

"No. No," Nina said, shaking her head, "I'm okay now."

After a few minutes she stood up slowly and tried to think what to do? She knew she wasn't able go out into the street. She wanted to go back up to the safety of Matt's apartment, but how was she going to get there? She couldn't get back into that elevator. Then she remembered that there were two elevators. Maybe she could use the other one. She turned to the woman, "Could you just wait here for a minute until I get into the elevator?"

"Where are you going to go?" The woman asked.

"I want to go back up to my boyfriend's apartment," said Nina.

"Oh. Okay," the woman said, doubtfully.

She watched as Nina went out into the hall and rang for the second elevator, nervously checking the front door. When the elevator door opened Nina turned and thanked the woman again and walked into the elevator. The door closed, locking her into the elevator again. It started to rise. Stay calm, stay calm, until it gets to Matt's floor, she told herself. When the elevator finally stopped at the top floor and the door slid open, she realized she had been holding her breath the whole way up.

She got out and rang Matt's bell, looking behind her. It took a long time before Matt came and opened the door, sleepy and confused.

"Nina?" he said, puzzled, "What...?"

As soon as she was inside the apartment, her knees buckled. She sank to the floor. Matt closed the door.

"Lock it! Lock it!" she begged.

"What the hell happened?" asked Matt, standing over her in his underwear. "Why were you outside?"

Nina wrapped her arms around his legs.

"I left...I wanted to go home," said Nina. "I didn't want to wake you, and...and...this guy was waiting in the lobby."

Nina started to tremble. Her whole body shook. She was finally safe enough to vent the emotions she had kept under control. Anguished sobs wracked her body and left her gulping for air.

"Oh, God!" Matt said, sinking to his knees to hold her, "Are you hurt? What happened?"

"I'm okay," Nina managed to say, struggling for breath. "He...he...just hit me."

"Shit!" cried Matt, standing and starting go to the door. "I'll fucking kill him!"

"Don't go! Don't go!" she pleaded as she clung to his legs.

"Oh, my darling," Matt said, turning back and kneeling again to clasp her in his arms.

"Why didn't you wake me? I never would have let you go out without me. I would have taken you home. Oh my God, Nina! Nina, darling."

He held her head to his chest with one hand and rocked her back and forth in a kind of a pietà.

All Nina heard was "darling." No one had ever called her that before. She closed her eyes and let the word warm her as though she had been placed under a heat lamp. Her sobs subsided.

"I'm really all right," she said, blotting the tears with the heel of her hand and sniffling. "I just got so frightened."

She tried to smile to reassure him.

"What can I do? What can I get you?" asked Matt, anxiously.

He held her face and gently swept the hair back from her hot forehead.

"Do you want a glass of water? A Valium?"

"No," said Nina, "I think I just need to lie down."

"I'm going to call the police," said Matt.

Nina nodded. He helped her up, brought her gently over to the bed, and put a box of tissues near her. Then he sat down on the bed, picked up the receiver, and dialed 911.

"I want to report a mugging," he said into the phone.

Nina blew her nose and lay down, listening to Matt's voice talking to the police. She could lie there and listen to his voice all night, she thought. Matt hung up and lay down next to her with his arms around her. Together, they waited silently for the police to arrive.

When the policeman came, he asked a lot of questions of Nina. Then he went out to the elevator. When he came back, he was carrying her purse, which he had found lying on the elevator floor. He also carried a man's black leather glove, which he put down on the bed. Nina gasped and shrank away from the glove. The leather fingers were curled inward and it looked to be alive. It looked as though it still contained the hand of the man who had hit her. The policeman put the glove in a plastic bag and said he would make his report and be in touch with them about coming down to the precinct to look at mug shots. Then he left.

"I have to go to rehearsal in the morning," said Matt, "but I don't want to leave you. I'll call Nick and tell him what happened. The understudy can go on for you."

"I...I think I'll be okay," said Nina.

"Nina, you've had a bad shock." said Matt. "Stay here. They can manage without you."

"But it's the first preview."

"It's a play!" said Matt. "It's not curing cancer."

"I know, but we're a team. I don't want to let everyone down."

"Everyone will understand. Is there someone I can call to come and stay with you while I'm at rehearsal?"

Nina thought for a minute, then said reluctantly, "maybe Tom."

"Good," said Matt, "I'll call him in the morning. Now why don't we try to get some sleep? Do you think you can sleep?"

"Maybe I will take that Valium," said Nina, weakly.

With the Valium in her, Nina soon fell into a deep, troubled sleep. Dark, surreal dreams tormented her: fists and faces, doors opening and closing, button panels…black gloves.

In the morning, she woke with swollen eyes, a massive headache, and bruises starting up on each wrist. Matt phoned Nick.

"Let me talk to her," Nick said.

"Nina! What an awful thing! I'm so sorry that you had to go through that. Whatever you need, just let us know. Rest and get better. Charlotte can go on for you tonight."

"Thank you," said Nina, "I'll…I'll let you know… Thanks…"

She handed the phone back to Matt and lay back down with her arm over her eyes.

"We'll see how it goes," Matt said into the phone. "See you in a bit." He hung up and asked Nina for Tom's number.

"Hello, Tom?" said Matt, "This is Matthew Ryland… yes. Yeah, I…Thank you. That was a while ago. Yes, um, the reason…Thank you. You're very kind. Uh, the reason I'm calling is that," he stopped and sighed, "Well…Nina, has had a…a scare. She is okay, but…I…I don't want to leave her alone. I've got to go to rehearsal, and I was wondering if you could possibly come down here to my apartment and stay with her for a while?"

Nina listened while Matt explain what had happened. Then he handed the phone to her.

"Nina!" Tom said. "My God! How horrible! I can't believe it. I'll be right there. I'll just walk the dog and get in a taxi."

"Thanks," said Nina

She hung up the phone. Her neck hurt. The punches had forced her head, violently from one side to the other and must have strained the muscles. Her hands hurt. She looked down at them. I must have hit him so hard...Matt brought over an electric heating pad and reached down to plug it in next to the bed. He folded it gently around her neck and plumped the pillow. The warmth felt good. How sweet he was! His tenderness contrasted sharply with the terror of the night before. With the heating pad on her neck and the Valium still affecting her, she fell back into a deep sleep.

The doorbell rang. She emerged from her sleep like a bubble rising to the surface from the depths of the ocean floor. She lay there for a moment trying to make sense of her surroundings until slowly it dawned on her where she was. Where was Matt? She raised her head to look for him and winced in pain. In a flash, it all came flooding back. The doorbell rang again. She got out of bed heavy with sleep and walked to the intercom. It was Tom. She rang the buzzer to let him in and waited by the door. When he came into the apartment, she melted into his warm bear hug.

"Oh, Nina," he said, shaking his head. "I can't believe it. Are you all right?"

"Well," she said, "my neck is sore, and I have an awful headache, but I guess other than that, I'm okay."

"Thank God he didn't hurt you more than he did!" said Tom.

"I guess he wanted to knock me out and...and...I don't know. He didn't take my purse..." She searched his eyes, questioningly.

"Don't think about it," he said. "It's over. It's passed and done with. It will never happen again. Do you want me to take you home? Or do you want to stay here?"

"Let's go home," said Nina.

Tom walked her to her apartment and came upstairs with her. Once inside she slumped into a chair at the living room table while Tom put up water for tea. Then he handed her a glass of water and two ibuprofen tablets.

"Thanks," said Nina. She drank in silence.

Tom put down two cups of tea and sat down at the table.

"Oh, Tom," Nina sighed, "I don't know what I'm going to do. I think I'm falling in love with him."

"Well," said Tom, "half the women in the world would agree with you, and more than a few of the men! He's a hunk. Don't you remember him on that series? Oh, right, you never watch Western shows. Well, he was so gorgeous and so talented. Is he in love with you?"

"I...don't know...He says so, but he's supposedly engaged to a girl in California."

"Oh, Nina," Tom said, his voice filled with distress, "I don't think I can go through another terrible time with you. He's engaged? Maybe you'd better think twice about this."

"Too late for that, I'm afraid. The genie is out of the bottle."

"Well, the genie better know what the fuck she's doing this time around," said Tom.

"All I know is I can't stop thinking about him, and I don't want to spend any time away from him."

Tom groaned.

"I've never felt this way," said Nina.

Tom gave her a sharp look.

"What? Oh, that last time was...I don't know...was a cry of loneliness," said Nina. "It wasn't like this."

"Well, you were pretty damned torn up," said Tom. "I must say, I never could understand that one. That hirsute creature? With the hairline down to his eyebrows? He proved Darwin's theory!"

Nina laughed.

"It's not like that. Matt is an actor. We speak the same language! I can't tell you how comforting that is!"

"Nina, honey," said Tom, suddenly serious, "I don't mean to throw cold water on your parade, but it seems to me that you fall in love every time you do a play."

Nina paused and looked at him.

"I get mad crushes," she said, defensively. "That's true. But this feels different—this feels like...family, this feels like home."

They sat silently, drinking.

"I once had a therapist," Nina remarked, "who suggested that I was afraid to really fall in love because I feared whomever I loved would be taken away in a flash, like my mother. I think he was right. I have had so many relationships, but I have never actually lived with anyone...or allowed myself to feel like this. It's a little scary."

"Honey," said Tom, "pain is the price we pay for love. You know that. But it doesn't mean it isn't worth it."

Nina kissed his cheek and looked at him, her eyes welling up.

"Thanks so much for coming," she said, "Thanks so much for caring. You can go home now. I'm okay. I think I'm just going to sleep."

Tom finished his tea, got up to leave, and hugged her.

"You know how to reach me," he said, as he went out the door.

She lay down on her bed and fell into a deep sleep. When she woke, it was dusk. She was groggy and her arm muscles ached. There was a tension knot on the left side of her neck, but her headache was somewhat less. She got up, staggered around, and looked at the clock. Picking up the receiver, she dialed the stage manager.

"Hi," she said in a voice thick with sleep. "It's Nina Landau. I'll be there at half-hour."

CHAPTER THIRTEEN

Previews

Previews had been going on for two weeks. Nick kept wanting to fine-tune the play. The cast and crew were exhausted from rehearsing during the day, performing at night, and doing two shows on Wednesdays and Saturdays. It seemed as if everything that could go wrong went wrong.

One Friday night, in the middle of Diana's scene with Matt, the prop phone suddenly rang. Both actors stopped talking abruptly and looked at the phone. After a moment, Diana turned to Matt and said, sweetly, "Aren't you going to answer it?"

Matt looked at her, got up, walked determinedly over to the phone, and picked it up.

"Hello?" he said gruffly into the receiver. He waited a second, then held the phone out to Diana, "It's for you," he said.

Glaring, but as imperious as a camel, Diana got up and walked over to the phone.

"I'm sorry," she said, tightly, "I'll have to call you back."

The audience seemed puzzled but didn't make a sound. They must have assumed all would be made clear at some point later in the play.

Leonard, the older man who was playing the lawyer, was

so nervous that the coffee cup he was holding rattled on its saucer. It rattled so loudly that you could hardly make out his words. Nick asked the prop people if they could pad the bottom of the cup in a way that wouldn't be seen by the audience. But after many unsuccessful attempts, Nick cut the coffee for the lawyer. Leonard's nervousness, however, persisted. During a Wednesday matinee, he went up on his lines. There was a long pause. Matt realized the man didn't know what his next line was and started to improvise.

"So…Will you draw up the necessary papers and mail them to me for my signature?" he asked of the flustered actor.

"Yes! Of course!…I…I that's just what I will do!" The lawyer, replied. You could hear the relief in his voice.

The beautiful green taffeta dress made for Renee Ballinger, who was playing Martin's wife, rustled when she moved. It sounded as if she were rolling in a pile of autumn leaves. A new dress of soft cotton was quickly substituted.

Opening night and the critics were two weeks away. For Nina it was a double-edged sword. She was dreading the arrival of Sharon, but on the other hand she was having more and more fun playing the part of the maid. With repetition she had perfected her comic timing, played around with different facial expressions and gestures, and now she always got her laugh. She was eager to have an understudy rehearsal for the part of Melanie, but that would have to wait until after opening night. There just weren't enough hours in the day.

Diana's onstage antics continued to be outrageous. If she didn't get her exit applause in the second act, she smacked her own hands loudly together as she cleared the sightlines in order to begin it. In the curtain call, her curtsey grew lower and grander each night. If her applause at the end of the play wasn't what she considered to be sufficient, Diana emerged for her curtain call affecting a distinct limp. Nick said nothing, but you could sense that he was seething.

The audiences fluctuated from raucous Saturday night laughers to Tuesday night stony-faced listeners. "I can't go back out there," Diana murmured under her breath, after the first act on one such Tuesday. "That's not an audience—it's an oil painting!"

So much depended on the audience reaction. "How are they?" was the first question Nina always faced as soon as she came offstage.

Previews continued. Technical problems were gradually being solved, and the cast was gaining a sense of confidence and cohesiveness. Then in the middle of a Wednesday matinee, the second-floor door stuck. It had worked perfectly for Nina in the first scene, but somehow when Diana was to make her entrance in the third act, she could not get it open. When her cue came, you could hear her pushing it gently, then harder, and then in a final desperate act, she shoved it so hard it flew open, banged against the opposite wall and made the entire set shake. As she came down the stairs, you could practically see the steam coming out of her ears. She carried on with the dialogue like a professional, but Demond and Matt, who were onstage at the time, spent an unusual amount of time facing upstage. They didn't dare meet each other's eyes. The gossip backstage was that Suzie had put glue on the door frame during the intermission, but nobody really believed it. The two had not spoken since the wig incident. Diana no longer allowed Suzie anywhere near her dressing room; Suzie's assistant, Naomi, was the only one allowed to enter and help her with her wigs. After the Wednesday matinee, Diana confronted Nick, yelling that she would have Suzie up on charges at Equity. Nick tried, without success, to calm her.

"They're fixing the door now," he said, patiently. "Let's remember that this is what previews are all about."

Indeed, two crewmen were up on the second floor of the set sanding and lubricating the door.

But Diana was not to be placated. She exited to her dressing room, slamming the door loudly behind her. Suzie remained in the wig room, quietly setting a curl.

The evening preview went smoothly. After the performance, an agitated Diana was waiting for Matt outside of her dressing room. When he approached her, she accosted him, "You are stepping on my laugh."

Matt's eyebrows shot up. "Oh? Which one?"

"When I say, 'I only want the baby, I don't particularly want the sex.' You come in too quickly with your line. Please wait for my laugh."

Matt bristled but said, "Sure."

At the next performance, Matt listened to Diana say her line. He waited a moment. There was silence. No sound came from the audience. So, he came in with his line.

"*I* only want the *sex*, I don't particularly want the *baby*."

It got a big laugh. When he passed Diana in the hall afterward, she grandly ignored him and floated into her dressing room.

On Saturday after the matinee, Nina and Matt went to Sardi's for their between-show dinner. Actors could eat for a special low price on the second floor. As they walked in, Nina recognized an actor she had once worked with in an Off-Broadway play and went over to the table to say hello. Matt spotted an actor he had worked with on the soap.

"Actors are like a deck of cards reshuffled over the whole world," he said as they finally sat down at a table together.

They both ordered Sardi's famous cannelloni.

"I've somehow managed to lose that laugh in the third act," Matt said to Nina.

"Which one?"

"The one I used to get when I'm talking to the lawyer."

Nina thought for a moment.

"Why don't you stop expecting it to be a laugh line and just say the words?"

Matt stopped eating and looked at her. "What do you mean?"

"Alfred Lunt and Lynn Fontanne used to critique each other's performances after their show every night. One night, Alfred complained to Lynn that he had lost a laugh he always got about a cup of tea. Lynn replied, 'Instead of asking for the laugh, why don't you try asking for the cup of tea?'"

Matt nodded, slowly.

"That's a great story," he said, "But what exactly does it mean?"

"What does it mean?" said Nina putting down her fork. "It means that you are telegraphing that you think the line is funny. Comedy has to have an element of surprise. There is nothing less funny than being told that now you are supposed to laugh."

"Okay…but what do you mean when you say I am *telegraphing*? I don't think I'm telegraphing."

"It's as subtle as thinking," Nina said. "If you are thinking about the fact that you know you are going to get a laugh, you won't get it. If you are thinking about the meaning of the words, you will! You have to play the reality of the moment."

Matt sat for a minute and studied her.

"You sound very cocksure of yourself. Are you sure this is going to work?"

"No. Of course, I'm not sure," said Nina, starting to eat again. "Comedy is…so fragile. If somebody on stage moves and draws the attention away, that will kill your laugh. If there is an extraneous sound. If the theater is too cold. Or too hot. And even if all that goes well, you might mess up your timing. Comedy is hard. Didn't you ever hear the quote, 'Dying is easy. Comedy is hard?'"

Matt laughed and shook his head.

"It was attributed to Edmund Kean, who supposedly said it on his death bed."

"Well," said Matt, skeptically, picking up his fork, "I'll try it tonight. We'll see…"

The cast had each been allotted one complimentary ticket to the opening night performance and the party afterward. The producers were throwing them a gala at Sardi's. Nina knew, of course, that Matt would be with Sharon. She wanted, more than anything in the world to invite Paul as her date. He cut such a dashing figure in his Pierre Cardin suit—slightly taller and broader than Matt but just as handsome in a darker, more sensual way. She wanted to make Matt jealous, but she knew it would break Tom's heart. She squelched her competitive inclinations and asked Tom to be her date for the opening night.

"Oh, God! Of course, I'll come! When you take your first Broadway curtain call, I'll be the one sobbing in the audience!"

"Oh, I hope not," said Nina, her heart sinking. "Do you have a suit?"

"You mean one that I can get into?"

"Oh, Tom! You have to look good! We're going to Sardi's after!"

"When is the opening?" asked Tom.

"December 2nd," said Nina.

Tom did some mental calculating.

"I'll look good by then" he said.

"Well," said Nina, doubtfully. "Don't starve yourself. Sharon is going to be there. I'll need you to support me if my legs buckle."

"I'll support you!" said Tom.

Previews continued. The technical aspects were going

more smoothly. The cast was responding to the audience's laughter and spirits were high.

After one matinee performance, Nick's voice came over the intercom, "Get out of your costumes, please, and come down to the auditorium for a few notes."

There were groans from the cast as this would cut into the short time they had between shows for their dinner.

Nina came downstairs in her kimono and sat next to Matt in the auditorium. As she waited for the note session to begin, she carefully pulled the bobby pins out of her pin curls and put them in a ziplock bag. Diana arrived late in her short makeup robe, her legs bare and her feet in high-heeled slippers. She was still in full theatrical makeup but had taken off her wig. She usually chose to stay in her makeup on a matinee day, so she could just do a quick touch-up for the evening performance. She preferred to eat her dinner in her dressing room and have a short nap between shows. As she stepped down the few stairs to the auditorium, her makeup robe snagged on something and pulled free. It landed in a silky puddle at her feet. She stood frozen on the spot, naked, except for a lacy thong, her high-heeled slippers and a stocking cap. The cast stared, open-mouthed. After a moment, she recovered her composure and said, "Thank God, I had on my face!" As she bent to retrieve her robe, she was given a huge laugh and some applause from the cast and crew.

Nina had virtually moved into Matt's apartment, stopping off at her home only to change clothes, water the plants, and pick up the mail. She had never really lived with anyone before. One night, when they were both sound asleep, Matt started whimpering. Nina woke and gently shook his shoulder.

"Are you all right," she asked?

"Huh?" said Matt.

"You were dreaming."

"Oh, God!" said Matt, sitting up. "I had the worst dream! I was on stage and I didn't...I didn't know...what play we were doing. I managed to get hold of a script, but all the lines were blurry, and I couldn't make out the words. The audience started to get up and walk out of the theater...I wanted to walk out with them. Then, I looked down and I wasn't wearing any pants!"

Nina burst out laughing.

"You had the 'Actor's Nightmare,'" she said. "It's a kind of occupational hazard! I'm afraid it comes with the territory. I'm sorry to laugh. I have it often. I know how terrifying it can be."

"Wow," said Matt, running his hand through his hair. "This business isn't for the lily-livered, is it?"

"If nature had meant us to get up in front of crowds of people and prance around pretending to be somebody else, she would have equipped us with better nerves," said Nina. "I sometimes wonder why we do it!"

"Thanks for waking me," said Matt, shaking his head. "Go back to sleep. I'm so sorry I woke you."

Opening night loomed large. The day before the opening, Nina reluctantly left Matt's apartment, taking with her any trace of herself. Sharon would be arriving late that afternoon. She paused as she put her perfume in her tote bag. She was tempted to spray a little on the pillow but thought better of it; she didn't want to cause any problems for Matt.

At her apartment, she busied herself writing opening night notes to each member of the cast. She would distribute them, along with an apple. Giving apples on opening night was a famous Barrymore family tradition, and they were, after all, in the Barrymore Theater.

That night she went to sleep in her own bed for the first time in weeks, missing Matt. Anxieties swirled in her mind. Was Sharon in New York? Was she with Matt? Had he kissed her? Oh, God! She lay staring at the ceiling.

Twice she sat up and reached for the phone to call him. Twice she lay back down. Would seeing Sharon after so long make him realize how much he loved her? Would his New York love affair be relegated to a dalliance, a brief fling that wouldn't stand the test of time—like a heady wine that was intoxicating but would never travel? Nina was used to disappointing love affairs. She had her share of men who said they loved her and six months later went back to their wives or girlfriends…or boyfriends; men who went to Africa or Europe to "find themselves" and sent back flowers or postcards that said, "I hope you find someone who deserves you." She had relationships with plenty of men, but she had always held something back. She knew in her heart that this was different. Here, finally, was a grown-up man—a smart, talented man she could admire. The little happenings of the day took on a special importance because she couldn't wait to run and share them with Matt. They would laugh over them together. He shared her passion for theater, he "got" her, understood her, and thought she was wonderful. She did not want to let him get away. She tossed and turned and tormented herself with thoughts of Sharon in Matt's arms, Sharon in Matt's bed. Sharon. When she finally fell asleep, it was well after two.

CHAPTER FOURTEEN

Opening Night

The morning began with dark, malignant clouds that blocked the sun, followed by fierce downpours that rattled the windows. It rained all day.

"Rain on opening is good luck," Tom called to remind her.

"We're gonna be a smash hit!" said Nina.

She got to the theater early. Once inside, the excitement was as thick as the bouquets of roses lined up outside of Diana's dressing room. Nina distributed her notes and apples. When she went upstairs to her own dressing room, she was surprised to find a bouquet of roses sitting at her door. It must be from my agent, she thought, stooping to read the attached card.

"On your Broadway opening. The first of many. See you on the ice. Love, Matt." She smiled, closed her eyes, and pressed the note to her heart.

As she opened her door, she noticed three telegrams on her makeup table. The first was accompanied by two dozen long-stemmed yellow roses. It was from Paul. "Break a Leg" it read. Nina smiled at his endearing attempt to speak the language of the theater. Another was from Tom and Brent: "Be brilliant! Why should you hold back?" The third was from Isabelle: "Go get 'em, Tiger," it said. Wonderful telegrams. Wonderful friends. They always came through for her. She felt particularly grateful for their love tonight.

She wondered if Matt had arrived at the theater. Spending the night alone had been so strange. A knock came at the dressing room door, rousing Nina from her reverie.

"Come in," she said. Kelly entered carrying a large, flowering pink Azalea.

"To our Broadway Baby!" the note read. It was from her agent.

Nina sat at the makeup table, surrounded by her flowers and telegrams, getting ready to transform herself into the character. It was part of the calming-down process to sit by herself and quietly prepare for her performance. She put her hair into pin curls and then slowly started to make up her face. Wetting a sponge, she applied her pancake makeup as a base. Then added eyebrows, eyeshadow, a slightly darker base to contour her cheekbones, rouge, lipstick, and the pièce de résistance, her black construction paper eyelashes. About forty-five minutes later, Wallace's voice came over the intercom.

"Half hour, please."

Then he asked, "Demond, are you here?"

Demond shouted from his dressing room, "Yes. Here."

"You didn't sign in," Wallace said.

"I was here before the sign-in sheet went up," called Demond.

"Doesn't matter," said Wallace.

"Sorry. It won't happen again," said Demond.

Nina felt a sudden frisson shoot through her. A Broadway opening! How proud her father would have been! She wished with all her heart that he could have been here to see it. Nick Travis had given everyone a copy of his latest book for opening night: *My Life in the Theater*. In Nina's, he wrote: "You are very good, you know," over his signature. She stared at the inscription for some time.

She carefully placed the wig on her head and secured it with long hairpins. She got into her costume and looked at herself in the mirror, assessing the completed work—she was ready! She went down the stairs. Passing by Matt's dressing room door, she decided against going in to wish him a good show. He had enough on his plate. She had left him an apple with a note that she had signed with love.

As she walked to the back wall of the theater, behind the set, to go to her ladder, she heard the muffled sounds and coughs coming from the audience as they filed into the auditorium. We've played for audiences before, she thought. Nothing new. Then she remembered the critics would be there, and her heart started to race. No. Better not think about that. In the dim light, she climbed the ladder and stood, like a trapeze artist, high above the ground on the little wooden platform just outside the closed door, waiting for the moment when the music would fade, the doorbell would ring, and she would turn the knob and run down the stairs into the limelight.

"Five minutes, please." Wallace's voice over the intercom. The tension in the theater ratcheted up.

Her mouth went dry. She took a few deep breaths. I can do this, she thought. Preparation, concentration, confidence. Those are the keys. I have prepared well. My father gave me confidence. That was his gift to me. All that is left for me to do is to harness my concentration. I can do that.

"House to half." That was Wallace over the intercom talking softly to the people in the lighting booth, followed by "House out."

She listened as the music started up. She felt a little dizzy. Her fingers twitched, nervously. She heard the curtain rise. The audience burst into applause for the set. She smiled quickly. They were in a good mood. As the music diminished, she sent up a silent prayer. The doorbell rang. Her heart was hammering so loudly, she thought it might be picked up by the microphone. This was it! With a trembling hand, she reached for the doorknob and opened the door.

From the dimness of backstage, she entered into the blinding lights of the set. She stood for a moment alone on the vast empty stage in the cavernous theater. She was acutely aware that all eyes were trained on her. How many people? Hundreds. Maybe a thousand. How many did the Barrymore hold? A rush of adrenaline pumped through her. Then she went blithely down the stairs. From the corner of her eye, she could make out the first few rows of the audience. She knew she had to keep them all in the back of her mind while she concentrated on the character. She understood how to split her concentration between the audience and the character, to strike a balance between the two, never losing track of the audience—never losing track of the character. She could not let the character "possess" her. She had to always have that "outside eye."

Noticing the box of chocolates, she did a double take, walked downstage to them, looked right and left, popped one in her mouth, and sprinted out into the wings. The audience laughed. Nina exhaled. Relief rushed through her like water from an opened dam. Thank God! she thought. Demond passed her, head down, tense and hurried, on his way to the stage. They were off and running!

The rest of the performance was met with great enthusiasm. The audience was enjoying the show, and their response acted as a spur for the cast. It was a symbiotic relationship. There was a sense of exhilaration, mixed with relief and pride, among the actors. Their hard work was paying off. By the end of the play, as they gathered for the curtain call, they all had broad smiles on their faces.

Nina went to her place in the wings, stage left. When her cue light came on, she walked out onto the stage accompanied by the curtain music. A sense of pride coursed through her. She could not keep from smiling. The audience was applauding. A few people started to rise to their feet. Out of the corner of her eye she saw Leonard, the actor playing the lawyer, come out from the stage right wings. More people stood up. As the actors continued appearing on the stage, more and more people got to their feet. Nina's hands were trembling. It was exhilarating!

Diana burst through the second-floor door and, like the goddess Athena descending from Mount Olympus, she floated down the staircase. The audience cheered. As she walked to the apron of the stage, there were whistles and shouts of "Brava!" She went into her deep, regal curtsy. Then she stood up, smiled, and blinked her eyelids rapidly to indicate humility. She applauded the audience and curtsied again. A bouquet of long-stemmed red roses was rushed out from the wings by a stagehand and she bowed, graciously accepting them. By the time she backed up and joined the rest of the cast, the whole audience was on its feet, applauding, whistling and shouting "Bravo." It was the most magical moment Nina had ever experienced! Now she knew why actors went through all the nerves and the rejections. Now she understood that this was one of the best feelings in the world.

She searched the left side of the balcony for Tom but couldn't locate him among the cheering crowd. Just then she saw someone frantically waving a white handkerchief. She wanted to wave back, but instead she just flashed a radiant smile in his direction. Three of the aisle seats in the orchestra were vacated, and Nina saw three men rushing up the aisle to the exit. The critics. The curtain came down and rose again. More applause. They took three curtain calls before the applause finally started to wane, and Wallace brought the curtain down for good. Backstage the cast wept and hugged each other. She caught Matt's eye, and they exchanged a silent smile. She went up to her dressing room. Her heart was high! It was time to get ready for the party!

CHAPTER FIFTEEN

The Party

Nina got out of her costume and took off her theatrical makeup and wig. Tonight, instead of dabbing on a little lipstick and running a comb through her hair, she carefully applied her street makeup. Then she undid her pin curls and brushed her hair out into soft curls. She got into her green silk dress and heels, added her mother's pearls and earrings, and looked at herself in the mirror. Satisfied, she went down the stairs to meet Tom, her raincoat slung over her arm.

As she passed Diana's dressing room, she could hear the sound of people talking and laughing. The producers and her agents were probably congratulating her. A crowd of people were jammed inside the small space by the stage door. Tom pushed his way through them and enveloped Nina into his arms. His eyes were moist with tears.

"You were wonderful!" he gushed.

Over his shoulder, Nina could see a slim, attractive girl with thin blonde hair and knew at once that it must be Sharon. She looked like a displaced person, hugging the wall and not taking her eyes off Matt as he greeted people and accepted congratulations. Tom took out a handkerchief and blew his nose loudly. He helped Nina on with her coat and guided her out of the theater and into the rain. There was a large crowd outside the stage door, waiting under umbrellas for Matt and Diana. Tom put his umbrella up and elbowed his way past them, with Nina in tow, finally reaching the curb where a lineup of limousines was waiting to take the cast to Sardi's. A driver jumped out to hold the door for them and then quickly got back behind the wheel.

Tom peered out of the rain-streaked window at the huge photograph of Diana Lawrence that stood on a billboard in front of the theater.

"Look at that photo!" he said. "I can't believe she's still using that bat mitzvah picture."

"Tom!" said Nina, laughing, "Diana is still beautiful!"

"Botox and fillers, honey, Botox and fillers," said Tom.

"Diana's only slightly older than I am," Nina protested.

"But, honey, she's so butch-looking. One has to wonder if she dresses right or left?"

Nina gasped and put a hand over her mouth.

"Besides," Tom added, "you are much more beautiful than she could ever hope to be."

The limo inched down Broadway. The streets were clogged with traffic because of the rain. It took twenty-five minutes for the limousine to finally pull up in front of the red awning at Sardi's. A doorman with a large umbrella came to open the door and help them out.

Outside Sardi's was another huge crowd. They were huddled under umbrellas waiting for the stars: Diana Lawrence and Matthew Ryland. They inspected Nina and Tom excitedly and then dismissed them. One autograph seeker thrust a pen and a piece of paper in Tom's face.

"Are you anybody?" he asked.

"Yes!" said Tom, angrily shoving passed him.

They entered the restaurant depositing their wet umbrellas and coats in the cloak room. Nina fluffed her hair, smoothed her dress, and looked around her. People were pressed three-deep at the bar, ordering drinks. A large

black-and-white photograph of John McMartin as Sga-
narelle in *Don Juan* hung over the bar, right above the seat
that Mr. McMartin usually occupied. Inside, in the large,
brightly lit dining room, the private party was in full swing.
People were milling around drinking champagne; some
were seated at tables and waiters were busy serving them
hors d'oeuvres and refilling their glasses. Nina and Tom
were ushered in by the maître d' and shown to a table right
under a caricature of Fred Gwynne. The walls were rife
with caricatures of theater celebrities: Bette Midler, Jason
Robards, Ethel Merman, Barbra Streisand, Christopher
Plummer and all the Broadway stars.

Tom turned to Nina, "Someday your picture will be
hanging here," he said.

A waiter came by and put two glasses of champagne
down on their table. Across the room, Nina could see Nick,
who was seated with his wife, Fiona. She looked like a
Vogue model wearing a bright red satin dress with a gold
filigree choker around her long, graceful neck. Her black
hair was slicked back into a chignon at the base of her head.

"Wow!" said Nina. "Fiona is gorgeous! I wonder how she
puts up with Nick and his affairs?"

"She knows what side her bread is buttered on," offered
Tom.

Suddenly there was a stir in the room. Matt entered with
Sharon. There was applause, and people stood up, clapping
as they made their way to the left side of the room, far
away from Nina and Tom. Sharon's head was turned toward Matt, and her eyes were fixed on his face. She smiled,
shyly. Nina stayed seated and squeezed Tom's hand under
the table.

"Yes, I see her," he replied. "She's no match for you. A
little mousy, I would say…"

Nina sipped her champagne and tried not to stare at
Sharon, but it was as though her eyes had been magnetized.

All of a sudden, a big commotion erupted from the bar area. Diana had arrived with her agent, Seth Williams. Mr. Williams was helping Diana out of her full-length, black mink coat, and they made their way into the dining room. Necks swiveled and people jostled each other to get a better look. Diana smiled, acknowledged the applause, and walked to the center of the room. She was wearing a dress that was the exact same shade of red as Fiona's with a neckline that plunged twice as deep. Her only jewelry was a pair of diamond chandelier earrings. Nina glanced over to Nick's table. Nick was standing and enthusiastically applauding. Fiona remained seated, looking into a small, round pocket-et-mirror and applying lipstick. Diana and her agent were shown to a table in the center of the room.

"I think she has that dress on backwards," murmured Tom. "Let's get something to eat! I'm starving! I haven't eaten since Thursday."

He signaled for a waiter, who came by and took their order. Nina was conscious of eyes being on her. She felt pretty in her green dress with her long, dark hair, wavy from the pin curls. Without the costume and wig, few people recognized her as the maid. She liked that. She liked being unidentifiable from the part she played.

They were enjoying their food and the champagne and discussing the evening's performance and individual actors, when Nick abruptly got up from his table holding a piece of paper that a producer had handed him. He had his glasses on and strode to the middle of the restaurant and called for quiet. Tom hit his spoon against his glass.

Nick cleared his throat and began to speak. "I've just been handed a copy of the *New York Times* review," he said. The restaurant quieted to an eerie hush. Nick began, "The team of Nick Travis and George DuPont has once again hit a home run!" The restaurant erupted in cheers. They cheered for two long minutes. Finally, there were shushes and Nick went on.

"Their new venture, aptly named *The Second Time Around*, just slid into home plate at the Barrymore Theatre. The team that brought you the Broadway hit *Spoiler Alert* added a definite home run to the score card." There was more applause and "hush, shhhhh" could be heard again. Nick went on.

"The play involves a divorced couple in which the ex-wife has reached 'a certain age' and does not want to remain childless. Unfortunately, the only man she wants to father her child is her ex-husband, who is more than willing. There is one caveat: he has to do it without his current wife knowing. The complications that ensue make for the kind of comedy at the Barrymore Theater that has long been missing from the Broadway scene." The crowd cheered again.

Nick went on. "The cast is superb, from the ravishing Diana Lawrence," Diana stood up beaming and lifted her glass of champagne as a toast to the applauding people around her.

Nick resumed reading. "Um...Diana Lawrence, who flawlessly does her star turn as Melanie, the childless, ex-wife, and the multitalented Matthew Ryland (of TV fame) as her eager-to-comply ex-husband..."

The applause broke out again as Matt smiled and nodded. Nina's heart inflated like a deployed airbag.

Nick went on "...all the way down to the maid, played with a saucy insouciance by Nina Landau."

Tom stood up, yelling, "Brava! Brava!" and clapped so hard that his hands and face turned red. The entire restaurant turned toward him. Nina blushed and laughed.

Nick read on. "Demond Daniels, Leonard Wallach and Renee Ballinger round out the talented cast, as the husband's best friend, his lawyer, and his beleaguered wife, respectively."

There were whoops and whistles and clinking of glasses. Nick shushed the crowd, once more.

"This Christmas season," he read on, "if you wish to make the holidays ring with laughter, set your sights on the Barrymore Theatre—it's the best game in town."

They were a hit! The diners rose to their feet as one. Applause filled the room. The producers were hugging each other and hugging Nick. Even the dour Sardi's waiters were smiling. Two men picked up George DuPont's chair, with him in it, and carried him around the room like a groom at a Jewish wedding. George gripped the sides of the chair crying, "Put me down! Put me down!" Tom hugged Nina, lifting her off her feet.

"My God, Nina!" he said, "You got a good mention in the *New York Times!* I said you were going to play the hell out of the maid, and you did! Can you believe it?"

"I can't quite," said Nina, shaking her head in disbelief and laughing.

Amid the noisy confusion, Matt caught her eye from across the room. He was glowing with pride. She flashed a dazzling smile in his direction and then quickly looked away. How she longed to share this moment with him! How wonderful life could be!

CHAPTER SIXTEEN

SRO

There was a line around the theater. People were waiting to buy tickets to the play. A sandwich board sat just outside the theater with a sign that announced, "Tonight's performance is sold out." "SRO" was plastered diagonally across the ticket booth for the evening's performance. Standing room only.

Nina had to walk out into the street in order to get around the crowd to reach the stage door. She had slept on and off for most of the day, talking on the phone, paying bills, and doing neglected housework. There was the usual letdown after the opening. The taut nerves and tight muscles could finally relax. She hadn't heard from Matt all day. She knew he had to sign in by seven thirty, so she got into costume and makeup early and at seven twenty-five went down to the stage door to check the sign-in sheet. She was relieved to see his initials there in the box next to his name. She went to the back wall of the theater and climbed her ladder to the second-floor perch. At seven thirty, Wallace called half-hour and opened the house. She could hear the sounds of the audience coming in and taking their seats. A full house was such fun to play to! She made an effort to focus her mind on the play, but she kept wondering what Matt was doing? What was he thinking? How long was

Sharon going to be in New York? Had he said anything to her about them?

She got her satisfying chuckle from the audience, as she did her bit with the chocolates, and she marveled how well actors could disguise their true feelings. Inside she was in a state of turmoil. Was Sharon in the audience, watching her? Was she judging her acting? Her looks? Nina hadn't planned to fall in love, but it had happened. It hadn't mattered to her at first that he was engaged to someone else. That was the chance she took. Those were the rules of the game, weren't they? She fell in love with the clear knowledge that he might go back to his girlfriend at any time. If it happened and she got hurt, she couldn't blame anyone but herself. Tom had said that pain was the price you paid for love. She understood that. She was willing to accept it. But how could she imagine her life without him?

The play went well enough, but not nearly as well as it had gone on opening night. Second nights were notoriously anticlimactic. The adrenaline was not pumping in the same way. The audience seemed to be in a "show me" mood. They had read the reviews, paid top dollar for their tickets, hired their babysitters, and eaten their dinners, and now they wanted their money's worth. The applause at the end of the first act was substantial. Maybe they were just that strange kind of audience that was quiet, but attentive? It was hard to tell.

She didn't see Matt backstage after her scene. The only time she made eye contact with him was on stage. And then, of course, it was Martin she was looking at, not Matt. There was not a hint, not a glimmer of recognition in Matt's eyes. Acting was so strange. She was eager to ask him a million questions, but all she could say to him was, "Sir, there is someone at the door who wishes to see you." By the end of the performance she was anxious to get out of her costume and see if he would be waiting for her outside the stage door, or if he would be taking Sharon back to his apartment. She dressed quickly and hurried down the stairs. If I make the first three steps before the dressing room door closes, she told herself, he will be there.

Matt was outside, signing autographs. He looked up at her. His jaw was tight, and he looked as though he hadn't slept. She didn't see Sharon.

"Joe's?" he asked.

"Sure," she said, with a sudden relief.

It was too crowded to get in the door at Joe Allen, so they walked to Charlie's. The hostess greeted them warmly, congratulating them on the show's success, and sat them in a quiet two-table in the back of the restaurant. They ordered wine and made small talk about the performance while waiting for their drinks to arrive.

"When I was a child, I thought SRO stood for "Sold Right Out!" said Nina.

Matt nodded but did not smile. Nina, sensing the tension between them, found it difficult to keep up the pretense of cheerfulness. A few people came over to congratulate Matt on the good reviews. Finally the drinks arrived, and Matt spoke.

"I'm sorry to be so uncommunicative today. I had to…a lot to…think about."

"That's okay," said Nina, rushing to absolve him. "I understand."

His demeanor was so solemn. She studied his face, searching for any sign of what was to come.

"She is a really good person," he said softly, looking at the table. "I hope you get to know her someday. She did nothing wrong. And I hurt her…deeply."

There was a long silence. Nina was afraid to breathe.

Matt sighed and looked up at her.

"Turns out she's allergic to cats," he said. "She had to stay in a hotel."

Nina's heart leapt. Oh, thank God for Murray! she thought. Then just as suddenly, trepidation gripped her. Don't ask, she thought, clamping her lips together and willing herself to be silent.

"I stayed at the apartment," Matt said answering her unspoken question.

"Sometimes I feel like I haven't learned all my lines for life," said Nina.

"There's nothing you can say," said Matt. "It has very little to do with you. And then again, in a way, I suppose, it has everything to do with you."

"Where is she now?" asked Nina, trying to make her voice sound casual.

"Back in California," said Matt. "I got a phone call right before the show...the plane landed safely."

"Oh good," said Nina, with relief. "I mean...that the... plane landed safely."

"And that she's back in California," Matt said, with a wry smile.

"Yes." Nina lowered her eyes. "That too."

A middle-aged couple approached the table. The man hesitated, but the heavy-set woman came right up to them. They had just seen the show and were raving about how good it was and how much they liked Matt's performance.

"How did you learn all those lines?" the woman asked astounded.

Matt shook his head, "It's not easy," he said.

The woman nodded, openmouthed, and turned to Nina.

"Were you part of the play?" she asked.

"She played the maid," said Matt.

"Oh!" said the woman, surprised. "You were wonderful! Tell me, my husband and I were arguing, were those real chocolates that you ate or fake ones?"

"Real," said Nina.

"You eat a real chocolate every night?" asked the woman.

"And two on matinee days!" said Nina, her eyebrows raised.

"Oh, right! I didn't think of that!" exclaimed the woman, turning to her husband to share the excitement.

"Thank you," she said, "I'm sorry to bother you."

"No bother," said Matt.

They walked away, chatting with each other.

Matt and Nina finished their drinks.

"I understand if you want to be alone tonight," Nina offered.

"I want to be with you," Matt said, "but I'm afraid I won't be very good company."

"You don't need to be," said Nina. "You never need to be."

Matt smiled for the first time that night and took her hand.

"C'mon, let's get out of here," he said.

The emotional roller coaster had left Nina so exhausted she could barely keep her eyes open. They climbed into bed and both fell almost immediately into a deep sleep. Sometime in the middle of the night, Murray the cat curled up next to Nina. Normally she would have shooed him off, but tonight she embraced him as her one true ally in the long, hard-won struggle for Matt.

CHAPTER SEVENTEEN

Diana

The following night at the theater, the bouquets of roses had already started to wilt, along with Diana's spirits. Withdrawal from the limelight and the champagne was starting to set in. Just before half-hour was called, she came out of her dressing room naked under her short makeup robe with her hair in pin curls and bellowed, "There is a miasma in my dressing room!"

The stage manager was dispatched to investigate and discovered the culprit: a dead mouse behind the radiator. The problem was quickly solved with the mouse's removal, but Diana refused to go back into the room. Matt graciously agreed to switch dressing rooms with her for the duration of the night's performance until the smell dissipated.

Friday night, during one of Diana's speeches, a bunch of latecomers arrived at the theater just after the first act had started. There was a frosty silence as Diana stopped speaking. Not wanting to break the fourth wall but unwilling to speak until the offending parties were settled, Diana busied herself brushing imaginary fluff off her sleeve and waited for them to find their seats. When they had settled themselves, she deigned to resume the scene.

By the Saturday evening performance, the house was packed, and people were standing in the back of the theater.

Diana made her first act entrance to applause, but during the scene with Matt, her words began to slur. Nina's face snapped up to the squawk box on the wall of her dressing room. Diana's speech seemed thick and sluggish. Something was wrong. She sounded like a tape recording that had been slowed down. Nina rose slowly from her chair and went warily downstairs, her heart in her mouth. This was not good. Most of the cast and crew were already gathered around the intercom in the costume room. Some were standing in the wings, peering out onto the stage. Matt was on stage trying to propel the scene forward, but he was conversing with a zombie. Wallace's voice was low and clipped, standing at the stage manager's podium just inside the wings and talking into his headphone. He kept looking out to the stage, trying to decide whether or not to bring the curtain down. Nick arrived breathless from his perch at the back of the theater. His face was dark with concern. Suddenly, Diana seemed to rally, and the scene went on. Everyone exhaled. But a few minutes later, her words became unintelligible again. Terror filled Nina's heart. What was happening? Matt was improvising like crazy. Somehow, they made it to the end of the act. The first act finale music began, and the curtain came down quickly. The cast and crew fell back and opened a path for Diana and Matt as they came off the stage. As soon as she cleared the sightlines, Diana swooned. Matt caught her and scooped her up in his arms. Nick rushed to help Matt. Together they carried Diana into her dressing room and lay her on the couch. Wallace, grim-faced, followed them into the room, turned once, glancing at the slack-jawed actors clustered around the entrance and closed the door. No one spoke. After about three minutes, Wallace came out, shutting the dressing room door quietly behind him.

"Get dressed," he said to Nina. "You're going on."

CHAPTER EIGHTEEN

Going On

Nina stood in stunned silence. She was led into the costume room by Teddy, who quickly stripped off her maid's outfit and her wig. She stood in her bra and panties as Teddy's assistant came rushing in holding Diana's second act costume. The two women helped Nina into the costume. It smelled of Diana's perfume. They zipped it up. Thank God it fits, thought Nina dully. There wasn't time to shorten the hem. Suzie came into the room, carrying Diana's second act wig.

"Sit down," she said. Nina sat. Suzie pulled the wig over Nina's stocking cap. As she centered it, she bent and whispered to Nina in her Caribbean accent, "She's on them drugs. He done broke up with her, and she must have taken one too many."

"Nick?" whispered Nina, astounded.

"Mmm-hmm," Suzie nodded as she secured the wig on Nina's head with hairpins.

"He had it with that bitch," she said. "That fancy behavior come back to bite her in the ass."

Charlotte Ways came rushing into the costume room, breathless. She undressed and put on the maid's costume. It was still warm from Nina's body. The wig that Nina had just taken off was placed on Charlotte's head. Wallace came into the dressing room.

"Nick has taken Diana home in a taxi where her sister will meet her. Are you guys okay?" Wallace asked, stone-faced.

All the color had drained from Nina's face, but she managed to nod.

"I'm about to call five minutes," he said, looking intently at Nina. "Is there anything you need?"

Nina had a moment's desperate longing to take the Valium she had upstairs in her purse, but after calculating how long it would take for someone to get it and for it to take effect, she dismissed the thought. She shook her head.

"I will be making an announcement over the loudspeaker," said Wallace in a steady and controlled voice, as though he were a newscaster explaining that the president was dead and the vice president was being sworn in, "that Ms. Lawrence has taken ill and that you will be assuming the role for the remainder of tonight's performance. And that Ms. Ways will be playing the role of the maid." His eyes glanced over to Charlotte.

Nina nodded and watched him leave the room.

Mayhem reigned backstage. It was like a triage center after a train wreck. Everyone was scurrying in different directions, dealing with the emergency. Diana's shoes were too small for Nina, and the pair that Teddy had put aside for her were not polished. Teddy spit on them and hurriedly ran a cloth over them, but they still looked terrible. Teddy sighed. They would have to do. She pressed her lips together and put the shoes down in front of Nina, who stepped into them. She looked at herself in the mirror and stuck a few extra hairpins in the wig to make it feel more secure, wishing she could do the same for the lines inside her head. She heard the words "five minutes, please," over the intercom and her hands began to tremble.

She turned to Teddy, silently asking for confirmation that she looked all right. There was a terrifying pause before Teddy nodded and said, "You look good!" and then gave her a nervous but encouraging smile.

Nina closed her eyes and exhaled loudly.

She walked out to the stage right wings from where Melanie made her second act entrance. The stagehands and the actors were all watching her. Across the stage, she could see Matt getting ready for his entrance from stage left. He was pacing back and forth and looking down. She heard the audience settling themselves into their seats. Wallace called "places" and then the sound of his voice came over the loudspeaker.

"Ladies and gentlemen, may I have your attention please. Diana Lawrence has taken ill."

A shock wave went through the audience.

"The part of Melanie will now be played by Nina Landau and the part of the maid will be played by Charlotte Ways."

The audience groaned and Nina felt her heart clutch. Let it go, let it go, she told herself. Concentrate on the part. Concentration, preparation and confidence. She had never had an understudy rehearsal. She had never even played the part on the stage, except for the one experience early on during rehearsals, and that had not been in costume nor in front of an audience! Put it out of your mind. Put it out of your mind, Nina thought, with desperation. Anchor yourself in Melanie's situation. Not Nina's. And remember to project.

The second act opened with a short scene between Renee, Martin's new wife, and Leonard, the lawyer. It usually got a few laughs, but tonight it was greeted with stony silence. The anxiety over Diana's illness and the change in the cast had clearly affected the audience's mood. A few had even gotten up to leave after the announcement was made.

In the following scene, after a quick blackout, Melanie was supposed to be discovered on stage, sitting on the couch, with Martin standing behind her. The lights went down as usual. Suddenly the realization struck Nina that she had never rehearsed getting to the couch in the dark. It's a straight-line, she told herself. There's nothing in the way. Oh, God! Why hadn't she taken that Valium? She felt her stomach lurch and for an instant thought that she might be sick. Panic seized her. Stop it! Stop it! She took deep breaths and talked to herself. Here is my chance to show them I can play this part. Remember how upset you were when Diana Lawrence was cast? Remember how you knew that you could play the part? Go out there and show them!

She heard the music cue. In the pitch-blackness, Nina walked out onto the stage. There was a tiny piece of glow tape on the floor marking where the back corner of the couch went, and she fastened her gaze on that as though it were the North Star. She moved forward, cautiously, and flailed around for the couch like a blind person. Her heart was beating wildly. As her hand hit the back of the couch, she bent, groped for the pillow and sat down. She felt light-headed and her hands were clammy. Then she heard Matt's footsteps as he walked onto the stage, and she felt his presence behind her, slightly to her left. Somehow his being there calmed her. She couldn't let him down. She had to stop thinking of herself and think about him. How nervous he must be for her. For himself. She had to look in his eyes and let him know immediately that she was in control, that he was in good hands, and that the play would go on.

The music ended, the lights came up and she said her first line. Matt answered. Suddenly it had a familiarity to it. It felt so much as if they were sitting in Matt's apartment, running lines. She could do this. They had done it so many times before. The words and his voice were so natural to her. Her diaphragm started to unclench. Her breathing started to calm. She lobbed the first laugh line over to him, and he sent it back with impeccable timing.

The audience laughed, faintly. They were beginning to let themselves forget the disruption and were getting back into the play. She could feel the shift in their attention. This added to her confidence. It's all about confidence, she reminded herself. Let them know that you are qualified to do this. Let them know they are in good hands. Broadway understudies can do the job. They were going to get a fabulous show! The show they deserved. The show they paid for.

She carried on with the scene, and when it came to an end and she exited, she got applause. The cast and crew had all been crowded around, watching from the wings. They clapped and greeted her with gleaming eyes. She smiled nervously at them and disappeared into the costume room to change for the third act. Matt knocked and poked his head around the door as she was changing.

"You are amazing!" he said and closed the door again.

She smiled to herself. Teddy patted her on the back as she helped her into the third act costume.

By the time the third act curtain was about to go up, Nina felt a bit calmer. She walked onto the stage with a new self-assurance. By the end of the act, she had done the emotional scene, with the tears arriving effortlessly and truthfully. It didn't matter that she had used her anxiety to produce them. Whatever worked! At the end of the play, the lights went down, the music came up, and the audience was clapping vigorously. She took her place in the stage right wings for the curtain call. She could not bring herself to come from the upstage, second floor door, as Diana did. She waited until the rest of the cast was on stage and came out for her bow. The whole cast turned and applauded her. Tears sprang to her eyes. One of the tech people ran out from the wings with a dozen roses. She looked out into the audience and saw that the entire crowd was up on its feet, giving her a standing ovation! She took her bow with goose bumps on her arms and mascara streaming down her cheeks. She had done it!

Nick had been watching from the back of the theater. Having left Diana in the care of her sister, he returned to watch the show. Now he came backstage as the cast was hovering around Nina. He looked at her for a moment and clasped her to his chest in a hug.

"Nice job!" he breathed into her hair. "Nice job!"

She was glad to have vindicated his faith in her. She climbed the stairs up to her dressing room, amid all the congratulations. As she got out of the costume, a knock came at the door. It was Teddy coming to collect the third act costume. She was holding a vase.

"This is for your flowers," she said with a smile.

She gathered up the costume and the shoes.

"I'll polish these for tomorrow's matinee," she said, pointedly.

"Diana might be back by then," said Nina.

"Diana has been let go," said Teddy. She opened the door to leave just as Nick was coming into the room. He sat down in a chair and sighed deeply. Nina sat motionless.

"Diana is having substance issues and plans have been made to send her to an excellent upstate rehab facility," he said. "I've just gotten off the phone with the producers. We want you to take over the role."

Nina was speechless. Nick looked at her. He got up and put his hands on her shoulders.

"Go home. Rest up. Just do what you did tonight. You're going to be fine. Matinee three o'clock tomorrow. Come at noon. We'll go over a few things. Okay?"

"Okay," said Nina, dazed.

"You have my home number. Call if you have any questions. You're going to be fine." Nick turned and left the room.

She stared at herself in the mirror. It was too much to take in. She slowly took off her makeup, combed out her hair, and dressed in her jeans and sweater. She put the roses into the vase and went downstairs in search of Matt. He was waiting for her, leaning against the wall by the stage door. The doorman, who never spoke, congratulated her.

"There are people outside," Matt said, smiling. "They want your autograph."

"No way!" said Nina.

"All right…but be prepared."

He opened the door. She walked out into a sea of people who surged forward, holding out pens and programs. Nina signed her name as Matt watched, enjoying her success. Finally, the crowd thinned.

"Do you want to go home?" he asked, "I think we have a bottle of wine."

"Oh, God, yes!" said Nina, gratefully.

In the taxi, Nina was pensive.

At Matt's apartment, she lay down on the bed, staring at the ceiling, while he poured them each a glass of wine.

"Do you really think it went all right?" she asked tentatively.

"You know," said Matt, "the play is much better with you in it than with Diana."

Nina laughed. "You don't have to say that," she said.

"No, I'm serious," said Matt. "Diana Lawrence was playing Diana Lawrence. That's what the audience came to see and that's what she gave them. You are playing Melanie. You are a better actor. You can assume the mantel of the character and disappear into it. You can become the character while also expressing something of yourself, and that is what I saw tonight and what was lacking in the play before."

Matt came over with the two glasses of wine and put one down on the bedside table.

"Also," he said, looking at her, "you listen on stage. God!

What a blessing it is to play a scene with someone who listens! Besides," Matt continued, sitting down next to her, "it finally gives you an opportunity to show how beautiful you are. That maid's outfit is attractive...but let's just say it lacks a certain *je ne sais quoi*."

Nina laughed, shaking her head in amazement. She rose up on one elbow and took a long sip of her wine.

"Well, I'm glad that you feel that way," she said, "because apparently Diana has been let go."

She looked up at him apprehensively, waiting for his reaction.

Matt leaned over and kissed her.

"I know," he said. "Nick told the cast when you were upstairs getting out of your costume. Congratulations, honey. I am so proud of you!"

They put down their glasses and looked into each other's eyes.

"I don't know how I found you," Nina said, "but I never want to let you go."

They undressed slowly, finished their wine, and soon they both fell into a deep, restorative sleep.

Sometime in the middle of the night, Nina was awakened by Matt gently shaking her shoulder and saying, "Nina. Nina."

"What happened?" she asked, sleepy and confused.

"You were crying in your sleep," he said.

Nina put a hand up to her face. Her cheeks were wet with tears.

"Oh, God," she said. "I remember. I...I was dreaming I was with my mother. She was holding out her arms to me, and my whole chest flooded with happiness. I ran to her and...just before I reached her...there was...a crash."

Nina stopped and her brow creased.

"I have never dreamt about the car crash. Never."

"My poor darling," said Matt. "What a horrible dream. Come here. Let me hold you."

He enfolded her in his arms and gently smoothed the hair from her wet cheeks.

"It was a dream," he whispered. "I'm here. I won't let anything bad happen to you. Go back to sleep."

Nina lay in his arms, staring blankly into the dark.

"But what if something happens to you?" she asked.

"Shhh," Matt said. "Nothing is going to happen to me. Go to sleep. You've had a very stressful day. I love you."

Nina fell asleep in Matt's arms.

By the time she arrived at the theater, Diana's things had been moved out, and Nina found herself surrounded by her own things in the star dressing room. Only two of Diana's plants remained, to attest to the fact that she had ever been there. Nina welcomed the chance to go over some of the scenes with Nick. Her shoes had been polished, and the costumes had been shortened and let out an inch at the waist. As she readied herself, standing in the wings, waiting to perform the part of Melanie from the beginning of the play, she watched Charlotte Ways play the part of the maid. Charlotte executed her part well, but Nina noted, with a certain amount of schadenfreude, that the bit with the chocolates did not get a laugh.

CHAPTER NINETEEN

Christmas Eve

The whole theater world was buzzing about the sudden absence of Diana Lawrence. The story given out was that she had been suffering from exhaustion after the opening and was taking a "rest cure." The producers had decided against making any permanent announcement. They wanted to give Nina a chance to perform the part for a while, so she could hit her stride and become more comfortable in the role before they unleashed the critics on her. The programs, the posters, the photographs outside the theater, all remained the same, listing Diana Lawrence as Melanie. However, according to union rules, two out of three things had to happen when an understudy took over: a sandwich board in the lobby had to announce the understudy, a slip had to be inserted in the programs and an announcement had to be made at the start of each performance. Wallace continued to make his announcement at the start of every show, there was a sign in the lobby, and an insert in the programs that stated "at tonight's performance the role of Melanie will be played by Nina Landau and the role of the maid will be played by Charlotte Ways." The cast knew this was not a temporary situation: a new actor had been hired to understudy the part of Melanie. She turned out to be Jean Moor, the lanky blonde who had been so nervous at the audition that her purse had fallen on the floor.

There was no decline at the box office because of Diana's absence. Houses continued to be sold out. On occasional afternoons, Nick would come in early to work some scenes with Nina. Things were falling into place.

She had been performing the role of Melanie for two weeks now with growing confidence. She was having the time of her life! It was wonderful to feel the audience's response when she timed a laugh line just right; wonderful to see out of the corner of her eye that their faces mirrored her own when she was playing the emotional scene. It gave her a sense of power. She loved going to the theater every day with Matt, penciling her initials in the sign-in sheet, and then going to their separate dressing rooms. "See you on the ice!" Matt would always say as he kissed her. Cast members would occasionally knock at her dressing room door and stop in to wish her a "good show." Sometimes they stayed and chatted about their day as she put on her makeup. She felt part of a large, loving family, which so often happens in theater—you go through a baptism of fire together and it fuses you. She was proud to be such an important part of the team and proud to see the smiles when she came offstage after a performance had gone particularly well. She loved the vibrations from a live audience when she was onstage, the electricity that flowed from her over the footlights to the audience and back again, the element of danger in a live performance, and the applause—it was intoxicating! She even loved the occasional tremors of the subway traveling deep underneath the floorboards, the stagehands who always had a poker game going in the basement, and the musty smell of the curtain. She loved everything about it. Some of the best moments of her life were spent holding for a laugh.

Tom had come to see the show three times. He never let her know when he was planning to be in the audience, in deference to her wishes, but Nina always recognized his loud laugh and it made her smile inside.

It was five o'clock on Christmas Eve. The Sunday matinee had gone well, filled, as it was, with people who had done all their Christmas shopping and needed a break before the family craziness began. A faint smell of wet wool and fur wafted over the footlights from the snow that had melted on the coats of the audience. By the time Nina and Matt got out of their costumes and headed out of the theater, the snow had stopped. Darkness was settling in quickly. The streetlights came on, throwing crystal-like sparkles onto the snow accumulated on the ground. The next day was a Monday, their day off. It was also Christmas. They were going to a Christmas party at Tom and Brent's. As they made their way over to Fifth Avenue from Broadway and Forty-Seventh Street, the snow muffled the sounds around them. They walked on, enjoying the languorous feeling of having no evening performance and no place they had to be.

Paul and Isabelle were now a couple. Nina was happy for them. She loved them both and was pleased they had found their own happiness. What could be more perfect than for Isabelle to end up with Paul? What Isabelle had always wanted was someone to love and take care of her and alleviate her constant anxiety about finances. Paul's whole joy came from caring for someone. It was a symbiotic relationship. Isabelle had recently moved into Paul's apartment, and Nina thought, ruefully, that it was only a matter of time before Isabelle would get pregnant. Both of them wanted children, badly. Paul, she knew, would more than willingly provide for a child, and Isabelle would have the love and security she needed. She could even continue pursuing an acting career…if, indeed, that was what she wanted.

As Matt and Nina strolled up Fifth Avenue, a light snow

began to fall again. Matt held out a hand and watched as a snowflake melted on his glove.

"What is this stuff?" he asked.

Nina rolled her eyes.

As they reached Fiftieth Street and Rockefeller Center, they stopped and looked down the long passageway bordered by trumpeting golden angels. At the end of it stood the towering art deco building, "Thirty Rock," rising sixty-six stories into the sky. At its base was the gigantic Rockefeller Center Christmas tree, gleaming with 50,000 ornaments and bulbs.

Matt looked at the tree, skeptically.

"Are we sure there's a real tree under all that?" he asked.

They decided to walk down the alley and watch the ice skaters making slow, graceful circles around the rink to the organ music. Perched above the skaters was the gilded statue of Prometheus about to hurl the stolen gift of fire to all mankind.

A father was helping his young daughter maneuver on her skates. She was dressed in a red plaid skirt and a matching beret. Her spindly legs were encased in thick, pink leggings and her ankles were bent inward over the ice skates.

"When I was little, my father used to take me ice skating here," Nina said.

"How old were you?" asked Matt.

"About her age...five or six."

They watched silently as the little girl tentatively let go of her father's hand and shakily skated for a few seconds on her own with her hands out before suddenly arching backwards and flopping down on the ice. Her father quickly skated over, picked her up, and was brushing off her leggings when she broke free from him and tried to skate on her own again.

"Good for you!" said Matt. "It's a hard world. When you fall, you have to get up and try again."

Nina looked at him.

"That's just what my father used to say."

Matt smiled.

"I got a phone call from Brooks," he said. "He reminded me that his directing gig will be over in the middle of January, and he'll be needing his apartment back.

He gazed out over the ice.

"We'll think of something," said Nina.

"I'm going to miss Murray," he said. "I've grown attached."

"We'll ask for visiting rights," said Nina.

They stood watching the young girl as she gradually got the hang of staying balanced on her skates.

"I have friends in California who have children," Matt mused. "She took about...um...two years off, I think, and then went back to acting. When she's working, he stays home and when he's working, she stays home."

Nina stood silent, watching the skaters. Matt went on as though probing an inner argument.

"He does movies that are mainly shot in LA. Sometimes he goes out of town, I guess, but not often. He's now got a directing gig doing a television series in Hollywood. I've always wanted to direct."

The skating music continued to play.

"My birthday is next month," Matt continued, lowering his voice so that Nina had to move closer to hear him over the music.

"I'm going to be thirty-five. Did you know that?"

"January eighteenth," said Nina, her eyes still on the ice.

The two of them stood watching the young girl. The father applauded every time she moved a few feet on her own, making Matt and Nina laugh.

After a while, Matt turned to her.

"What are you thinking? You are a thousand miles away."

Nina kept her eyes on the little girl.

"I was thinking…I wish I could talk to that young girl I used to be. I wish I could tell her, don't worry. Everything's going to be okay. Not only is it going to be okay, but it is going to be so much better than you could have ever imagined!"

They watched as the little girl made it halfway around the rink before falling. Her father skated up to her and clasped her in a triumphant hug.

"I knew, even then," continued Nina, "that somewhere love was out there, and I'd find it if I just kept searching."

She looked up at Matt and smiled.

Across the street, the windows of Saks Fifth Avenue were decorated with reindeer and red sleighs. They walked up Fifth Avenue. On the corner opposite St. Patrick's Cathedral, a man with thick gloves was roasting chestnuts in a metal pan. The smell of the chestnuts permeated the air. Matt stopped to buy a bag of them. The doors to the cathedral were flung open, and you could see into the massive, lit interior and hear the organ music. They continued up Fifth Avenue, eating chestnuts. The entire Cartier building was wrapped in a three-foot-wide red ribbon and glittering, miniature silver Christmas trees stood in each of the windows. At Fifty-Fourth Street, a Salvation Army Santa Claus rang his bell. Matt stopped, pulled off his gloves, and put a contribution into the red kettle. Christmas music was piping out of the speakers on the street: "It Came Upon a Midnight Clear," "Adeste Fideles," and "Oh, Little Town of Bethlehem." The lampposts were festooned with silver garlands, and at one intersection, a huge electric snowflake was strung across the street. The trees along Fifth Avenue were wrapped in tiny, white lights all the way to the tips of their graceful branches, making the world look like a fairyland. At Fifty-Ninth Street, the Plaza Hotel stood as an example of timeless elegance. Huge green Christmas wreathes with red ribbons were in every window and bright red poinsettias were in the window boxes.

At Central Park South, five horses stood in a line with blankets over them, harnessed to carriages, waiting patiently to take sightseers for a loop around the park. The gold statue of William Tecumseh Sherman on his horse stood proudly with a pigeon on his head. Occasionally four or five pigeons would swoop low and land on the ground near the horses and peck at the spilled grain next to the feed pails. Their iridescent feathers gleamed. Matt walked over to a horse.

"Hey, buddy," he said, stroking the horse's flank, "How ya doin'?" The horse snorted. Steam came out of its nostrils.

Matt bent and picked up something from the ground. He came back to Nina grinning, with his palm out. "Look what I found!"

There in his palm was a bright, copper penny.

"It was heads up!" said Matt, delighted with himself.

Nina laughed. "Have I made a convert out of you?"

"I'm covering all my bases," said Matt. "Don't want to take any chances with my luck."

A girl in her late teens approached them, shyly. Nina smiled and glanced up at Matt, but the girl moved toward Nina.

"I saw you in the play last night," she said. "You were wonderful! You were so funny. My mother and I were laughing like crazy."

"Thank you!" said Nina, pleasantly surprised.

"Could I have your autograph?" the girl asked.

"Of course," said Nina.

She removed a glove and signed the piece of paper the girl held out.

"Merry Christmas!" the girl called over her shoulder, as she went on her way.

"Merry Christmas," said Nina and Matt together. They looked at each other and laughed.

It was getting colder. Matt, shivering, put his arm around Nina and pulled her close.

"Looks like the show is going to run for a while. Guess I'd better buy some warmer clothing," he said.

"Guess you'd better," said Nina.

They continued walking up Fifth Avenue, at a slow pace, unwilling to break the spell. Lights twinkled, music played, sleigh bells jingled. On their left was the vastness of Central Park, bordered by a low stone wall. A sudden snow squall sprang up. Heavy flakes landed on the sidewalk in front of them and clung to the trees in the park. They looked up and watched them falling in the light of the streetlamp. Matt held Nina close, with the snow swirling around them. He kissed her—a long, impassioned kiss, broken only by their laughter.

CHAPTER TWENTY

Winter

Winter continued and darkness fell with a sudenness by five. Temperatures plummeted. The trees in the park, stripped of their leaves, resembled dark ballet dancers posed against the snow. Occasional snowstorms frosted the cars and the sidewalks making everything look white and crystalline for a while, until it turned to mounds of dirt-flecked snow that piled up on the curb.

Matt, who had moved into Nina's apartment, sat fascinated by the living room window as the heavy flakes came down, muting the sounds of the city and forming a large, white crescent on the bottom of the windowsill.

"How beautiful it is!" he said.

"Yeah, but it's going to be hell trying to get to the theater!" said Nina.

The radiators in their small, rent-controlled apartment clanged and hissed and poured out steam at an alarming rate. They didn't dare complain for fear of having no heat at all.

At five thirty Nina started to get nervous and suggested they leave for the theater to allow enough time to get there before seven, which was the time she liked to be sitting at her makeup table. They bundled into their gloves and hats, coats and scarves and headed out the door. There were no taxis to be had. Matt trudged over to Fifth Avenue and tried to hail one there, with no luck. Finally, after about twenty minutes, a taxi turned onto the street with its windshield wipers working overtime and stopped halfway down the block, letting off a fare. Matt waved his arms and struggled toward it. He held the door open for Nina.

"Thank God!" she said, as she settled back in the seat, stamping the snow off her boots.

As they drove, the windshield wipers kept getting stuck, and the driver had to continually get out of the cab to brush the snow off the windows in order to see. By the time they made it to Sixty-Fifth Street, the traffic was bumper to bumper, and the driver suggested taking the transverse to get to the West Side. It was six forty-five. The transverse was clearer because the heavy buses had blazed a trail, and their spirits rose, but once they reached Broadway, they sat in traffic for ten minutes without moving. Matt looked at his watch, anxiously.

"We'll never make it at this rate," he said.

It was seven fifteen.

Nina's chest tightened.

"I'm sure Wallace will hold the curtain," Nina said. "I mean, how is the audience supposed to get there?"

"By subway, which is what we should have done!"

The taxi inched a few feet further down Broadway and then stopped dead.

Nina's lips were pressed tightly together. Matt started drumming his fingers on the back of the driver's seat. He was sitting hunched forward and trying to peer out the front window through squinted eyes. All he could see were red break lights. As they approached Fifty-Seventh Street, Matt sighed.

"We'd stand a better chance walking than sitting in this traffic. Come on!"

He paid the driver, and they got out of the cab. With the snow coming down hard, Matt took Nina's gloved hand and pulled her along after him, tromping down Broadway through half-a-foot of snow.

It was seven thirty.

"We'd better stop somewhere and call Wallace," Nina said, anxiously. "It's half hour."

"That would take too much time. Let's just keep going!" said Matt, "The sooner we get there, the better."

They continued walking as fast as they could, the snow stinging their faces. Nina kept her head down, with her hood up and her scarf covering most of her face and held on to Matt's hand. Snow had gotten into the top of her boots. Her socks were wet and had inched their way down her ankles. Every once in a while, she would have to stop to catch her breath. Her anxiety mounted. She had never been late for half-hour. They kept trudging forward but, as though in a dream, they seemed not to make any headway. Finally, at ten minutes past eight, they arrived at the theater. They pushed against the heavy stage door and collapsed into the backstage area, as though they had just run the Iditarod. Matt went to find Wallace.

"We're here! We're here!" he said, gasping for breath.

"Good," said Wallace. "Hurry and get into your costumes! The understudies are ready to go on. Demond isn't here yet. Shawn will have to go on for him. I can hold the curtain for...maybe another fifteen minutes. That's all."

Matt and Nina went to their respective dressing rooms. Nina pulled off her boots and threw her heavy coat and her wet outer gear over a chair. She got out of her jeans and sweater and sat in the makeup chair shivering in her kimono. After a sharp knock at the door, her dresser came in carrying the first act costume that she had just taken off Jean Moor. Wallace's voice came over the intercom.

"We are holding the curtain for fifteen more minutes.

Matt and Nina have arrived. Shawn will be going on for Demond."

Nina threw her hair up into a bun and put the stocking cap over it. It would be lumpier than the pin curls but there was no time. Then she went over her face quickly with the sponge, applying the pancake makeup. She added eyebrows, false eyelashes and rouge, some lipstick and eye shadow, and stood up. The dresser helped her into her first act suit and then secured the wig on her head. She had about ten minutes into the play before she appeared in which to calm herself down.

"Breathe, breathe, breathe," she told herself.

Wallace knocked at the door and stuck his head in.

"Matt is ready. How are you doing?"

"I'm ready!" she said.

"Good," he answered. "The front-of-house people tell me that the theater is only about half filled, but we have to give those who made it here the performance they deserve."

He left, closing the door after him. A minute later the call came over the intercom: "Five minutes, please."

Nina sat at the dressing room table trying to calm her jangled nerves. By the time "places" was called, she was breathing more normally, but her heart rate was still elevated. She listened as Wallace made the announcement to the audience that the part of Tony would be played by Shawn Johnson.

The familiar music started up and the dresser handed Nina her shoes. She stood up and slipped into them, listening as the music faded and she heard the sound of the doorbell. She knew that Charlotte was opening the second-floor door and coming down the staircase. She heard the audience chuckle at the bit about the chocolates. She listened as Shawn came on stage and called into the stage left wings to Matt.

"Martin, are you here?"

It was strange not to hear Demond's voice. This was the first time an understudy had gone on except for the time that she had been abruptly swept into the part of Melanie. She checked herself in the mirror. One of the false eyelashes had come unstuck and she added a tiny dot of glue to it and pressed it back firmly, holding it until it adhered. She tucked in a stray curl on the wig, added more rouge and went to take her place in the stage right wings. The first scene between Matt and Shawn sounded good. They were getting all their laughs. Thank God the stage manager had held understudy rehearsals, and Shawn knew all his lines! She marveled at how calm Matt sounded. Matt exited into the stage left wings. She swallowed and looked down. The doorbell rang and Shawn went to let her in. She walked out into the bright lights.

"Hello, Melanie," Shawn began, "I didn't expect you today."

"I wanted to stop by and see how the patient was doing," she said, crossing to the center of the stage.

Her voice was strong and assured, belying her pounding heart. She knew how nervous Shawn must be. Poor Shawn! This was his first time in front of a Broadway audience. She had to be strong for him. She had to be the rock—the one to drive the scene forward.

"That's fine," Shawn said, "but I'm afraid he's asleep. Won't you sit down and let me get you a drink?"

She sat on the couch and knew they could do this. They were professionals.

They managed to get through the play, quite smoothly and at the curtain call, the cast applauded the audience. There was a warm feeling of fellowship between them, a bond the inclement weather had created. By the time the actors left the theater, the snowplows were hard at work making loud scraping noises on the asphalt and piling the snow onto the curbs where pedestrians stomped down narrow passageways to cross the streets at the corners. Matt and Nina were able to make their way back to their apartment where they collapsed with relief, warmed a can of soup for dinner and crawled, exhausted and grateful, into bed.

CHAPTER TWENTY-ONE

Goodbyes

N ow that they no longer had rehearsals during the day, Matt and Nina could enjoy some of the New York City nightlife. After the show came down, they often went to Charlie's or to Joe's to unwind with a glass of wine and a late-night dinner. If there was no matinee the next day, they might decide to go to Bemelmans Bar at the Carlyle Hotel and listen to music or to go down to the Village and hear some jazz. They would then take a taxi home and sleep until noon. On Monday, the theater was dark.

On one day off, they rented a car and drove upstate to the Catskill Mountains where Nina had spent summers as a child. They stayed overnight at a stone inn where a crackling wood fire blazed in a huge stone fireplace. Shivering under the down quilts, they peered out the window at the moonlight sparkling on the snowy ground. A Bernese mountain dog belonging to the innkeeper befriended them and slept curled up on the braided rug on the floor of their room.

By April it was still cool, but the daffodils and the bright yellow forsythia were already starting to show color in the park. In May, there were buds on the apple trees, and the Callery Pear trees on Nina's block were bursting with white flowers, forming an enchanting bower over the street. Spring in New York was Nina's favorite season.

June would signal the end of the play's contract for both Nina and Matt. As much as they loved performing, after six months a bit of weariness had crept in.

"God! It's hard to keep repeating the same lines over and over and over again and make them sound like you are saying them for the very first time," complained Matt.

At the start of one Wednesday evening show, Nina heard the strains of Kiri Te Kanawa's beautiful soprano start up once again and felt as though it were some kind of Chinese water torture. How much is too much, she wondered? Everything starts to cloy after a while, like too much sugar, she thought. She and Matt worked hard to keep the lines fresh and their concentration sharp. But at one matinee, during a long speech of Matt's, Nina's mind wandered. She was hungry and found herself trying to decide between the chef salad and the liver and onions at Joe Allen's. The stage got eerily quiet. She was startled to realize that Matt had finished his speech and was looking at her intently, waiting for her response.

They made the decision to leave the show when their contracts were up in June and to take some time off. Nina knew that her understudy was hoping to inherit her part. The producers, however, wanted a "name." Nina, familiar with the syndrome, felt great empathy for Jean Moor. She wished that she could call in sick for just one performance, so that Jean would have a chance to show how well she could do the part, but her professional ethics would not permit her.

Two weeks before the end of their contract, as they were making plans to take a trip out to Amagansett and introduce Matt to the Atlantic Ocean, Matt's agent called. They were asking for his availability for a supporting role in a TV mini-series. He was thrilled to be wanted again in the television world after being absent for so long.

"Will you come with me?" he asked Nina.

"Well," Nina said, "Are you sure you're gonna want me around when you're busy working?"

"Of course," said Matt. "I won't be working all the time. I'll introduce you to my agent. I'm sure he will submit you for things. You're a Broadway leading lady!"

There was silence. They both knew this wasn't how it worked.

"That sounds lovely," said Nina, smiling. "I would love to come."

There wasn't a lot of time before Matt would be needed on the set, so they cancelled their Amagansett trip and made arrangements to leave for California instead.

Nina could not conceal her excitement.

"So—what can I expect in California?" she asked as they were heading home from the theater one night.

"Well," said Matt, considering, "everything comes with avocado."

"I love avocado!" said Nina.

"You're gonna be a natural. I think you will like my place. It's a small house on Norma. It has a living room, a sort of galley kitchen, a bedroom, a swimming pool, and lots of bougainvillea."

"A what? A pool?" asked Nina, "You have your own, private swimming pool?

"Of course, I have a pool—it's California!"

"Oh, Matt, it sounds incredible, but how am I going to get around?"

"You're going to take driving lessons," said Matt, confidently.

Nina sat quietly, thinking.

"I guess if everyone else can learn how to drive, I can too," she said with some apprehension.

"You'll take to it like a duck to water." said Matt.

Two days before their last night of the show, the phone rang. It was Susan, her agent.

"The Cameron Mackintosh office called. There is interest in you for the part of Amanda in *Private Lives*."

Nina sat mute on the other end of the phone.

"They are mounting a revival of Noel Coward's play, taking it out on tour for the summer to see how it does. If it goes well, the plan is to bring it to Broadway in the fall."

"The Gertrude Lawrence part?" asked Nina.

"Yes, honey, the female lead. The starring role," said Susan. "The director is Norman Roberts. He saw you in the play and asked for you, personally. There's a good possibility of money in this one. If it goes to Broadway, you'll be able to pay off your student loans. Looks like there's going to be a nice cast. They've got Harry Marino for the male lead."

"I…don't know what to say…" said Nina.

"Say yes" said Susan. "Unless you're an idiot."

"Yes," said Nina, with unease.

"Good! It plays the Eastern Seaboard circuit: a week in Pennsylvania, Cape Cod, uh…Maine…I think…like that. Let me find out specifics and get back to you." And she hung up.

Nina sat for a long while with her hand still on the receiver. What would she say to Matt? The door opened and Matt came in balancing a bag of groceries on his knee while he retrieved his key from the lock. He looked at her.

"What happened? You look strange."

"Susan called," she said. "They…they want me for a play."

Matt closed the door, put down the groceries, and walked over to her.

"That's wonderful, darling," he said.

"What about California?" asked Nina, looking up at him.

Matt paused for a moment. "It'll be put on hold for a while." He sat down at the table. "Tell me more about the job offer."

"It's a revival…of *Private Lives*. Someone named Norman Roberts is directing. They're going to tour it for the summer with the hopes of bringing it to Broadway in the fall. They have signed someone named Harry...Savino...or Marino for the male lead."

"Harry Marino?" said Matt, "Christ! I'll have to take out a restraining order to keep him away from you. I know Harry. We worked together on the soap. He is a notorious womanizer."

"Don't be ridiculous," said Nina. "That's what they warned me about Nick Travis and nothing ever happened."

"Nick Travis had other fish to fry."

"What's going to happen with us?" asked Nina, looking up anxiously into Matt's eyes.

"Others have had long distance relationships before. It can work. We'll make it work."

Nina got up, unconvinced, and started to put the groceries away.

"I love our life together," she said from the kitchen. "I don't want to lose that."

"What we're suffering from is too much success," Matt sighed. "Not such a bad thing for two actors."

"God, you're amazing!" said Nina. "You can put a good spin on anything!"

Their last night of the show arrived. There was a standing ovation from the audience for Matt and Nina, and the whole cast turned and applauded them. Tears sprang to Nina's eyes. There were hugs and heartfelt goodbyes. They had become a family. But the show would go on...the following Tuesday with two new actors playing the leads.

The night before Matt was to leave for California, they went out to dinner at their favorite Italian restaurant. They were both feeling melancholy. There were long gaps in their conversation. That night they made urgent love as though to forestall the separation.

The next day Matt woke early to get ready for his flight.

When Nina woke, she had a heaviness around her heart that she couldn't shed. As she turned her face up to the showerhead, she thought again about what she was doing. She wasn't naive. She knew Matt wouldn't lack for female companionship. She had seen how women's eyes followed him whenever he walked into a room. They'd be all over him like iron filings on a magnet. How long would it be before Sharon resurfaced in his life? The thought of Sharon made her heart feel like it had cracked open, and she found herself pressing her hand to her chest as though to stem the bleeding. Later, as they sat drinking their morning coffee, she looked across the table at his familiar face. The pensive sadness in his eyes made her cringe, and she wondered for the hundredth time if she had made the right decision.

At ten o'clock, Matt got up from the kitchen table, took the framed photograph of Nina at the zoo with the sea lions from the bedroom bureau, and put it in his suitcase. They brought the luggage downstairs and waited by the curb. With a loud whistle through his teeth, Matt hailed a taxi. When it pulled up, the driver got out, put Matt's suitcase in the trunk, and got back behind the wheel. Nina and Matt stood looking at each other.

"I want you to know something," said Matt, measuring his words. "No matter what happens, I will always love you."

Nina's eyes started to well up.

"No, no. No crying," said Matt. "You've got a rehearsal to get ready for."

She smiled but couldn't prevent the tears from trickling down her cheeks. He took her by the shoulders roughly, kissed her hard on the mouth, and quickly disappeared into the taxi, shutting the door and looking straight ahead.

Nina stood at the curb, gripping her elbows as if she were holding something inside that was determined to follow Matt. She watched as the taxi turned the corner of Seventy-Seventh Street and headed up Park Avenue on its way to Kennedy Airport. She watched until it was lost in the New York traffic. Then she climbed the two flights of stairs back up to her apartment. Matt's coffee cup was still on the table. She stared at it and felt the ache of his absence like the phantom pain in an amputated limb.

She knew she would always love Matt, too. Maybe they could keep a long-distance relationship going. Others had done it…hadn't they? Maybe he would come back East after the TV series was in the can. But even as she was thinking this, she knew in her heart that Matt was a California boy. He was the epitome of the all-American boy, with chiseled features and blond hair. He belonged out there in the film and television world—the world of sunshine, and cameras, Mercedes convertibles, pools, and bougainvillea. To love and be loved in return…that was…everything… Wasn't it? But she loved the theater too. That was her passion, the thing she did well, the thing that gave her her self-esteem. She wasn't ready to trade it in for a sound stage. Did they even have theater in Los Angeles? Not a lot of it. Could she stop now and be a California housewife? No. Not now. Maybe sometime in the future, but not when things were just beginning to break for her, when all her hard work—years of acting in little theaters and struggling to pay her rent—was finally beginning to pay off. In the back of her mind another thought nagged her: she knew she was a third-generation New York City girl, and the realization pained her. I'd be a fish out of water in California, she thought. I know I would. I'd probably get arrested the first week for jaywalking or get hit by a car making a right turn on a red light.

Her head hurt. Her heart hurt. She ran her fingers through her hair, sighed and reached across the table and pulled the script toward her. It was going to be a challenge to play this part. First of all, she had to perfect her English accent. Then she had to find something of her own to invest this part with, this part that had been done by so many other actors. She would have to work hard and dig deep to make it true to her own personality because only then would it be a unique characterization, different from all the hundreds of portrayals that had gone before.

She opened the script to act one, scene one.

She glanced down to Amanda's entrance. With her eyes still on the script, Nina reached for the red pen and started to underline her lines.

CHAPTER TWENTY-TWO

Tom and Isabelle

It was almost a month since Nina had seen Isabelle when she called wanting to meet for lunch.

"Sure," said Nina. "Where?"

"Um…our usual salad place? Say…one o'clock?"

"Great! See you then."

She had a feeling she knew why Isabelle wanted to meet. Nina had been invited to dinner at Isabelle and Paul's many times, but she had always declined. It would have been awkward, she thought, to sit in the living room sipping wine and making small talk within clear sight of the door to the bedroom where she and Paul had had such steamy sex. Isabelle probably guessed at the reason, but Paul always responded, "Nina! You are always so busy!"

Nina was already seated at the table at their favorite lunch place on the Upper East Side when Isabelle arrived, late as usual, her blonde hair pulled back in a ponytail. The moment she walked in the door Nina's suspicions were confirmed.

"How are you?" Nina asked. "You look luminous!"

"You think?" said Isabelle. "I'm exhausted! I guess you're busy getting ready for rehearsals?"

"Yes. They begin in a little over a week."

"That is so exciting! But I bet you are missing Matt."

"Oh, God, yes! It's hard. We speak almost every day, but I miss him terribly!"

A waiter came by, gave them menus, and asked them what they would like to drink.

"I'll have a glass of pino grigio, please" said Nina.

"Just water, thanks," said Isabelle.

The waiter left.

"So," said Nina, "What's going on?"

"Well," Isabelle sighed, looking down at the table, "we're not actually telling anyone yet but," she raised her eyes to meet Nina's, "I wanted to let you know. I'm pregnant."

"I knew it!" said Nina, a little too quickly.

Isabelle's head jerked up sharply. She looked at Nina quizzically.

"I mean…you look so…glowing."

"Oh," said Isabelle. "Thanks. I don't feel glowing."

"Morning sickness?"

"Indigestion." Isabelle put her hand on her abdomen. "It feels like nine hard hats are jackhammering in my stomach."

Nina smiled, sympathetically.

"How's Paul taking it?"

"He is over the moon! He follows me around like a nervous hen and calls from the office at least ten times a day."

Nina thought how grating that would be.

"How sweet," she said. "When are you due?"

"Well, by my calculations, sometime in February."

"Oh, so you are very early on."

"Yes, much too early to tell anybody, but I had to let you know."

"Oh, Isabelle. I am so happy for you!"

"You are?"

"Of course, I am! It's wonderful news! A baby? I'm happy for both of you!"

"Thanks," said Isabelle, visibly relieved.

"You know, we thought we might start trying, just in case it took a long time but bingo! I got pregnant on the very first shot!"

Nina sent up a silent prayer of thanks for the effectiveness of her birth control pills.

Once she was reassured of Nina's acceptance, Isabelle poured out her plans and dreams in a flurry of words. She was flushed with happiness. It was contagious. Nina found herself smiling broadly just listening to her.

"Let's face it," Isabelle said, "I was getting nowhere with my acting career. I was a hazard as a waitress, and I don't think I could have taken another year at the Harris Poll. God! It's been so wonderful not to have to go to work there! I am so happy! I have to pinch myself to make sure it's real."

"Are you thinking about turning one of the bedrooms into a nursery?"

"Well, I was, but Paul is so superstitious. He said it would be bad luck. He won't even set up a crib until after the baby is born. Can you imagine?"

When they finished their lunch, Isabelle got up with a protective hand on her abdomen. Nina hugged her gingerly.

"Please tell Paul how happy I am for you both" she said.

And she was. It wasn't until she got home that a twinge of jealousy crept in. *Isabelle was going to have a baby.* But she was too busy learning lines to dwell on it for long.

Unlike her Broadway experience, the summer tour only had a two-week rehearsal period. With Isabelle busy with Paul and Matt in California, she called on Tom to help her with her lines. Tom had been overjoyed that the California trip had been cancelled and that Nina was going to be a working actor again. Just as she sat down to call him, the phone rang.

"Oh, Tom!" she said, "I was hoping you'd call!"

"What's the matter with *your* finger?" asked Tom.

"I'm sorry. I've been meaning to call you. It's been a crazy couple of days. Matt left for California, and I've been working hard on the script. I want to have all my lines learned before I arrive at the first rehearsal. I hate that, don't you? I'd so much rather learn them as you're getting to know the character...but the rehearsal period is so short."

"Honey, I'd be so happy to have lines to learn. I wouldn't care when I had to learn them!"

"Oh, Tom. I'm sorry. Didn't you have an audition last week?"

"Yes, for a mute Alzheimer patient in a wheelchair."

"How did it go?"

"I didn't get it."

"Oh. I'm sorry."

"Anyway," said Tom, "What can I do for you?"

"Would you have any time to cue me?" asked Nina.

"Of course! Come on up! Brent is busy working on a new Broadway musical. Gus and I are just sitting here watching *The Price is Right*."

Nina took the bus up to Tom's that evening. Gus, the Schnauzer, could be heard howling his high-pitched welcome all the way down to the vestibule, as soon as she rang the bell. It was cozy and pleasant in Tom's apartment. She sat in the den which was a small room walled with bookshelves and had an L-shaped couch that you could sink into. Tom disappeared into the kitchen to get them drinks. Gus followed. Nina could hear the dog-biscuit tin being opened. Tom returned with a glass of wine for her and a Tab for himself. Gus walked behind him, noisily licking his chops, and plunked himself heavily down at Nina's feet with an audible sigh.

"Isabelle's pregnant," said Nina. "I'm not supposed to tell you, as it is very early, but I couldn't spend the whole evening here without your knowing. Please don't say anything—even to Brent."

"I won't," said Tom, sitting down in the desk chair. "That will be good for her, I think, don't you? She needs a little stability in her life."

"Yes. I think she will be very happy. Both of them will be. Paul was never right for me, as you pointed out so often."

"Bet you have mixed feelings about that, though," said Tom.

Nina looked at him for a long minute.

"Let's get started," she said, putting down her wine glass.

She opened her script to the first scene and handed it to Tom.

"I think I'm pretty much off book for the first act. If you could just cue me on that, I'll work on the second act tomorrow. I want it verbatim, please. If I mess up a word, correct me, okay? I have no desire to rewrite Noel Coward."

"Okay," said Tom. He cleared his throat and began to read the first scene between Victor and Amanda. His English accent was dreadful, but Nina made it through the first act, asking for a line only twice. After a short break, they ran it again.

"You were word-perfect that time!" said Tom.

"Good enough to go to Broadway, I hope," sighed Nina.

"Oh, honey, that's what they always say about these tours. I don't want to burst your bubble, but only about one percent actually make it to Broadway."

"Well," said Nina, slightly miffed, "we can always hope to be that one percent."

Tom smiled.

"What do you hear from Matt?" he asked, changing the subject.

At the sound of Matt's name, a wave of warmth washed over her.

"Oh, working hard," she said unable to conceal a smile. "Enjoying being back in front of the cameras. I miss him."

"Brent said a guy at the theater told him that the new actor, Jasmina somebody is going to be in that TV show."

"Oh, really? The one they're making all the fuss about?"

"Yeah," said Tom. "She was in this season's crop of new actors on the cover of *TV Guide*. Her father is that gorgeous, black jazz guitarist and her mother is a Chinese beauty queen."

"Santiago?" asked Nina.

"That's it!" said Tom, "Jasmina Santiago."

Nina nodded and finished her wine. She put her glass down, smiled at Tom, and got up to leave.

"Well...I better get home and start learning act two," she said. "Thanks so much. It really helps to have someone cue me."

"Any time," said Tom. He walked her toward the door. Gus struggled to his feet and wobbled after them, wagging his tail.

"If you wait a second, I'll get the leash and Gus and I will walk you over to Broadway."

Tom hailed a taxi for her on Broadway and they hugged goodbye.

On the ride home, Nina stared out of the window and thought about Jasmina Santiago.

"I can't spend my life being anxious and jealous," she thought. "There are a ton of actors out there who are much more beautiful than I am. I just have to trust that things will work out."

But the seed had been planted.

CHAPTER TWENTY-THREE

A New Rehearsal

Nina was eager for rehearsals to begin. She had spent three weeks memorizing all of her lines and felt confident that she knew them. She was going to be a working actor. She could put aside, for however long it lasted, the anxiety about never working again. She had a job. How exciting it was to be playing Amanda and to once again transform herself into someone else! Nina felt sure she could do justice to Amanda's witty lines. She was also eager to be in a new cast and work with a new director.

She had chosen her rehearsal outfit carefully, recalling her first day of rehearsals for *The Second Time Around*. How anxious she had been...and how humiliated to be playing the maid. Now she approached the upcoming rehearsal with an enthusiasm mitigated only by the pressure of taking on a leading role, and one played many times before by many accomplished actors.

As the play *Private Lives* begins, Amanda and her new husband, Victor, are on their honeymoon in Switzerland. In the next-door suite, enjoying his own honeymoon, is Amanda's ex-husband who has just married Sibyl. When Amanda and her ex-husband, Elyot, meet by accident on their adjoining balconies, they realize they are still in love and rekindle their passion.

As the taxi traveled along Fifth Avenue, Nina rolled down the window. It was late June, and the scent of summer permeated the air. Central Park was green and lush with a sprinkling of pinks and yellows.

She entered the building on Broadway, took the elevator up to the fourth floor, walked down the hallway, and opened the door to the same room they had rehearsed in for *The Second Time Around*. The ghosts of Nick and Diana seemed to hover everywhere. There was the old scratched up piano, the mirrored wall, and the metal folding chairs set up in a semicircle.

Harry Marino rose to his six-foot-three inch frame to greet her. He was smiling and all of his Hollywood caps gleamed. He was everything that Matt had said and more—well-built and extraordinarily handsome. His luminous brown eyes searched hers as he extended his hand.

"So glad we'll be working together," he said.

She could smell his aftershave lotion.

"I caught your performance at the Barrymore. Wow. Terrific!"

"Oh, thank you," said Nina, placing her hand in his and smiling up at him.

"Yeah. I'm a...friend of Matt's. We worked together on a series."

"So he told me," said Nina, nodding.

"Yeah. I hear he's got a spot on the new CBS thing," said, Harry. He had not yet relinquished her hand.

News travels fast in this business, thought Nina.

"Mmm hmm," she said as she nodded and extricated her hand with some difficulty.

Harry Marino bore a strong resemblance to a young Frank Langella. He had the same dark hair and large brown eyes. He was probably in his mid-to-late thirties and was one of those people who radiated charm. Or was it sex appeal? He had a full, sensuous mouth. You couldn't look at him and fail to wonder what it would be like to kiss him. She would find out soon enough, thought Nina, as there was a lot of kissing called for in the script.

"I'm glad we'll be working together, too," said Nina, and there was a slight flutter in her stomach. She smiled, again, and turned her attention to the director, Norman Roberts, who was waiting patiently to greet her. He was a small, thin English gentleman of about sixty with thinning hair and a trim mustache.

"Ms. Landau! Welcome! Welcome!" he said in his clipped, English accent. "I see you have met Harry! Come! Let me introduce you to the rest of the cast."

He led her over to two actors, Pamela Middleton and Nigel Dermot, both English, who were playing the spouses, Sybil and Victor, respectively. The door opened and Laurie Dunbar, who was playing the French-speaking maid, arrived late and breathless. She smiled nervously as she apologized and was introduced to everyone. Norman Roberts indicated that they should take their seats in the small semicircle of chairs. He gave a short speech explaining the style of the production and the history of the play. Then he proceeded to describe the set.

"All right. Shall we begin?" he asked.

Nina's heartbeat quickened as she took her script from her tote bag. She cleared her throat, licked her lips, and sat up straight. The English actors were intimidating for her. She and Harry were the only Americans in the cast, and she was nervous about her accent.

The reading seemed to go well. The cast chuckled at most of the laugh lines she delivered, increasing her sense of confidence. When rehearsal was over, they all said cordial goodbyes. She piled into a taxi, along with two other actors in the cast, to go to Eaves for a costume fitting. Then she took a taxi home, poured a glass of wine, settled herself on the couch, and called Matt.

"How did it go?" he asked.

"Well," Nina said with a sigh, "I guess it went…okay."

"You don't sound very enthusiastic. What's wrong?"

Nina thought for a moment. "I guess…I'd rather wait and see how it goes tomorrow when we get up on our feet. I'm getting vibes but I don't want to verbalize anything yet, in case that will somehow jinx it. I think I'm just nervous."

"Got it," said Matt.

"How are you, sweetheart?" asked Nina. "How's the filming going?"

"Going well. Nice accommodations on the set. The trailers keep getting smaller, but mine is comfortable. My horse nearly tried to unseat me yesterday by rubbing me against a tree. They offered to get me a replacement, but I think I'll just try to sweet-talk her tomorrow. Maybe bring an apple. It's going well, though. Except I miss you."

Nina closed her eyes. How lovely it was to hear his voice! They talked for a long while, Nina reluctant to let the conversation come to an end.

"Get some sleep," Matt said, finally. "I know it's getting late there, and you have a rehearsal tomorrow."

"Thank you. I miss you."

"I miss you too, darling."

Nina went to bed, but like a water strider on a pond, she skimmed the surface of sleep, never going under.

The following day, Norman Roberts started blocking the first act.

"Ms. Landau, do you think you might cross stage left on that line?"

"Please call me Nina."

"Oh, quite. And you must call me Norman."

Nina smiled and nodded, but the name sat uneasy in her mouth. He was a formal man who seemed to keep people at a distance. As the rehearsal progressed, Nina slowly realized he was the kind of director who preferred actors to come equipped with marionette strings, so that he could move them around at will.

"When you come up to Victor," said Norman, "Why don't you try plucking a piece of lint off his collar? Such an intimate gesture, don't you agree?"

Nina bristled. She resented a director who gave her specific gestures, especially this early in the game. This was only the second day of rehearsal! She wanted to have a chance to find the bits of personal business for herself, for them to evolve naturally during the course of discovering the character. It seemed stiff and arbitrary to her, but she did the bit of business as Norman had directed her to. She was not one to make waves.

As she thought about Amanda, Nina came to the conclusion that she would be the type of person to wear Arpège. It was a perfume with a sophisticated scent that had been created for Lanvin in 1927. It must have been all the rage three years later, when the play was written. As she often did, Nina searched for some small morsel—some personal characteristic—to make the role come alive. Just as she had made those black, construction-paper eyelashes that helped transform her into the part of the mischievous maid, she bought the perfume and sprayed it cautiously on her wrists. Closing her eyes and enveloping herself in the scent, she could easily imagine herself as the sophisticated Amanda. She brought the iconic black circular bottle to rehearsal with her, and whenever she felt the characterization in jeopardy, she reached into her tote bag and surreptitiously sprayed herself with Arpège. At least this would be something that Norman could not object to. She hoped.

It soon became obvious that Norman had a crush on Harry. He was all smiles and flustered whenever he talked to Harry, as opposed to the clipped tones he reserved for her.

"They can't all be experiences like the one we had with *Second Time Around*, Matt counseled on the phone that night. "Just try to do the best you can."

"I feel like a trained bear," said Nina. "There is no artistry involved. I'm counting on my technique to get me through, but I don't just want to give a technical performance. Oh, Matt, I'm so used to rehearsals being full and alive and productive."

"I understand," said Matt.

Nina sighed. "Thank God it's only a two-week rehearsal. And then Norman will be gone. I guess I can get through anything, if it's only two weeks."

Rehearsals dragged on. Norman would interrupt, constantly, to give Nina line-readings. The other cast members avoided her eyes. It was shocking for an actor to be given a line reading. They knew. Norman persisted. One afternoon, in the middle of one of Nina's speeches, he stopped rehearsal abruptly and got up from his chair.

"Nina, darling. No, no, no, no, no. It is not, 'I was brought up to believe it was beyond the pale for a *man* to strike a *woman*.' What we need to hear is: 'I was brought up to believe it was beyond the pale for a man to *strike* a woman'. Do you understand the difference? Do you? The emphasis is on the word *strike*. We are doing a period English piece, not a contemporary American play about your women's lib."

He spat out the words "women's lib" with such contempt that one of the English actors inadvertently gasped. Nina stopped. She blinked her eyes rapidly as though someone had thrown acid in her face. She could feel the blood tingle in her spine and rush to her head, and she knew her face must be red. The humiliation turned quickly to anger, and she had to clamp her lips shut not to let it out. The new line reading made no sense to her. But she swallowed once and nodded her head. Still smarting from the rudeness, she managed to say the line as he had requested.

"I was brought up to believe it was beyond the pale for a man to *strike* a woman." She looked at Norman, questioningly. The entire cast was glancing at Norman from the corners of their eyes. He mumbled something, turned around, and resumed his seat.

Everything Nina did Norman hated. Every line. Every gesture. She felt her characterization of Amanda melting away like a snowman in the sun. Everything felt unsupported. Nothing was organic. It was becoming impossible for her to make the character "real." Her anxiety mounted. She was playing the notes that Norman gave her, rather than playing the character. She had heard about directors who ruined performances because their vision of the character was so completely different from the actor playing the part. It seemed clear to Nina that what Norman Roberts wanted was a totally different actor. She reminded herself that she had never auditioned for the role. He had hired her after seeing her perform on stage, but that had been a very different part. Maybe he felt he had made a big mistake, and now he was stuck with her. Whenever she stopped rehearsal to question Norman about a direction, he would patiently listen and then patronizingly respond.

"Ah, yes, my dear, but you can't see the whole picture as I can, now can you?"

There was nothing to do but nod, press her lips together, and look down. It was useless to complain.

She hated every second of rehearsal. She dreaded waking up in the morning and getting dressed to go to work. She tried to reassure herself that once she got in front of an audience, Norman would be gone, and she might have a little wiggle room in which to breathe again. She plunged onward, without complaining. She knew the cast felt sorry for her.

One afternoon, emerging from the ladies' room, she overheard Norman talking on the pay phone at the end of the hall. She quickly closed the door, leaving it open only a crack so that she could hear the conversation.

"Yes, yes. I quite agree," Norman was saying. "But she cannot do the *accent!*"

Suddenly all the insecurities that Nina had experienced as a child rose to the surface and threatened to suffocate her. A feeling of such inadequacy flooded her; she felt dizzy and her knees started to buckle. The disinfectant smell of the bathroom overwhelmed her, and she thought she might throw up. She put a hand up to her mouth. She wanted to cry, but the feeling of shock transfixed her. She closed the door and stood leaning against it. Her hands felt clammy. Was she going to be fired? After a few minutes someone pushed against the door and a woman walked in. She looked at Nina.

"Are you all right?" she asked.

Nina swallowed and nodded. She breathed deeply to calm herself, took a Valium from her purse, and walked over to the sink to swallow it with a handful of water from the tap. She reapplied her lipstick, combed her hair, and walked, shakily, but determinedly back to the rehearsal room. Thank God rehearsal was almost over for the day! She sat quietly watching a scene between Harry and Pamela without seeing it. By the time they were released for the day, Nina was completely drained.

She hailed a taxi, and as soon as she got home, she called Matt. He did not pick up.

"Call me. Please!" she said into the answering machine, trying to hold back her tears.

She poured herself a glass of wine and the phone rang.

"What happened? Are you all right?" asked Matt, alarmed.

"I feel like an idiot. An amateur. A stupid, unprofessional...novice. I don't know what to do."

Tears sprang up in her eyes and rolled down her cheeks. She sat down at the table.

"Hold on, hold on, what happened?"

"Oh, Matt, I'm embarrassed to tell you."

"Nina! Why? You can tell me anything. Were you fired?"

"Oh God! Not yet, but…I may be."

"Why, for Christ's sake?"

She told him of the phone conversation she had overheard in the hallway.

Matt thought for a moment.

"Can Harry do the accent? he asked.

"Oh, Norman is in love with Harry. He could be speaking Swahili for all Norman cares. Oh, Matt, what am I going to do? I'm so upset. I feel like he has stripped me of all my confidence. I want to quit and never look back."

"You know, I asked around about this Norman Roberts guy," said Matt. "Apparently he always has a whipping boy in his rehearsals. He's a prissy little shit. God! I wish I was there. I'd fucking crush his tiny balls!"

"Oh, Matt. I want to give my notice," Nina moaned. "I have never felt this way. I have always been the darling of the directors! I am completely at a loss."

"Nobody's giving their notice," said Matt. "And for God's sake don't be so hard on yourself. All actors have accent problems at some point in their careers. That's why there is a whole industry called Accent Coaching. I had to have a coach once, myself, to teach me how to do a Texas accent. It isn't a crime. What you'll do is hire a coach!"

"You think so?" asked Nina, suddenly seeing a glimmer of hope.

"Of course! That's the thing to do! I may have someone out here who can refer you to somebody good in New York. Let me call you back…in an hour. Okay? Okay?"

"Okay," said Nina, weakly.

"Nina! Stop this! You are a magnificent actor. You were an unqualified success in a lead role on Broadway. You need a little help with the accent. That's all."

"Okay," said Nina, softly. "Thanks."

She put down the phone and gave vent to her wounded pride, sobbing into a paper towel.

The next day after rehearsal, Nina went directly to the apartment of the accent coach. They worked for an hour and a half. She spoke into a tape recorder, feeling much like Eliza Doolittle. But it was definitely helping. This routine continued throughout the week and for the rest of the rehearsal period. Nina worked around the clock. When she wasn't rehearsing, she was working with the accent coach. By the end of the week, she had crossed a threshold and could speak with a credible English accent. She was starting to feel more confident in the role. A fragile détente had been established in the rehearsal hall.

CHAPTER TWENTY-FOUR

Harry

Nina had played many love scenes on stage, but the love scene in the second act of *Private Lives* made her uneasy. She was aware that it had nearly gotten the play censored when it opened in London in 1930. She approached the scene philosophically. It was a job... but Harry was extremely sensual. It was a little unnerving to kiss him for the first time. When the moment came in rehearsal, Nina gamely put herself into Harry's arms. He bent his head and pressed his lips to hers. She closed her eyes. It was like sinking into soft pillows. Nina felt her pulse quicken. When they pulled apart, she was certain her face was red. What a curse it was to have a blood system that betrayed you at every moment! Harry had an amused grin on his face that was not part of the character. Everyone watching was slack-jawed. Clearly, they all wanted to be kissed like that by Harry—including the men.

Nina carried on with the rehearsal, but Harry was someone she needed to handle with caution. He was a very physical person, the kind who touched you when he talked to you, laying a hand on your shoulder, or squeezing your arm, ensnaring you in his web and rolling you over and over to set aside for his future enjoyment. His handsome looks were not the only thing that attracted Nina. He also had a sense of humor—something that acted as an aphrodisiac for her. Plus, he didn't take himself too seriously.

"I was working out at the gym this morning," he announced at the start of rehearsal one day. "Two old guys were looking at me. I figured they recognized me and wanted an autograph. But when I was toweling off after a shower, I heard them talking on the other side of the lockers 'Hey,' one said to the other, 'Did you see that Harry Marino? He didn't look so hot.' 'Nah,' the other guy said, 'He's gotten flabby.' I wanted to go up to them and say, 'Hey, guys, gimme a break. I'm in the gym! I'm trying! I'm trying!'"

Harry entertained the whole cast with his stories. Arriving late to rehearsal one morning, he apologized, explaining that he had just come from a commercial audition.

"How did it go?" Pamela asked him.

"It was crazy," said Harry. "They wanted us to improvise farm talk. I didn't know what the hell they meant. But I was there with this other guy, and the other guy looks at me and starts: 'Cow still sick?' he asks me. 'Nah,' I said, 'He's all right.' Everyone laughed. Turns out all cows are female. What the hell do I know about cows?"

It was all too easy to be caught in his spell.

Harry seemed to have no problem with the English accent. He sounded as if he had been born a stone's throw from Trafalgar Square. He had an ear for accents perhaps because he was a singer. When Harry was feeling good, he serenaded them. He had a wonderful deep baritone voice and had performed in a number of musicals.

One morning, as Nina entered the rehearsal room, Harry burst into song.

"If ever I would leave you…" Nina rolled her eyes but smiled. She stood still and everyone sat mesmerized until he had finished the song. They applauded. How could you resist a man like that? It was going to be hard. He had talent and a sense of humor, two of the three things that had always attracted her to a man—the other was intelligence. Well…two out of three was not bad. Harry was not the sharpest knife in the drawer. He was smart, but he couldn't hold a candle to Matt, who could answer ninety percent of the questions on *Jeopardy* and do the *New York Times* crossword puzzle in half an hour. Also, it was apparent that while Matt was interested in everything, Harry was interested only in Harry.

However, Harry was sweet, funny, and extremely charming. As they all gathered for notes after rehearsal one afternoon, Nina looked down at Harry's feet.

"Look," she said, pointing to his socks, "You have on one black sock and one blue one!"

Harry looked down and studied his feet solemnly.

"That's funny," he said, full of wonder. "That's the second time this week that's happened!"

Dating Harry would be like dating Frank Sinatra. He could have any woman he wanted, and he had wanted plenty of them. No one was going to change him. And Nina had no intention of being one of his multitude. He obviously had been told that she and Matt were in a relationship, but it didn't stop him from trying. He asked her out for a drink after rehearsals. She was tempted but decided it would be best to nip anything in the bud. He asked if he could take her home in a taxi. He invited her to his apartment to run lines after rehearsal. She refused, smiling. It became a game: Harry persisted; Nina resisted.

Finally, the two weeks were up, and rehearsals were coming to an end. The entire cast was bused to a little theater in Woodstock, New York, the site of their first performance. Matt had sent her an opening night gift, a beautiful silver Tiffany pin of the theater masks, comedy and tragedy. The cast settled themselves into a nearby motel, unpacked, and headed out to find a restaurant for dinner in the charming town. Dress rehearsal was called for the following morning, so they could get used to the stage, the costumes, and the music cues. Norman had chosen "Someday I'll Find You," for the music, which Noel Coward had written specifically for the play.

Nina was aware that women in the 1930s would never go out without wearing stockings. Hosiery in the 1930s came with a seam down the back. Instead of sending out the wardrobe person to track down the hard-to-find stockings, Nina decided to paint a dark brown line on the back of her bare legs with a liquid eye liner. This trick worked well for her onstage, just as it had for many women in the 1940s when stockings were in short supply because of the war. In the makeup room, she sprayed herself with Arpège and painted her legs with a dark brown line. She was ready!

Opening night arrived. The audience seemed to enjoy themselves, and Norman Roberts was grudgingly pleased. They were disappointed to find that the reviewers gave them a lukewarm reception. Nina was aware that the production hadn't quite jelled in the same way that *The Second Time Around* had. But it was hard to put your finger on exactly what had gone wrong. The actors were good; the script certainly had stood the test of time…Was it the direction? Was it her? Even though she got a good review, Nina couldn't help but feel a gnawing sense of responsibility, and a feeling of depression descended on her.

"Productions sometimes just don't work," counseled Tom, on the phone. "Look at all the Broadway shows where millions of dollars have been spent—musicals with massive sets and lights and gorgeous costumes and wigs and stars and the whole thing fizzles out after opening night. You'd think the producers or the directors would have an inkling that something wasn't working and fix it. Just as in a relationship, sometimes the chemistry isn't there. Theater is an intangible thing, honey. Forget it. The magic was just missing."

Harry was philosophical, "Well, at least it didn't open and close on the same night," he said. "I've been there and done that!"

What was obvious to the cast and the producer was that they would not be going to Broadway. Nina joined in a lackluster opening night celebration and went back, exhausted, to her motel room. They would finish out the week in Woodstock, then the company bus would take them to Connecticut for a week at the Westport County Playhouse, then on to the Bucks County Playhouse, the Pocono Playhouse, then Rhode Island, Massachusetts, New Hampshire, and they would end the tour in Maine. And that would be the summer.

CHAPTER TWENTY-FIVE

On the Road

By the time they reached the Cape Playhouse in Dennis, Massachusetts, the summer was on its last legs and so was the cast. They slogged through the week, thankful for some attentive audiences. One more venue, the Ogunquit Playhouse in Ogunquit, Maine and the tour would be over.

They would leave for Maine in the morning. Another bus ride, another theater, another stage to adjust to, another motel room, another threadbare carpet, and another mattress that sagged in the middle. Nina was weary of packing and unpacking her things. She was weary of spending isolating days in her room. When there wasn't a matinee, there was little to do but read and walk. The English members of the cast were friendly, but they had formed a clique that excluded her, and she tried to steer clear of Harry. She was sick of the coffee-shop meals and the mosquitoes. She missed Matt. Phone calls were a poor substitute for being with him, and the time difference made them inconvenient.

As soon as the last performance on the Cape ended, the cast left the theater, laden with their towels, tote bags and makeup kits. Nina knew she should go back to the motel to pack, but she was too tired. She would do it in the morning. Instead she decided to join the rest of the cast and some of the crew at the local bar to celebrate the final performance. It was so pleasurable to sit with the people from the show and let the wine relax her. The performance had gone particularly well that night, and they had a respite the following night as it was Monday, a travel day.

At each stop along the tour Harry had managed to hook up with a pretty summer-stock apprentice just a hair's breadth away from jailbait. He would spend time with her after the show and into the next day. He left a trail of broken hearts in his wake. As the bus pulled out of every little town, a swollen-eyed teenager could usually be spotted watching forlornly as the bus turned the corner and disappeared out of sight. Tonight, however, Harry had decided to join the rest of the cast at the table in the bar.

"Could you believe that audience?" asked Nina. "They talked all through the first act!"

"Really?" said Pamela, "I thought they were good. What did they say?"

"They were good, but those two women in the front row—I think they thought they were in their living room watching television—one turned to the other and said, 'Do you think that's a wig she's wearing? Or her real hair?' Loud enough for me to hear! I almost stopped and took my wig off to show them. In the second act they talked about my shoes and kept pointing to them. They seemed to be enjoying the play, and they laughed a lot, but as soon as the lights came up for the curtain call, they got up and walked out. No applause. No nothing. It's as if they turned off the television and went to bed."

"You think that's bad," said Harry. "I once did this political play—it was a two-hander by some Polish playwright and one night, after the other guy finished a long, boring speech, there was a pause and I said, 'Shall I speak again of politics?' A mournful voice from the back of the audience said, 'Noooooo.'"

The table erupted in laughter.

"I was once in a play," joined in Pamela. "Oh, God! it was a dreadful play, and it got the horrid reviews it deserved. But this one poor actor, his name happened to be Guido Nuzzo. The reviewer said four words, 'Guido Nuzzo: Nuzzo Guido.' I'm not sure what ever happened to Guido Nuzzo. Poor devil."

The cast and crew were laughing again.

Nigel chimed in.

"I once did a production of *Julius Caesar* at a Shakespeare festival in Toronto," he said. "It was during the scene where Caesar is stabbed—the scene in the senate. It was dramatically directed. We were all in stark white and the set was white. There was strobe lighting as the blades struck and then the white was suddenly sprayed with red. There was a moment of silence and in that moment the stage manger's phone rang. *Ring. Ring.* We all froze. You could hear the footsteps of the poor stage manager running behind the scrim to answer the phone. The actor playing Casca said under his breath, 'What do we do if it's for Caesar?' None of us could speak for ages. I was jolly glad I didn't have the next line!"

The cast was doubled over with laughter. It was so good to tell the funny theater stories and relax. Everyone had experienced them.

A man sitting at the bar was eying Nina. He had been in the audience that night and had waited backstage to meet her. Now he appeared to be a little drunk. He stared at her and when she looked back at him, he grinned, broadly and saluted her with his glass. He bought a round of drinks for the table. They toasted him. A little while later, he bought a second round, and they all looked at each other, but politely accepted. When he tried to buy a third round, Nina put up her hands, "No thanks, I'm good."

She started to get up.

"You're leaving?" asked Harry.

"Yes, I'm exhausted, and I have to pack in the morning."

"I'll walk you to the motel," he said, standing up.

"No need. Thanks, Harry, but…I'm fine."

"I cannot let a lady go out by herself after dark."

Harry came around the table and held her chair. She did not resist. She was feeling a little nervous about the man at the bar and also a bit unsteady on her feet. They headed out of the bar together and down the dark path to the motel.

"Jeez! The mosquitoes are as big as blue jays!" said Harry, swatting one on his arm. Nina could hear their high-pitched whine amplify and then recede as they zipped past her ear. She shook her head to keep them from landing. It was hot and muggy and difficult to breathe. Now that they were out of the air-conditioned bar, the sweat started to drip down between her breasts. Her blouse stuck to her chest. She gathered up her long hair and held it on top of her head hoping to feel the breeze on her neck. But there was no breeze. Harry said something that she didn't quite hear, but she laughed anyway. She stumbled and they bumped into each other which caused them to laugh again. The cicadas were as loud as an oncoming train, and a surprising sweet scent of honeysuckle perfumed the air, adding to the sultry atmosphere of the night. When they finally reached the motel, Nina tripped going up the porch steps. Harry grabbed her arm to keep her from falling. Moths fluttered around the dim, yellow lights on either side of the front door. Dead ones had piled up in the bottoms of the glass fixtures and cobwebs connected each light to the wall. They walked down a hall that smelled of a combination of mildew and Lysol. Harry helped her with the key to open the door to her room and pushed it open for her. She lurched into the dark as he tried to catch her.

The room was cooler. She had left the air-conditioning

on low. She put down her theater belongings and plopped down on the bed trying to steady herself.

"Whew! I didn't realize how much I had to drink."

"It was that last one," said Harry, "I think it may have been spiked. I'm feeling the same way, and I can hold my liquor. Are you okay?"

"I will be," said Nina, without much confidence. "I think I just have to sit for a minute."

"I bet that "stage-door Johnny" bribed the bartender to slip a mickey into that last drink," said Harry. "I think he had a case on you."

He sat down next to her.

"Whoa! Don't rock the boat," said Nina, bracing herself with her hands on the bed.

"Sure you're all right?" asked Harry.

"The room is spinning, but I think I'm just going to go to sleep."

Nina lay down on the pillow and closed her eyes. Harry moved over to make room for her legs. The room spun faster, but she didn't say anything because she wanted Harry to leave.

"I'm okay now," she said. "You can go." Then she murmured, "Thanks. Thanks a lot, Harry." Before she finished talking, she had fallen into a drunken sleep.

At some point during the night she was kissing Harry. Was she dreaming? Or was it real? She had kissed him so often in the play, she couldn't be sure. His lips were fleshy and clinging. She could feel her body respond to him. They were sailing through the sky on a magic carpet. On a mattress. On a carpet. On a mattress. It was a dream! She had just come offstage. Someone was unzipping her costume. She was so tired! She felt Harry's tongue plunge into her mouth. Then it didn't matter. Nothing mattered. She wanted him. She wanted him with a red-hot desire. Harry kissed her breasts; he kissed her thighs, his mouth lingering between her legs. She moaned. He slipped into her, and it was only moments before their passion mounted and exploded. She fell back into a deep sleep.

A few hours later she woke, disoriented, and consumed by a sense of unease. Her mouth was dry and the pain in her head was intolerable. Then she realized that her clothes were off, and Harry was lying naked beside her in the bed. The air conditioner was making a whirring sound, and the digital clock glowed and pulsated with a blood-red number that she couldn't quite make out. She focused on it, narrowing her eyes. 3:14. She sat up and looked around. A slow horror filled her. Her jeans and her blouse were in a heap on the floor, and her underwear was nowhere to be found. She reached down for her blouse and put it on. She needed to pee. Putting her arms out to steady herself, she got up and gingerly walked to the bathroom. When she got inside, she closed the door quietly and switched on the light. The light was harsh and blinding. She stood and looked at herself in the mirror through squinted eyes. Her eye makeup was smudged, her hair was in disarray, and her face was ashen.

"Oh, God. What have I done?" She whispered to the image in the mirror.

She sat down on the toilet and stared at the tiled floor. As she gazed, the little white hexagons shifted into three-dimensional forms and then shifted back again. She had to think. The first thing she had to do was to get Harry out of the room. Then she could deal with the rest. She left the bathroom, turning out the bright light, and waited until her eyes adjusted to the dark again. When she could make out the bed, she walked over to it and sat down.

"Harry! Harry! Wake up!" she said, shaking him.

"Mmmmm? What?"

"Harry. It's Nina. You have to get out of here!"

"Nina? What are you doing here?"

"No. You are in my room. You have to get dressed and get back to your own room."

"Ohhhh, no. Too tired, too mmmmmmm." Harry turned over and snored softly.

"No!" said Nina, emphatically, shaking him again.

Harry groaned and sat up.

"What? Oh man! What the hell was in those drinks?" He held his head.

"I don't know but you have to leave. Quickly. Before anyone sees you," she hissed, urgently.

"Okay, I'm going. I'm going."

He looked around and ran his fingers through his hair. He stood up. In the dim light she could see his naked silhouette. He groped for his jeans and pulled them on, hopping around as he tried to balance on one foot. He searched the floor, found his socks, and sat back down on the bed to put them on.

"Don't bother about your socks," said Nina. "Go!"

"But I…"

"Here. Here are your shoes." She handed him his loafers. "Now go. Go!"

She opened the door and pushed Harry out into the bright hallway, barefoot and naked from the waist up, clutching his clothes, his shoes, and his makeup kit.

Nina closed the door and collapsed onto the bed.

"What the hell am I going to do now? Oh, God! What have I done?" she whispered aloud.

With a pounding heart she decided that the best thing to do was to try to get some sleep. Things would be the same in the morning, she reasoned, and she might be better able to deal with them.

CHAPTER TWENTY-SIX

The Following Day

By ten thirty, the August heat was already so palpable that objects in the distance appeared to ripple. Nina stood outside the motel with a scarf over her hair, her sunglasses on, and her suitcase by her side. Her head throbbed, her stomach roiled, and her chin was chafed from Harry's unshaven cheek. One by one the rest of the cast and crew straggled out of the motel and onto the bus, glancing furtively at each other. Most were pale and also wearing sunglasses. Nina walked to the back, collapsed in the seat by the window, put her sweater over her like a blanket, and closed her eyes. Harry arrived late and in disarray and slumped down in the front seat not looking at anyone. The bus was eerily quiet. Nina slept all the way to Ogunquit.

At the new motel, she unpacked only her toiletries and a nightgown and left her suitcase open on the floor. Then she collapsed on the lumpy bed and slept some more. When she woke, it was getting dark. She dreaded facing Harry, but she was too hungry to settle for the stale peanut-butter cracker sandwiches in the vending machine down the hall. Reluctantly, she joined the rest of the cast who were being driven in the company van to a local restaurant for dinner. There was only one place that was open after eight on a Monday night in Ogunquit. It was a dump that served bar food. A strip of flypaper hung by the door, swaying gently in the air-conditioning.

She sat down at the cast table next to Nigel Dermot, and as far away from Harry as she could and did not make eye contact with him for the entire evening. After a greasy hamburger and cold fries, Harry waylaid her on her way back from the ladies' room.

"Nina, I have to talk to you."

"Stay away from me, Harry."

"Nina, that's ridiculous. We have to play opposite each other."

"How can you talk to me after what happened?"

"That's exactly what I want to talk to you about," said Harry. "What happened? I don't remember. We were both so drunk. Maybe...maybe nothing happened." He looked at her with his face scrunched up.

Nina's heart leapt for a moment. *Could it be possible?*

"What do you mean?" she said, immediately wary. "I went to bed fully clothed, and when I woke up, I was..." she looked around her, moved closer to him and lowered her voice, "...I was naked."

"I know!" said Harry, with astonishment.

"How did I get that way?" hissed Nina, angrily.

"I'm...I'm not sure. I swear. I don't remember very much of it."

Nina looked around sharply. The rest of the cast was busy at the table, trying to divvy up the check.

"Look," said Harry, "I'm sorry for whatever my part was in it. I know I probably tried...I mean, c'mon." He held both his hands out, palms up and tilted his head to the side. "But I was...um...too drunk." He shrugged and smiled, apologetically.

Nina studied him for a long minute. Then she lowered her head and walked back to the table looking at the floor. Maybe it had been a dream?

When she got back to her room, she ran a hot bath. She lay in the steaming water and tried to force her mind to remember what had gone on the night before. She remembered walking back to the motel with Harry. She remembered him helping her to open the door…and then…what? It was a blank. Had she been unfaithful to Matt? Or did she dream it? What constituted infidelity? Was it just sleeping with someone? Or…was it the sex? Or was it enough just to want the sex?

She got out of the tub as pink as a boiled shrimp, toweled herself off, and tried to look in the mirror, but it had fogged over. She rubbed it with her towel and stared at herself. Her eyes were puffy and the dark circles under them attested to the amount of liquor she had drunk. Remembering her water cure, she unwrapped one of the plastic-covered glasses by the sink and filled it with water from the tap. Then she sat down on the bed and dialed Tom.

"Tom? It's Nina. Is it too late to call?"

"Nina, honey! No! It's only ten o'clock. I know in those little towns you're playing they roll up the sidewalks at eight thirty, but here in the Big Apple we're still alive and kicking!"

"Can you talk? I need to…to talk to you."

"Oh. Hold on. Let me get a drink and turn off the TV."

He put down the phone, and Nina could hear the canned laughter from some TV sitcom spilling into the room. After a moment it stopped, and Tom came back on the line.

"What's the matter, honey? You sound like death."

Nina haltingly told him the story of what had happened with Harry.

"I'm pretty sure it wasn't a dream," she sighed.

There was silence on the other end of the phone. Finally, Tom drew a long breath in through his teeth and then exhaled loudly.

"Well…you know…there are the rules of life and then

there are the rules of the road. The two are different. You happen to be on the road, and you are playing by those rules. I wouldn't be too hard on myself, if I were you."

"Oh, God, Tom. I am miserable. I'm consumed with guilt. It's like a horrible dream that I can't wake up from. I don't deserve Matt. He is so trusting and...and sweet and...I screwed up so badly." She started to cry.

"Nina. Honey. It was a mistake. You were on the road. You were drinking. It will work out."

Nina blew her nose.

"Has this ever happened to you?" she asked.

"Oh, honey. Don't go there," said Tom. "It's different for me and Brent. We are not like you and Matt. Brent cannot be monogamous. Having one sexual partner for all of his life would be to him like...eating only celery for every meal. He just can't do it. If I got upset at every man he ever slept with, I'd have been put in the looney bin years ago. No. He does his thing, and I turn a blind eye. It no longer bothers me. It used to...but no more. I don't touch his thing...so to speak. Our sexual relationship is long over. Long over. Now, if he were to form an emotional attachment, well... that would upset me. But sex? Oh, no, honey. Brent would fuck a snake if it would hold still long enough."

Nina sighed, "I guess I don't know as much about life as I thought I did."

"Well, all I can tell you is it doesn't come in those little boxes you always like to put things in. You have to grow up a little, honey. I know you, Nina. You always finish a chapter before you put a book down for the night. You pay your bills before they're due. You never enter a door marked Exit. Perfect is only found under P in the dictionary. Life is a messy affair. And sometimes you have to break some of the rules, tell a few white lies." Tom paused for a moment, "For instance, you don't have to share this with Matt, you know."

There was silence on the other end of the phone while

Nina considered what he had said. Tom continued, "Go to sleep. You have a show tomorrow. When are you coming back from this cockamamie tour? Where the hell are you, anyway?"

Nina sniffled.

"Ogunquit. Maine. This is our last week. Thank God! I don't think I could survive another motel room. The other night I got up to go to the bathroom and walked straight into a wall. I stood there in the dark wondering which fucking motel room it was that had the bathroom on the left?"

Tom chuckled.

"Get some sleep," he said. "I love you. You are not a horrible person. You are a person who made a mistake. Think of that, Nina, you are human!"

CHAPTER TWENTY-SEVEN

Back Home

After the week in Ogunquit, the tour came to an end. It had rained for most of the week, and the audiences were sparse. The air was uncommonly cool for Maine in August, and Nina caught a cold. She had a choice between playing the part while sneezing and blowing her nose or taking cold medicine. She took the medicine. It dulled her mind. As she stood backstage with Nigel waiting to make her entrance for the penultimate performance, her first line flew right out of her head.

It'll come to me as soon as I step on the stage, she said to herself with false bravado. But she panicked.

"What's my first line?" she whispered urgently to Nigel.

He was so disconcerted that his mind went temporarily blank.

"Uh…uh…let's see," he whispered, "I say, 'Come outside, the view is wonderful,' and you say…"

"Oh, 'damp from the bath,'" Nina cut in, immediately. "Right! Of course! I'm so sorry. I…I've got it now." She exhaled sharply.

She was relieved, but a thin layer of flop sweat remained on her skin. What if that happens while I am on stage? Panic gripped her, but she was afraid to take a Valium on top of the cold medicine and end up like Diana, slurring her words. Anyway, it was in her purse in the dressing room and there was no time. She would just have to do this cold turkey. What is the worst that could happen? she thought. What if I won't be able to think of a single line? I'll have to apologize to the audience...Oh God! Don't go there! I'll never be hired to act again. Stay positive! She breathed deeply and forced her mind to concentrate. When she heard her cue, she tossed her chin up and went out onto the stage like a thoroughbred. You're a Broadway leading lady, she reminded herself. Act like one! She managed to make it through a competent, if tense performance, but now she was more eager than ever to put the whole terrifying experience behind her.

The following day, the last day of the summer tour, she packed her belongings in her motel room leaving out only her toiletries, a nightgown, and the jeans and T-shirt that she would be wearing on the bus ride home.

They had a full house for the last performance, and the show seemed to go well. After the final curtain came down, she placed her theater possessions in a tote bag and snapped her makeup kit closed with a deep sense of relief. It was over. Harry had brought his suitcase with him to the dressing room because he was taking a red-eye to California as soon as the last performance was over. He had a job out there that started immediately.

The next morning, on the long bus ride to New York, Nina slept with a large box of tissues on the seat next to her. By the time they reached New York, it was dusk. The bus pulled into the Trailways terminal at Eighth Avenue and Forty-First Street and stopped with a prolonged hiss of the air brakes. It seemed to Nina that it too had heaved a big sigh of relief. The fluorescent lights clicked on. She stood up stiffly, collected her belongings, and stepped down into the hot, clammy terminal. She said a nasal goodbye to the cast and crew and walked to the Forty-Second Street exit.

Most of the taxis she tried to hail were occupied, and the ones that weren't went whizzing past her to pick up fares further down the avenue. Despite this and despite her cold, Nina was happy to be back in New York. She was home! The city energized her. She walked up Eighth Avenue, dragging her suitcase behind her, breathing in the city. As she reached Forty-Seventh Street, she felt a magnetic pull to turn down the block and stand in front of the Barrymore Theatre, the site of her tremendous success. Perhaps that would serve as balm on the open wounds from the Norman Roberts experience.

A new play was on the marquee, and photos of the actors were up on the outside wall. She stood there astonished. How fleeting it all felt, how achingly transient. All the laughter, the perfectly timed lines, the meticulously honed technique, and the prodigious talent that had been up there on that stage—gone, evaporated, like so much mist. What did she have to show for it? Memories. There must be something in this world that you can hold on to—that you can build on. Something sturdier, she thought. You can't just be left with a few inflamed mosquito bites and a miserable cold.

A taxi stopped a few feet away from her discharging a woman. Nina waved frantically at the driver. He pulled up, got out, and put her suitcase in the trunk. She got into the cab and gave him her home address. As the driver restarted his meter and continued down Forty-Seventh Street, she sat back and watched the Barrymore Theatre recede in the distance. The business is so unstable, she thought. Now what? I'll have to start looking for another job immediately and go back on unemployment. I need to get new head-shots and print up a new résumé, but that costs money. God only knows when I'll work again. Maybe never. She closed her eyes and sighed. Suddenly she missed Matt. She missed Matt with all the force she could muster in her exhausted, ailing body.

She paid the driver and bumped her heavy suitcase up the two flights of stairs to her apartment. At the top of the stairs, she rummaged in her purse for her keys and opened the door. Home. The apartment was dark. She switched on the light by the door and looked around. All seemed pretty much the way she had left it. It was dusty, and she had to step over a half dozen Chinese menus that had been slipped under the door. The air was mildewy and stale. She crossed over to the front window and turned on the air conditioner. Tom had been there once a week to water the plants and collect her mail which now sat in a precarious heap on the kitchen table. Nina put down her purse and collapsed into an armchair. Her cold was full-blown, and the frigid air-conditioning of the bus hadn't helped. She knew she should call Matt and Tom to let them know that she was home, but she had a headache and was too tired to talk. She had to prioritize. She needed to get herself something to eat, take a hot bath, and get into bed.

She dragged herself up, got her purse, and went across the street to the all-night convenience store. A bell jingled as she opened the door. The only thing that appeared to be at all edible was a cellophane-wrapped American cheese sandwich on white bread. She took it off the shelf and looked it over, dubiously. She got a quart of milk from the dairy case and an apple and brought them all up to the counter. The Pakistani clerk rang them up on the cash register without looking up at her. She paid and turned to leave. The bell sounded again as she opened the door. She got partway out when she noticed a rack of tabloids to her left. On the front page of one there was a small photo of Matt sitting in a restaurant with a woman. "Hollywood hunk and up-and-coming actress spotted in LA hot spot," read the caption.

Nina stood frozen. After a moment, she slowly approached the rack, clutching her paper bag of food, and pulled out a copy of the tabloid. She stood reading the article.

"Miss. You want to buy the paper or not?" asked the clerk.

Nina looked up sharply, pulled a dollar bill from her purse, and put it down on the counter.

"Keep the change," she said, giving him a surly look. She left the store.

Once outside, she stood in the glow of the store's neon light and stared at the photo. She read the short article again. "Mathew Ryland and Jasmina Santiago were spotted having dinner in a trendy new restaurant in Downtown LA. Can it be love?" the tabloid queried. Oh, great! thought Nina. The perfect ending to a perfect day.

She climbed the stairs to her apartment and put the kettle up for tea. Then she sat down at the table and stared at Jasmina's face. Don't jump to conclusions, she told herself. It's probably a publicity stunt. But a knot had formed in her stomach. She poured herself a cup of tea and ate her sandwich and her apple looking out the window at the lights of the traffic in the darkening evening. She ran herself a steaming hot bath, submerged herself in the water up to her chin, and closed her eyes, letting the warmth soothe her. Afterward, she turned off the phone and climbed into her own bed for the first time in two months. It was musty and slightly damp from the humidity, but it felt good.

She woke after eleven to horns honking in dissonant tones, clanging garbage trucks, and wailing ambulance sirens. She felt thickheaded and achy, but the racket was more welcoming to her ears than the chirping of the chimney swifts in Maine. She blew her nose and went into the kitchen, opening the refrigerator and peering into it hopefully, as though it might have somehow magically replenished itself during the night. There was nothing in it but the quart of milk, a bottle of ketchup, soy sauce, Dijon mustard, and half a jar of English marmalade. The mound of mail sat on the table waiting for her to deal with it. Her suitcase was still standing upright in the hallway where she had left it, the phone machine was blinking, and on the table was the tabloid photo of Matt and Jasmina.

"Oh God!" she breathed, as she sat down at the table and put her head in her hands, "Where do I begin?" She turned the tabloid face down. The hardest thing was going to be calling Matt. She listened to his anxious message on the phone machine.

"Where are you? Are you all right? Was the bus delayed? Call me."

She put up the water for tea and dialed his number. Her heart raced as she listened to the phone begin to ring. Then a click. His voice on the recorded message.

"Matt here. Leave a message. I'll get back to you."

Gratitude washed over her. She didn't have to talk to him. Not yet.

"Hi. It's me," she said in a throaty voice. "The bus got in. I'm home in the apartment. I have a miserable cold. I miss you. Talk to you later."

She poured herself a cup of tea, dumped a spoonful of honey in it, and dialed Tom.

"Hey!" said Tom. "Home is the sailor, home from the sea."

"The sailor is sick," she said. "I have a wretched cold. But that's not the bad news. Guess what I saw in a tabloid last night?"

"Oh," said Tom, his voice dropping, "I was hoping you wouldn't be reading those rags."

"It kind of accosted me as I was buying a sandwich last night. What the hell is that about? What am I going to do now?"

"Well, it's probably some trumped up publicity thing…

Or not. But what you're going to do is go out there and claim him!" said Tom.

"You really think I should?"

"Well, if you don't, somebody will."

"Apparently," said Nina, wryly.

"Well what did you expect?" said Tom. "Look at him, for Christ's sake! Is he supposed to remain monastic while a thousand beautiful girls fling themselves at him and you're flouncing around on a stage in Bumfuck, Alabama?"

Nina suddenly felt as fragile as a dried leaf.

"How do I know he still wants me?"

"We'll cross that swaying bridge when we come to it," said Tom. "Meanwhile, I wouldn't stand around wondering."

There was a beep on the phone line. "I'll call you back," said Nina, hurriedly.

It was Matt, returning her call.

"You sound awful. So sorry you're sick," he said.

"Thanks. I'll get over it. I went straight to bed last night. That's why I didn't call. God! It's so good to be back! To have that wretched show done with! How are you? How is work going?" She was aware of trying to make her voice light, despite her cold. She thought it best not to mention the tabloid.

"Just winding up. But...I think I may have another job. I put in a request to direct one of the episodes, and I have a feeling they are going to say yes!"

"How wonderful!" said Nina, happy for him.

"Yeah. It's the kind of thing I've always been interested in doing," he said, enthusiastically. "I'd like to give it a shot. But...I'd have to start in a little over two weeks after this job ends. So, it means I won't...have time to come to New York."

"Of course, you can't come to New York," said Nina. "You'll be working!"

But her heart sank.

"I was wondering…" said Matt, "if you might come out here?"

"To California?" asked Nina, with such amazement that Matt assumed he had overstepped his bounds.

"I mean…when you feel better, of course," he added, hastily.

"I would love to!" she said, flooded with relief.

"Oh, good!" said Matt.

By the end of the week her cold had subsided, her clothes were unpacked, washed and put away, and the bills had all been paid. She called the airlines to arrange a flight to California.

"Will this be one-way or round trip?" the agent asked.

"One-way!" said Nina.

CHAPTER TWENTY-EIGHT

California, Here I Come!

The voice of the flight attendant speaking over the intercom roused Nina from her sleep: "We are approaching the Los Angeles Airport. Please stow your trays, make sure your seat is in the upright position, secure your carry-ons under the seat in front of you, and fasten your seat belt. The captain is preparing for landing."

Nina closed her book and put it in her tote bag, unread. She could not focus her mind on anything except Matt. Had he seen Sharon? Should she tell him about Harry? And then there was the nettling question of Jasmina…

It was almost three months since she had seen him. How would he react to seeing her again? Excitement and apprehension in equal measures jockeyed for prominence in her mind. She took a mirror from her purse and checked her face. She applied some lipstick, zipped her purse, and pushed it back under the seat in front of her. After a minute, she bent down and reached for the purse again, took out the mirror, and ran a comb through her hair. How would he feel about sharing his house with her? They had lived together happily for almost six months in her little East Side apartment, but now the thought of her toiletries crowding the space in his bathroom, her clothes taking up room in his closet made her anxious. When he had moved in with her in New York, he had brought hardly anything with him. Men take up less room, she thought. And anyway, it was her apartment, and she was sharing it with him. Now she was the interloper. What about his California friends? Would they accept her? Or would they feel resentment that some New Yorker had shown up to monopolize his time?

She stared out of the window. Snow-covered mountain tops peeked through a layer of white clouds, and then the plane descended into a clear, robin's egg blue sky. She watched as the lines became freeways and the dots became houses. Now she could make out trees and cars. She had been to California once before, as a child, but not since.

The landing gear came down with an alarming, grinding noise, and the plane bumped twice as it hit the tarmac. She sent up a silent prayer of thanks, undid her seat belt, and stood hunched over, waiting for the line of passengers to clear her aisle and inch its way toward the exit. As she struggled to dislodge her carry-on suitcase from the overhead compartment, a tall, handsome man stopped and asked if she needed help.

"Oh, yes, thank you!" said Nina, gratefully.

He retrieved the small suitcase with ease and set it on the aisle in front of her. She smiled her thanks, and he winked and gestured for her to go before him. At least I've still got it, she thought. She slung her large tote bag over her shoulder along with her purse and dragged the carry-on suitcase behind her.

Emerging from the air-conditioned plane, she walked into a wall of heat and sunshine. California! Palm trees like giant feather dusters stood tall in the sun. She took her sunglasses from her purse, bumped her suitcase down the metal stairway, and followed the signs to the baggage claim. That's where they had agreed to meet. As soon as she stepped onto the escalator, she saw him. He was standing there, alone, at the bottom. His head was tilted to one side, his hands were dug deep into his jean's pockets, and there was an uncertain smile on his face. She had forgotten how handsome he was with his long legs and broad shoulders and strong jaw. He was wearing a blue shirt that made his eyes look twice as blue. She loved the sexy way his top lip slanted down on the left side. Her pulse quickened as she took this all in while the escalator descended. When she reached the bottom, she was enfolded into his arms. She buried her face in his shirt, inhaling the familiar scent of him.

"Finally!" he said.

They stood hugging, as people made their way around them. Then they walked, awkwardly, with their arms around each other to the baggage claim, carrying the travel bags. After they retrieved her large suitcase from the baggage carousel, they left the terminal for the parking lot and got into Matt's Mercedes.

They took the 405 to the 10 and headed up La Cienega, talking over each other in their eagerness to share information. Finally, Matt pulled into a red-brick circular driveway that fronted the house on Norma and stopped the car. Nina peered out of the window. The house was white stucco with curved, terra-cotta Spanish tiles on the roof. An orange tree, laden with oranges, stood just to the right of the front door.

"Are you kidding me?" exclaimed Nina. "You mean... when you want an orange you just go out and pick one?"

Matt laughed.

"Welcome to California!" he said.

Once inside, he put down her suitcases, closed the door, and kissed her—a long, gratifying kiss. How wonderful it was to feel his arms around her, to feel his mouth on hers! All the doubts that had bubbled up to the surface on the plane were assuaged at the touch of his lips and the familiar sensation of his body pressed against hers.

"God! I have missed you!" Matt whispered into her hair.

"I don't ever want to be away from you again," said Nina,

her heart pounding. She looked up into his eyes, "Let's never be apart again. Please."

Timidly, she began to explore her surroundings. The house was small, basically only three rooms. The spacious living room was awash in sunlight from the skylight over the center of the room. It contained a couch, a coffee table, and a few easy chairs. There was a fireplace at the far end. At the opposite end was a galley kitchen with a tiled counter that served as a place to eat. Just off the kitchen was an alcove with a washer-dryer and a large bathroom.

"Oh! It is charming!" gushed Nina.

She walked down two steps into a bedroom. Matt followed. The bedroom was cool and dark in contrast to the sunny living room. It had a king-size bed, a dresser, and two night tables. On one of the tables, Nina recognized the framed photo of herself with the sea lions. She moved cautiously toward a wall to her right that was covered in blue drapes.

"What's behind here?" she asked, turning to Matt.

Matt indicated with a lift of his chin that she should look.

Nina parted the drapes like a child opening a birthday present. Behind them was a sliding glass door that led to a pool. Nina gasped. The blue water of the pool sparkled in the sun. It was bordered by blue and white delft tiles. Bright red bougainvillea clung to the white stucco wall that enclosed the pool area.

"Oh, Matt! It's just spectacular!" she said, turning to him and smiling broadly.

"I'm glad you like it," said Matt, as pleased as a schoolboy.

"I love it!" said Nina, breathlessly. "How can you ever bear to leave it?"

Matt was smiling as he brought her suitcases into the bedroom and put them up on the bed. He went into the kitchen to pour them some wine. As she began to unpack Nina's shyness returned. She placed a few of her things tentatively among the sparse, masculine setting. It was totally different from when she had moved into Matt's apartment in New York. So much more was at risk. There she could have simply sprinted the four blocks back to her own home. Now, she thought, as she put her cosmetic bag down on the countertop in his bathroom and stashed her box of tampons in the cupboard, she was a complete stranger in Los Angeles. She didn't even know how to hail a taxi.

After hanging up a few blouses, she dropped her arms and sighed, apologetically, "I'm afraid I'm going to have to leave the rest for tomorrow."

"Of course!" said Matt, appearing in the doorway, "You must be exhausted. Come and sit down. There is no rush. You can do it all tomorrow. Come have some wine."

Nina sank into the soft pillows of the living room couch and closed her eyes while Matt placed two glasses of wine on the coffee table.

"I can hardly believe you are here," he said, sitting down next to her and running his hand down her arm. "I have to touch you to be sure you're real. Are you hungry?"

"Starving!"

Matt laughed.

"There's a great Japanese restaurant not far from here, that I think you'll like. It's early for dinner, but it's eight o'clock New York time."

"Sounds fabulous!" said Nina.

"Or, if you're exhausted, we could just order a pizza and you could go to bed?"

"The restaurant sounds great," she smiled.

She sipped the wine and leaned back in the couch, listening to him talk about the new job he was about to embark on, directing an episode of the series in which he had guest-starred. He had gotten along well with the rest of the cast, most of whom were regulars, and with the crew, so he was looking forward to working with them as a director. He was animated and eager to share it with her. It was wonderful to hear his excitement, listen to his voice, and feel his body so close to hers.

They drove to the restaurant with the convertible top down. The air was perfumed with night-blooming jasmine. Nina held her hair with both hands to keep it from flying all over.

"Too much wind?" Matt asked.

"Oh, no, I love it!" she replied.

They drove passed bright yellow hibiscus, banana plants with leaves large enough to wrap yourself in, and cactuses, lots of cactuses, some bulbous and prickly, some pointy and sharp, some tall and slim like twisted signposts. There were exotic trees that Nina had never seen before: red bottlebrush, pink floss-silk trees, blue jacaranda, and on the ground, pink succulents that resembled coral. And, of course, looming above them all, like giraffes, were the palms: fan palms, king palms, the majestic royal palms and palms that looked like giant pineapples.

"It's a tropical paradise!" Nina laughed.

Just outside the restaurant, there was a small cluster of bird-of-paradise plants.

"Oh!" Nina cried, going up to a flower and touching it, "I have always wanted to see a real one! I've only seen pictures of them!"

The interior of the restaurant was serene and uncluttered in the Japanese style with shōji screens made of translucent white paper near the walls. It was empty except for a Japanese family. Matt and Nina were seated at a table near the family, and as they waited for their drinks, they observed the children. The toddler was fascinated by Matt. She smiled at him and he smiled back. He waved and she ducked her head, shyly. The parents glanced up, looked around and then continued eating, bent over their chopsticks. Matt took his napkin and held it up, hiding his face. A look of intense curiosity lit up the toddler's face. When he lowered the napkin, she broke into a delighted laugh. The father turned in his chair, still holding his chopsticks, and inclined his head in Matt's direction. Matt smiled at him and nodded. The mother continued eating with her eyes on her plate.

Any self-consciousness Nina had been feeling dissolved in the wine and the laughter. They ate their meal, eagerly regaling each other with stories of things that had happened while they were apart.

After a while, the toddler started to fidget in the highchair. Matt took his napkin and folded it into a kind of origami. When he opened it out, it had turned into a pair of cat's ears which he put on top of his head. Both the five-year-old and the toddler stared at him. The toddler reached out for the napkin, and Matt got up from the table and handed it to her. Nina couldn't help but recall the moment when she had fallen in love with him, at his friend's house, when he had amused the crying baby in the playpen. A man who loves children can't be all bad, she remembered thinking, and a new wave of love swept over her. What would it be like to have his child, she wondered?

When the Japanese family got up to leave, the father returned the napkin to Matt and bowed. The mother was occupied helping the children into their sweaters and speaking to them in Japanese. When she finished, she bowed to Matt and Nina and gently nudged the back of the toddler's head to do the same.

Matt returned the bow.

"Are you about ready?" he asked Nina.

She nodded.

"Let's get out of here," he said.

They drove back to the house. Once inside Matt leaned against the closed door and took Nina in his arms. They kissed and clung to each other. Matt started to unbutton her blouse. She stopped him, gently, whispering, "I'll be right back."

She went into the bathroom, taking with her, the new silk nightgown that she had bought for the trip. When she emerged with her face scrubbed free of makeup, she was as nervous as a bride on her wedding night. She walked barefoot into the bedroom and stood at the door.

"Ah! There's my girl!" said Matt.

He was waiting for her in the bed.

"Come here. Take that thing off," he said, grinning.

Nina pulled the new nightgown off over her head and let it fall to the floor. She stood before him naked.

"My God, Nina, you are a beautiful woman."

He reached out his hand. She came to him and slipped under the covers. He took her in his arms, and she felt his lips opening and the tip of his tongue searching for hers. He moaned with pleasure.

"Oh, I've waited so long for this," he murmured.

The wine, the jet lag, the time change all combined, and suddenly nothing existed except Matt and his hands and his mouth and his body. As he knelt over her, she closed her eyes and abandoned reason for instinct. Her back arched of its own accord, and sounds emerged, unbidden, from her lips. She let her whole body move with his in a primordial rite. The noise of their coming together and pulling apart, again and again, accelerated in a steady rhythm—an ancient song of love. Afterwards she fell asleep with her head on his chest and his arms encircling her. She had come home.

CHAPTER TWENTY-NINE

The House on Norma

They had ten days before Matt's new job began. He was eager to show Nina all of Los Angeles. They began at an outdoor restaurant in Malibu, overlooking the Pacific Ocean, with a brunch of lobster salad. Afterward they walked barefoot on the beach, their arms around each other. They spent a day at the Griffith Park Observatory and dined at Yamashiro taking in the magnificent backdrop of a sprawling Los Angeles spangled with lights. Along with the rest of the tourists, they went to Grauman's Chinese Theatre and looked at Marilyn Monroe's handprints in the cement. They shopped at the Farmers Market, bringing home fresh fish and vegetables to cook for dinner. At the classic Hollywood restaurant Musso & Frank, they toasted each other with the famous martini. They window-shopped in the trendy stores on Rodeo Drive. Almost everywhere they went, people recognized Matt. Nina could tell by the sideways glances and the whispers, but no one ran up to him asking for his autograph. Here, they were used to stars. It was a company town.

Nina sunbathed and swam in the pool almost every day.

"I feel like I'm on a tropical vacation!" she told Matt.

"You are!" he answered, as he watched her from a lounge chair by the pool's edge.

They planted a large barrel of red geraniums and then bought a hummingbird feeder to hang over it. Nina joined the library and indulged in her favorite pastime, reading novels. Matt arranged for her to have driving lessons. Occasionally they would dine with Matt's friends, but most often they stayed home where Matt showed her videos of *The Crescent Moon Café*, the television series that she had never seen. Away from the excitement of theater and the roar of the applause, they delighted in the simple, everyday things—the sudden emergence of a bright yellow sunflower poking its face in the living room window, a frenetic hummingbird at the feeder, or the sweet scent of honeysuckle in the air. They were passionate lovers and the best of friends. If Nina had any residual concerns about Jasmina, she repressed them. But looking at Matt's beautiful body as he slept, the thought of Harry rose up to irk her, like a splinter under the skin, and she knew at some point she would have to tell him.

About a week after Matt had started his job, Nina stood at the kitchen sink in her nightgown, putting the breakfast dishes into the dishwasher and humming to herself. She went to replace the cover on a can of coffee and realized they were running low. She looked around for a pad to write on. Not finding one, she dried her hands on the dish towel and went in search of one in the bedroom. She opened the drawer of the bedside table, found a small white pad, and took it out. Just as she began to close the drawer, she noticed a gold bracelet. She froze and looked at the piece of jewelry with confusion. She sat down on the bed and cautiously extracted the bracelet as though it was alive. It was a delicate bracelet, studded with ruby chips and had an Asian design tooled on it. She suddenly felt light-headed. Don't jump to conclusions she told herself. She put the bracelet back, closed the drawer, and sat on the bed, staring into space. The worst-case scenario was, of course, that it belonged to Jasmina, and she had taken it off while she was in that bed. But she tried not to let her mind go there. It was hard, however, to shake the images the bracelet evoked: Matt's body—the body she knew so intimately—entwined with Jasmina's. She shook her head, got up from the bed, and went back into the kitchen with a heavy heart.

Throughout the day, the vision of the bracelet stayed on her mind, like the afterimage on your retina when you have stared too long at the sun. She and Matt had lived together in New York for a blissful six months. She had assumed they had a committed relationship, but it was an implicit understanding. Nothing had ever been put into words. Did three months apart signal to him that he could have other sexual partners? Suddenly she started to question everything. Why had he never asked her to marry him? Marriage had never been a necessary component of a long-term relationship for her, but now her insecurities began to soar. He had been engaged to Sharon, hadn't he? Jealousy seized her. Her idyllic world started to crumble. What should she do?

She spent an anxious day taking her driving lesson and attending to paperwork, trying all the while to convince herself that she was overreacting.

When the phone rang at six, she jumped. She answered in a high and unnatural voice.

"What's wrong?" Matt asked, immediately.

"Nothing. What's happening with you?" she asked with a studied cheerfulness.

Matt paused for a moment.

"What are you thinking about for dinner?" he asked.

"Up to you," said Nina.

"Is there any of the pasta left?"

"I ate it for lunch," she said.

"Well, we might try that Mexican restaurant on Beverly," he said, "That is, if you're in the mood for Mexican food…?"

"Sounds lovely," said Nina.

Matt was unconvinced.

"I could pick up a pizza…"

"No. Mexican is fine."

"Great!" said Matt, but without conviction. "I'll be home in about forty-five minutes…Sure you're okay?"

"Sure. See you then."

He paused for a moment as though he were about to say something else and then hung up the phone.

Nina showered and dressed. She chose a light green blouse that she knew was Matt's favorite. She poured herself a glass of wine to steady her nerves. At seven she heard the familiar sound of his car in the driveway. She smoothed her blouse and checked her face in the bathroom mirror. He came in, kissed her, and smiled, taking in the green blouse. Then he plopped down on the sofa.

"Whew!" he said as he sank into the cushions, "Good to be home!"

"Beer?" asked Nina.

"Please!" said Matt.

Nina went to the refrigerator and took out a beer. It hissed as she opened it.

"How did it go?" she asked from the kitchen.

"By the time we set up in Griffith Park, the light was already going, but thank God, Marty had a few tricks up his sleeve. When I saw the rushes, I was amazed! The damned thing looked pretty good!"

She poured the beer into a mug and poured herself another glass of wine wondering when she should broach the question of the bracelet. She knew she couldn't get through a dinner pretending that everything was all right. As good an actor as she was, they were too tuned into each other. He would know that something was wrong. She walked into the living room, handed Matt the beer and put the glass of wine down on the coffee table. Then she walked into the bedroom. He looked after her, questioningly. She took the bracelet out of the drawer and slowly walked back, holding it behind her.

"I wanted to ask you about something…" she said.

She could see the concern in his eyes.

Holding it by two fingers as though it was a pair of soiled panties, Nina placed the bracelet on the coffee table and sat down on the edge of a chair facing the sofa. Matt stared at the bracelet.

"I was looking for a pad to write a grocery list on, and I found it in the drawer of your bedside table." She looked up at him with hopeful eyes, willing him to tell her that it was nothing.

Matt sighed and put the beer down on the coffee table next to the bracelet.

"Yeah," he said, looking at the piece of jewelry, "It be-longs to…a girl. A woman."

Nina let the silence hang in the air.

"I guess Freud would say I left it there for you to find. I was planning to tell you anyway…I just…wanted to give you a little more time to get accustomed to…to fall in love with being here."

His voice dropped. "I was afraid you might go back to New York."

Nina's heart sank. It was going to be bad.

"We both had too much to drink at the wrap party. She ended up coming back to the house. I barely remember it. I'm sure she barely remembers it. It meant nothing to either of us. I swear."

He looked at her with haunted eyes.

Inside Nina something broke. She got up from the chair taking the wine glass with her and walked over to the glass wall that looked out onto the pool. Ice had formed around her heart. She wanted to ask if the bracelet belonged to Jasmina, but she couldn't bring herself to. She stared out at the bougainvillea for a long minute, sipping the wine and recalling the drunken night with Harry. Was she any less guilty than he was? "Do you expect him to remain monastic while thousands of girls fling themselves at him?" Tom had said. But the pain of the betrayal was too great.

Finally, Matt broke the silence, "Please say something. I have to know what you're thinking."

Nina spoke. Her throat was tight.

"I don't know what I'm thinking. I'm thinking..." There was a long pause. "I don't know what I'm thinking."

Now would be the time to tell him about Harry, she thought. But she hurt too much to let him off the hook so easily. She wanted him to feel the pain of the guilt. Maybe he never needed to know about Harry? That's what Tom had said, hadn't he? After all, it may never have even happened...

Matt got up from the sofa and walked over to her but stopped short of touching her.

"I swear to God, Nina. It was nothing. I told you once that I had to be careful with alcohol. There were drugs at the party, too. Bowls of cocaine. I was trying to stay away from the drugs. Successfully, by the way. I kept refusing the drugs, and people kept pouring me drinks. I got drunk. It meant nothing."

Nina whirled on him. "Is that supposed to excuse you? People kept pouring you drinks? You resisted the drugs? Does that give you license to go to bed with someone? I trusted you!"

"Ah, Christ, Nina! It could've happened to anyone. It doesn't mean I don't love you. You're so judgmental. Everything has to be perfect for you. There's no room for human error. I walk on eggshells around you, always worried that I'm not going to measure up."

Nina reeled as though she had been struck. She had heard it before. Her anger flared and her face turned red.

"Perfect? Excuse me? Perfect? I'm sorry if I can't spend my whole life worrying that, just because you're...just because you're catnip to every girl that walks by...that every time you have two drinks you are going to end up in bed with one of the thousands of beautiful women who fling themselves at you! If that's what you call perfect...maybe we'd better just...just...better end this now. Because, I've got news for you—I don't need this!"

The second glass of wine started to surge through her bloodstream, emboldening her—giving her the courage to say the one thing she most feared.

"Maybe you should have just taken the goddamned drugs. Then Sharon would have to come and save you again."

Matt clamped his lips together in a straight, hard line.

She drained her glass and headed for the door. She put the wine glass down on a small table by the door and picked up the keys to Matt's Mercedes.

"What are you doing?" Matt asked, alarmed.

"I have to get out of here. I need to clear my head."

"You're not driving!"

"I'll be okay. I just need to be by myself for a while, okay?"

"But not...in the car. You...you don't know how to drive."

"Yes, I do," she responded smugly. "I had a lesson today."

"But you don't have a license! And it's getting dark. Besides you've been drinking. Don't be crazy!"

"I need to get out of here!" Nina said forcefully, reaching for the doorknob.

"I can't let you do that."

He started toward the door.

She turned on him. Her back was against the door, her face just inches from his. The wine had now filled her with bravado. She kept her voice low, but insistent.

"Suppose you tell me how I am expected to get into that bed when I know you've been in there fucking Jasmina Santiago?"

At the sound of the name Matt's face drained of color and he drew back, blinking. Nina looked at him. She nodded, slowly. It was apparent that the name had hit home.

"You don't have to worry," she laughed, wryly, "I'll be back. I don't know anyone in California except you."

Then a thought struck her. "Wait a minute! Wait a minute! Yes, I do! *Harry's* out here. I have his phone number. He'll be happy to see me!"

"Marino?" asked Matt, confused.

Now all bets were off. Revenge tore through her like a wildfire. She had only one thought, the need to hurt him as much as she had been hurt. She was breathing hard and couldn't stop herself.

"I might as well tell you," she said. "You're not the only one who had a drunken night." She stopped and stared at him, defiantly.

There was a long pause while Matt stood very still and looked at her. Then he slowly lowered his jaw, like a boxer who was expecting to be hit.

"You're saying that just to get back at me. To hurt me. It's not true."

"No," she said, relishing having the upper hand. "It's the truth. I thought I knew everything there was to know about myself…but," she shrugged her shoulders, "apparently I was wrong."

"With Harry?" Matt said. She saw the revulsion in his face as he backed away from her.

"Yes. Just like you. It was nothing," she said, mocking him with his own words. "A silly, stupid, drunken night."

She turned and opened the front door.

"You are not going out of my house to see fucking Harry

Marino!" Matt said through clenched teeth. There was a fury in his eyes she had never seen before.

"Stay away from me!" shouted Nina, and she turned and struck his chest with her fists.

He grabbed her wrists, ripping the keys from her hands. Nina flinched. He pulled her forcefully back into the living room. The wine glass wobbled on the table and fell, breaking into pieces. He went out, slamming the door behind him.

Nina lost her balance and fell hard on the living room floor. In the silence that followed, she could hear the car start up.

"Oh, God! No! Please, don't go! Don't leave me."

She started to sob; deep wrenching sobs that wracked her body.

Pain shot up her left hand, and she realized that she was bleeding. Her hand must have come down on a shard of glass. She raised her arm and watched, mesmerized as the blood dripped down her arm and onto the green blouse. She got up, unsteadily, and went into the bathroom to find something to stop the bleeding. She just made it to the medicine cabinet when she suddenly knew she was going to be sick. Kneeling over the toilet, she retched and gagged until all the contents of her stomach had emptied into the toilet. She stayed there for a moment, breathing hard and trembling, her head hanging over the bowl. As she sank down onto the cold tiles, the thought came to her that she had hit rock bottom. There was no further down that she could go. She had ruined the most beautiful thing that she had ever had. Why couldn't she have just forgiven him quietly and asked forgiveness for herself?

She rose, slowly, bracing herself on the sink and looked at herself in the mirror. Her cheeks were blotchy, and her eyes were smudged with mascara. The green blouse was ruined. She blew her nose and rinsed her mouth out with water. She tore off a long piece of paper toweling and wrapped it around the cut. Then she found some white first aid tape and wrapped her entire hand with it. With her right hand, she splashed water on her face, dabbed at the smeared mascara with a tissue and looked for some mouthwash in the cabinet. Getting the wine out of her system had completely sobered her. She took off the blouse, leaving it in a heap on the bathroom floor and walked into the bedroom.

The sound of a car outside made her heart leap, and she turned and looked quickly toward the door. But the car went passed the house. She sat down on the bed, picked up the phone, and dialed the operator. When a woman's voice answered, she said, "Could you give me the number for American Airlines, please?"

"Hold for the number," said the operator.

She dialed.

"Hello…yes…I wonder if…if I can get a single ticket on a flight from Los Angeles to New York City?"

"I can help you with that," the agent said. "When would you like to travel?"

"Tonight, if possible," Nina said. "As soon as possible."

There was a pause.

"I'm sorry, but the red-eye is totally booked," she said. "The soonest I can get you on a plane would be…ah…tomorrow morning at…let's see…six.

Nina's disappointment was clear in her voice.

"Are you sure?" she asked. "Nothing tonight?"

"No, I'm sorry. You might try TWA."

"Never mind," said Nina. "I'll…I'll take the one tomorrow morning."

She reasoned, sullenly, that she could sleep at the airport.

"Good!" said the agent, "That's a single seat on a 747 leaving LAX at six tomorrow morning. Do you prefer a window seat or the aisle?"

"It doesn't matter," said Nina.

"All right," said the agent, writing something down, "and is that going to be one-way or round trip?"

"One-way."

"Very good." She gave Nina the details of the flight and told her to be at the airport by five and that the ticket would be waiting for her at the check-in counter.

"Thank you," said Nina, "Oh, one more thing. How do I get to the airport? I'm...I'm not from LA. I...I don't even know how to hail a taxi."

The agent chuckled sympathetically, and said, "Why don't I give you the name of a very reliable car service? I use it myself, sometimes when I don't want my car sitting at the airport for a long time."

"Oh, thank you!" said Nina, jotting down the number.

When she hung up, Nina rose from the bed, took a sweater out of the drawer and put it on. Then she went to the closet and pulled down her carry-on suitcase. She could have the other things sent later on.

She busied herself taking clothes off hangers and placing them in the suitcase, going back and forth between the closet and the bed. She must not have heard Matt come back into the house, but when she turned, he was standing in the bedroom door. She stood stock still, her heart racing.

"What are you doing?"

"Packing."

"What happened to your hand?"

"I...The glass broke. I must have landed on it."

"Are you hurt?"

"I...I think it's just a superficial cut," said Nina, looking at the bandage. She saw that the blood had soaked through the paper toweling. "It just bled a lot."

"Nina. What the fuck are we doing to each other?" His voice was filled with pain. "When are we going to start appreciating what we have? We are two of the luckiest people in the world. Of every gift in life—all the extraordinary things—we have been given the most wonderful one. This love. I sometimes think we've been blessed with this because we've both paid our dues. But…" he shook his head and closed his eyes…"whatever. We have it. It's ours. And we throw it away."

Tears ran down Nina's face. She had hurt him so. They had hurt each other.

"For Christ's sake," continued Matt, "what does a drunken fuck mean compared to a family? A home? A life? I love you. I want to build a life with you. Nothing else means anything to me!"

There was silence for minutes, broken only by Nina's sobs.

"I'm sorry," Matt said. "I was wrong. I promise you it will never happen again."

"No. *I'm* sorry," said Nina, coming to him. "Believe me, I never, never meant to hurt you. Oh, God! That was the last thing I wanted to do. I tried so hard and then—this one dumb, drunken night—"

Tears were pouring down her face.

"Shhh," said Matt, putting his arms around her. "Stop crying. I love you."

He held her close and gently rocked her. She quieted, somewhat, and then a sudden eruption of new sobs overcame her, and he could feel her jagged breaths against his chest.

"What? What is it?" he asked.

She mumbled something unintelligible into his shoulder.

"What?" asked Matt, tilting his head, trying to make sense of what she was saying.

All sense of decorum had left her, and she was sobbing, convulsively.

"You asked Sharon to marry you," Nina blubbered like a child, "and you never asked me."

Matt pulled back and looked at her.

"I was afraid you'd turn me down," he said. "Like you did Paul."

"Paul?" said Nina, trying to make sense of his words. She looked at him, uncomprehending. "I never loved Paul."

"Do you love me?"

"Of course, I do!"

"You never told me."

Nina blinked. "I never told you that I loved you?"

Matt shook his head. She looked down.

"I...I have a hard time with that word."

She looked back up into his eyes. "But I do!"

"Would you marry me?" Matt asked.

"Oh, Matt! You are just saying that because I am crying."

"I am not. Will you?"

Nina sniffed and blotted her tears on Matt's shirt and looked up at him.

"Of course, I will! *I love you!*" she said, and she sobbed anew.

They held each other tightly until Nina's sobs finally subsided.

They could hear the clock ticking in the kitchen.

"Come, let's get a proper bandage for your hand," said Matt, "That one is a mess!"

He led her gently toward the bathroom.

"Be careful. Don't step on the glass."

The shadow of a banana palm could be seen through the front window. The clock struck nine.

CHAPTER THIRTY

A Full Moon

They tried to put the pieces of their lives back together again, but not all of them fit. They had to learn to live with their imperfections—to store the painful memories next to the pleasurable ones. There was no turning the clock back to the way things were. Occasionally Matt grew unexpectedly quiet and a wistful look filled his eyes containing a sadness she could not assuage. Some nights, looking at Matt's sleeping face, Nina thought how much he looked like a little boy, and the realization of how she had hurt him made her cringe inside. The violation of trust had shaken them both, but their love for each other, their mutual respect, spoke louder than the pain.

The fact that Matt wanted to marry her acted like a salve on Nina's heart. No longer did she feel a nagging inferiority to Sharon. No longer did she feel there was a tenuous quality to their relationship. She had never given much thought to marriage. Now, suddenly, the idea had a permanence she found herself moving toward as a sunflower follows the sun. She had decided to wait before telling Isabelle, who was so high about her baby, because she didn't want to steal her thunder. And she would tell Tom when the time was right.

California continued to seem like an exotic land to Nina, but she was happily adjusting to it. Every morning, as she opened the blue drapes, she was greeted by brilliant sunshine. Leaning against the open bathroom door, she watched as Matt shaved, gazing at his muscular torso. The thrill of going outside and picking an orange from the tree each morning did not diminish. She was immersing herself in the classic novels she had always wanted to read. She swam almost daily, took driving lessons, and scoured cookbooks for new recipes to try on Matt, who was deeply immersed in his directing job. After a month she lost her New York pallor and was developing an attractive tan. She had also finished two novels, executed a credible coq au vin, and was confident enough about her driving skills to take her driver's test. When she passed, she was proud and thrilled! It gave her a whole new independence.

The first thing the following morning, she phoned Tom.

"Guess what? I passed my driver's test!"

"Uh-oh. Stay off the roads, Los Angelenos!" said Tom.

"Matt says he's is going to buy me a red Mustang convertible," said Nina.

"Ha! I gotta hand it to that guy, he knows how to treat a lady! You sound good. What's going on?"

Nina hesitated.

"Nothing. Nothing's going on," she said. "I feel like I'm on an extended vacation. For the first time I can remember in a long time, I am not working. I'm not looking for work. I am just...enjoying life. I swim almost every day for exercise. I'm afraid I'll get arrested if I walk. Nobody walks here."

"Well, it's about time you relaxed!" said Tom. "You have been working so hard for so many years—you deserve to float. Floating is good. In my experience, sometimes when you stop trying so hard to get somewhere, good things have a chance to come to you. Speaking of good things, Brent knows someone who is looking for a sublet in New York. Do you want to sublet your apartment?"

Nina paused, "I'm…not sure yet. I might. Can I think about it?"

"Sure," said Tom, "Don't wait too long."

"Tom?

"Yes?"

"I told him about Harry."

"Okay…" said Tom, drawing out the word.

"He didn't take it well."

"I'm sure he didn't."

"We're trying to get past it," said Nina, "Trying to make it count, somehow, to make us stronger, instead of letting it be a wedge between us."

"You know about the Japanese art of Kintsugi, don't you?" asked Tom.

"No."

"When a vase shatters, they repair the broken pottery with a special lacquer dusted with powdered gold. It makes the repaired piece stronger and more beautiful than the original."

Nina thought for a moment.

"I like that," she said.

She had not intended to tell Tom about Matt's infidelity. The hurt was still too raw, and more importantly, she didn't want Tom to think badly of Matt. But suddenly, she had a need to confide in him.

"As it turns out," she said nervously, "Matt had his own drunken night. So, I guess we're even."

"Well, I can't say I'm surprised," said Tom. "But I know that doesn't mitigate the pain it caused you."

"You once told me that pain was the price we paid for love," said Nina.

"Yes, that's true," said Tom. "You could choose to live your life without love and insulate yourself from any pain, but what would be the point? Love is always painful, but usually worth it. Look, temptations are all around—especially in this goddamned business where there are a lot of good-looking people and you're working in close contact with them. It's easy to fall into a relationship. Attractions are exciting and that sex urge is very strong. It's a life force! If you have made the decision that Matt is the one for you, I think you have to decide to stay near him."

There was a moment of silence.

"Matt thinks we should get married."

Tom paused. "And? What do you think?"

"I think so, too. He is my best friend—except for you, of course."

"Well, I think that is a terrific idea! Are you going to let me walk you down the aisle?"

"Oh, there's not going to be an aisle. Probably just a chair for a witness in a clerk's office. Matt's been estranged from his family for years and, as you know, both my parents are dead."

"I'll be the witness, then."

"Really? You'd fly out to California? But you hate to fly!"

"To be there when you get married? Of course, I will!"

"Oh, Tom! That would be wonderful! You are my only family. I wish you weren't so far away."

"I'm always there for you, honey. All you have to do is pick up the phone."

Nina hung up, wiped her eyes with the heel of her hand and went into the kitchen to make herself lunch.

The phone rang.

"I felt the baby kick!" said Isabelle. "I had to tell somebody! Nina! There's a baby inside me!

"Ha! That is great, Isabelle!"

"I sing to her."

"You know you're having a girl?"

"Oh, not from any test. I just know."

"She is going to be so beautiful."

"You think?" said Isabelle. "I hope she has Paul's green

eyes. Paul wants us to get married before the baby is born. He feels it's important for her to know that her parents were married when she was born.

He would, thought Nina wryly.

"Isabelle! Am I going to miss your wedding?"

"Oh, it's not going to be a big deal," said Isabelle. Then she laughed, "Paul felt it wouldn't be appropriate to have a big white wedding with a pregnant bride! We're just going to city hall. Paul's mother will probably come up from Palm Beach, and my parents will come in from Indiana. Paul says he'll take us all to The Four Seasons for lunch afterward."

"Still…" said Nina, "I wish I could be there."

"I'll send pictures," said Isabelle. "Paul says he'll take me on a honeymoon to Puerto Vallarta! Can you imagine?"

Nina's mind flashed, briefly, on the Puerto Vallarta trip that Paul had invited her to go on.

"That sounds like fun," she said.

"You think? Wait until you see me in a bathing suit! I'm gonna look like an olive on two toothpicks. Paul keeps saying, 'You're supposed to eat for two, not five!' Last night at ten o'clock, we were watching television, and I had a sudden craving for Mallomars. Paul got dressed and went down to the all-night convenience store and bought me a box. I ate all but three!"

Isabelle dissolved in laughter.

"Oh, Nina! I wish you were here! We would have so much fun! Oh! I almost forgot; I have his mother's engagement ring!"

"Wow!"

"Paul flew down to Florida to tell her about the marriage, and she gave it to him. Me in diamonds! Are you ready? I've never even seen a diamond close-up, and now I'm wearing one on my finger! I keep looking at it to be sure it's really there."

"Nothing sparkles quite like a diamond!" said Nina.

There was a click on the line.

"Oh, that must be Paul calling. Gotta go."

When Nina hung up, she instinctively put a hand on her abdomen.

A baby. Isabelle's going to have a baby!

Late that afternoon, she decided to take a quick swim in the pool before getting dressed for dinner. She dove in, touched the blue-painted bottom, came up and swam a few laps. Then she lay on her back buoyed up by the water and looked up at the sky. The late afternoon sun was warm, and she closed her eyes and floated for several minutes, listening to the birds and musing about Isabelle and Tom. The pool phone rang. Annoyed, she almost let it go to voice mail, but thinking it might be Matt, she rolled over and swam to the edge of the pool, pulling herself up onto the tiled perimeter to answer it.

"Hold for Susan," said the voice on the other end.

Oh no! She probably has a job for me in New York, Nina thought, with a mixture of hope and fear. *What am I going to do?*

"What the hell time is it out there?" bellowed Susan. "I never can remember if it's three hours ahead or three hours behind! Why don't all the states have the same time, for Chrissake?"

"Hi," said Nina. "It's four o'clock."

"Anyway," said Susan, "I wanted to run something by you. I just got a call from Nick Travis's agent. Nick is directing a revival of *You Can't Take It with You*, and he wants you to play the daughter. It doesn't pay a whole lot. Those guys at the Mark Taper Forum think that artists can live on air alone. But since you seem to love it out there so much, I thought I'd let you know. What do you say?"

Nina's heart leapt! The Mark Taper Forum? To be able to stay in California and work? Nick Travis?

"Yes!" said Nina. "Tell him yes!"

"Yeah, I figured," said Susan. "It's a four-month deal. Rehearsals start next month, and the show is scheduled for a twelve-week run. It'll play through the holiday season. The good news is that casting agents out there usually go to see these shows, so you might get something out of it. Who knows? I'll call you tomorrow to firm up the particulars. Wear your sunscreen."

Nina hung up, stood, and toweled herself off. The faint smell of chlorine clung to her. She dialed Matt.

"Hi. When will you be home?" she asked, breathlessly.

"I'm just finishing up," he said. "Why? What's up?"

"I'll tell you when you get home."

She peeled off her bathing suit and got into the shower. As she held her face up to the water she thought, "I'm going to be working! A comedy! With Nick. Oh, my God! And I can stay and live with Matt! I should ask Tom to sublet the New York apartment, so I have a little extra money."

She dressed in a new white outfit and tied a peach sweater around her shoulders. When she heard the car pull into the driveway, she ran out to greet Matt. She told him the news, trembling with excitement. He hugged her, lifting her off her feet.

"I told you you'd work in California!"

"I can hardly believe it!" said Nina. "Can you believe it, Matt?"

"I can!"

Matt insisted they celebrate by going to their favorite restaurant, high in the hills, overlooking a sparkling panorama of nighttime Los Angeles. He ordered a bottle of champagne.

That night, in the darkness of the bedroom, Nina lay looking up at the ceiling.

"Thank you for dinner—and the champagne," she said. "That was unnecessary, but I loved it! You are the best thing that ever happened to me."

Matt reached for her hand.

"I love you more than anything in this world," he said.

"I always get frightened when I'm this happy. I'm afraid something will happen to you."

"I'll do my best to stay around for as long as I can," said Matt.

"I need more than that," said Nina.

She got out of bed and went over to the glass door that led to the pool. Matt rose up on one elbow and watched her.

"I need to know that if something happens to you, I will always have a part of you."

It was a warm night, and she drew the drape and slid the glass door open. There was a full moon.

"I want to have your child," she said, looking out at the night sky.

Matt was silent for a moment and then he spoke.

"I'd like a little girl if she looks just like you."

Nina turned and looked at him.

"Is that a yes?" she asked.

"It's a yes." said Matt.

She approached the bed, slowly.

"But I want it to be a little boy who looks just like you!"

Matt sighed.

"I guess we're going to have to go for twins," he said, with a resigned shrug.

"Hold on! Let's not get carried away!" said Nina, with amused alarm.

"Well? What are we waiting for?" said Matt. "We'd better get started. This is going to take a lot of practice!"

Sometime during the night, Nina woke. She was chilled and got out of bed to close the sliding door. The moon was high in the jet-black sky and the summer night was sown with stars. They looked like diamonds spilled out onto a jeweler's black velvet cloth. There was Orion—just back from the hunt, his sword at his side, his shoulders shimmering with sweat. The white light of the full moon glinted off the water in the pool and silhouetted a palm tree against the cloudless sky. Looking up at the craters of the moon, Nina thought she could see an embryo in a womb: there was the curved spinal column and there the large head! She smiled, closed the door, and slipped quietly back into bed.